Omega Morales

and the Legend of La Lechuza

Omega Morales
and the Legend of La Lechuza

LAEKAN ZEA KEMP

ILLUSTRATED BY VANESSA MORALES

LITTLE, BROWN AND COMPANY
New York Boston

Text copyright © 2022 by Laekan Zea Kemp
Illustrations copyright © 2022 by Vanessa Morales

Cover art copyright © 2022 by Vanessa Morales. Cover design by Karina Granda.
Cover copyright © 2022 by Hachette Book Group, Inc.

Little, Brown and Company
Hachette Book Group
1290 Avenue of the Americas, New York, NY 10104
Visit us at LBYR.com

First Edition: September 2022

Little, Brown and Company is a division of Hachette Book Group, Inc. The Little, Brown name and logo are trademarks of Hachette Book Group, Inc.

The publisher is not responsible for websites (or their content) that are not owned by the publisher.

Library of Congress Cataloging-in-Publication Data
Names: Kemp, Laekan Zea, author. | Morales, Vanessa, illustrator.
Title: Omega Morales and the legend of La Lechuza / Laekan Zea Kemp ; illustrated by Vanessa Morales.
Description: First edition. | New York ; Boston : Little, Brown and Company, 2022. | Audience: Ages 8–12. | Summary: "A girl must learn to trust herself—and her ancestral powers—when she comes face-to-face with the Mexican legend La Lechuza."
—Provided by publisher.
Identifiers: LCCN 2021056721 | ISBN 9780316304160 (hardcover) | ISBN 9780316304481 (ebook)
Subjects: CYAC: Empathy—Fiction. | Emotions—Fiction. | Witches—Fiction. | Magic—Fiction. | Supernatural—Fiction. | Family life—Fiction. | Hispanic Americans—Fiction. | LCGFT: Novels. | Paranormal fiction.
Classification: LCC PZ7.1.K463 Om 2022 | DDC [Fic]—dc23
LC record available at https://lccn.loc.gov/2021056721

ISBNs: 978-0-316-30416-0 (hardcover), 978-0-316-30448-1 (ebook)

Printed in the United States of America

LSC-C

Printing 1, 2022

Para mis primos.
Blood and beyond.

CHAPTER 1

THE TREES ARE TALKING TO ME AGAIN. Mami tells me it's because I'm too willing to listen. My cousin Carlitos tells me it's because I don't practice controlling my empathic abilities enough. But I think it's because I'm cursed.

It's not the trees' fault they're so chatty. You try standing in one place for hundreds of years without anyone to talk to, collecting memories since you were just a tiny seed. The moment you finally have an audience, it makes sense that you'd want to put on a good show.

"Excuse me." One of the pecan trees lining the park path tosses an unripened shell at me. "But are you trying to say we're making this all up?"

Did I mention trees can also read minds? At least the ones in Noche Buena can, and that's not even the strangest thing about this place. Which is why our family has been practicing magic here for centuries. On this little patch of dirt where horny toads grant wishes, cats have way more than nine lives, and the ghosts are more obnoxious than the living.

"You think you see with eyes stronger than mine?" The pecan tree hurls one at Carlitos next.

"Ouch!" He rubs his scalp. "¿En serio? I'm not the one who thinks you're lying." He turns to me. "Why do you keep letting them in, Omega?"

I jam an elbow into his side. "Gee, thanks for your help." *And I can't help it*, I want to tell him.

Carlitos has always been better at controlling his powers. Ever since he woke up on his ninth birthday and was suddenly able to stop his little brother Chale's crying with the touch of his hand. When my ninth *and tenth* birthdays came and went, I didn't even think I had powers. But it's been almost a year since they finally showed up and I'm still trying to figure them out.

I turn my attention back to the trees, pretending to be interested. "Okay, we're listening. Describe it again."

"It was a curse incarnate." The oak tree above me splays its leaves, stretching and twisting its gnarled branches into shadow-puppet shapes. "First the breeze blew in, so cold that in an instant I knew it didn't belong here. Not under the harvest moon."

"Then that disappeared too," the pecan tree says, "covered up by something giant, its wings black as oil."

"It landed right on one of my branches. Almost snapped it in half."

"Swooped down like a storm cloud." The pecan tree shakes its leaves, shivering. "I thought I might burst into flames."

"And its *face*." The bark of the oak tree turns pale. "It was vile. Hideous."

"The face of a monster," the pecan tree adds.

"The devil!" the oak tree wails.

This time Carlitos is the one who shivers, the trees' whipping branches creating an unnatural breeze that shouldn't exist in the middle of September in south Texas.

I just roll my eyes. "Okay, so you're telling me you think you saw el Diablo last night...."

The pecan tree slaps a branch against the trunk of the oak tree. "She still thinks we're making this up!"

"I don't think you're making it up," I say. "I just think you spook easily. Remember that time you swore a demon was stuck in one of your branches and it turned out to be a cat?"

"Cats *are* demons," the oak tree corrects me, twisting its trunk to flash me a patch of scratched bark. "It tried to kill me!"

Carlitos and I both laugh, but it only makes the oak tree angrier.

Its leaves stretch like it's throwing up its hands. "Fine. Don't believe us." It jabs a branch at us. "But you've been warned."

"Ya," I wave a hand. "Hasta luego."

"Adiós, árboles," Carlitos adds once we're far enough away. "If we took every one of their 'warnings' seriously, we'd be stuck in the same place for a hundred years just like they are."

"Yeah," I say, even though I still feel their fear like a pit at the bottom of my stomach.

I reach for the moonstone I always carry in my pocket, enchantment keeping it cold like a block of ice, and I squeeze it in my palm until the fear lets go of me.

But it's quickly replaced by dread.

"Oh no, there's Abby." Carlitos nods up ahead.

Next to her, Naomi Davis and Joon Lee are taping flyers to the accessible parking signs, the word MISSING beneath the black-and-white photo of a calico cat.

"Maybe she won't see us," I say, lugging Carlitos behind me. "Just don't look in her direction."

As Carlitos and I pass, all three of them look up, laughing at us, and I get that fire-in-the-belly feeling like they've been talking about me.

Few people in Noche Buena know my family's...*special*. But all of them think we're strange. Despite the fact that Noche Buena has a reputation for the supernatural, it's not one the townspeople carry with pride. According to my abuela, there was a time when those of us marked with magic could be more open about it, but over the centuries invisible borders have fenced us in, turning us into something to fear.

I should be used to the whispering, but being an empath, a mediocre one at that, means it's a lot harder for me to just brush it off. Instead, every snarky comment, every paper taped to my locker scribbled with the word *freak*, sticks to me like glue.

That's how the bullying started with Abby. First, she taped mean things to my locker.

Then she made an entire Instagram of photos of me doing perfectly ordinary things while looking absolutely hideous to prove I'm the spawn of Satan. Me drinking from the water fountain and replacing the water with blood. Me eating lunch and replacing my sandwich with human guts.

Things so cruel, I seriously don't even know how she thinks of them. Unless it's *her* who's actually the spawn of Satan.

I've tried talking to teachers about it. Abuela even marched down to the principal's office one day to complain. But the problem is, it's not just the other kids who treat us like we don't belong, and when it's adults who are the bullies, who do you call for help?

Abby clutches a stack of flyers to her chest and bats her lashes. "Well, what do you know? Returning to the scene of the crime, Omega?"

Naomi and Joon move on to taping flyers to a park bench.

She glances at them and I can tell she wants their attention. That's when I realize what this whole thing has really been about. She just wants an audience. For someone to *see* her. And it's so pathetic that I almost feel sorry for her.

Almost.

Abby clears her throat, raises her voice. "You know, there's only one way to get rid of that guilty conscience." She holds up her phone, recording Carlitos and me like she's some kind of modern-day witch hunter.

Carlitos turns to me and gags. "I can't believe she used to spend the night at your house."

"Just tell us what you did with them."

This time she's flanked by Naomi and Joon, their arms crossed.

"What is she talking about?" I hiss.

Joon silently shoves the flyer at me.

"It's Doña Maria's cat," Carlitos says, pointing out the spots.

"Mrs. Villarreal's went missing too," Naomi says, her eyebrow raised.

Abby crosses her arms to match her posse. "Yeah, any idea where they might have gone?"

Naomi smirks. "Maybe their family ate them for dinner." She turns up her nose. "You two do always smell like boiled meat."

Abby laughs like it's the funniest thing she's ever heard.

Joon just yawns. "I'm bored." He grabs Naomi by the wrist. "Come on, I need some more photos with these flyers for my Insta before my makeup melts off in this heat."

Abby scrambles for her things. "Wait up, guys."

They don't, laughing together as they head in the opposite direction, leaving her behind.

"Guess they're not in need of a third wheel," Carlitos says with a smile.

"I'm *not* a third wheel," Abby shoots back.

"It's not always so bad," I say. "You used to not mind it."

She narrows her eyes at me. "Yeah, until I found out there

were actually four of us." She means Clau. My best friend who also happens to be a ghost.

When I first told Abby the truth about my family and she didn't run away scared, I was so relieved. I thought I could trust her. But then her mom died, and when she begged me to help her communicate with her, I said no. I told her it was against the rules. The truth was, I didn't know how.

Maybe if I'd told Abby that she could have forgiven me. Maybe if I hadn't lied, she wouldn't constantly be trying to get back at me. But...maybe I shouldn't want a friend who's only nice to me when I do what she wants anyway.

"It's not right, the kinds of secrets your family keeps," she says. "It's not right what y'all *are*."

"It was all right when you thought I could help you. When you wanted to use me to..." My throat clenches.

She's misty-eyed as she says, "And now I know that your family doesn't use magic for good." She shoves another flyer at me. "Your family uses it for things like this."

I look her right in the eye, searching for the girl who used to braid my hair. Who used to pass me notes in class. Who used to laugh at my jokes. But all I see, all I *feel*, is how much she hates me. And buried even deeper, how much she dislikes herself.

"Forget her." Carlitos grabs me by the arm.

As he leads me toward home, all I can think is, *I wish I could.*

"It won't be long before people start putting two and two together. They're going to find out it was you." Abby huffs, trying to keep up just so she can keep tormenting us. "You and your weird family!"

We finally reach my front door, Abby still going on and on about the cats. But when I push it open, cold air rushes out, the draft so strong it knocks Abby back onto the street.

It swirls in her hair, her eyes wide. "What's happening? What are you doing to me?"

"Don't worry, Abby." Carlitos laughs, holding up his phone. "I got you. Everyone at school's going to love this."

The breeze musses her hair, making her scream. She finally runs off, yelling something about our house being haunted.

I roll my eyes. "Clau...get back here."

Clau can't help but sneak up on Carlitos next. He shudders as she traces an invisible hand up his back.

"Clau!" He scrapes at his arms. "I thought we had a deal. No sneaking up on me when I can't see you."

Her edges soften, fuzzy, before getting sharper and sharper. She slips into her less invisible skin and leans against the door as if this is her house and we're just some guests she's having over for dinner.

"All right, all right," she says. "Now take off your shoes before you come inside."

We do as we're told, even though this is my house and

Clau only lives here because she's dead. The reason for which is still a mystery—even, it seems, to Clau.

All we know is she showed up in our living room one day nine months ago and once she realized we could all actually see her, she has made absolutely zero effort to leave.

Inside, my abuela is watching *Amor Eterno* while she pretends to dust. Abuelo snores in the recliner by the window, probably having another one of his prophetic dreams.

"Hola, mijitos." Abuela comes over and gives me and Carlitos each a kiss on the cheek. "I'm glad you're home. Clau has been driving me up the wall."

Everyone in my family is strange, but our empathic abilities tend to manifest a little differently. My mother can shift a person's energy through potions she forms into candle wax. Abuela can do the same thing through food. Abuelo influences people through their dreams, and my tía, Carlitos's mom, channels emotions through her embroidery.

Like the rest of them, Carlitos has the gift of Touch and can shift people's emotions just by resting a hand on them, but it's weak without a tool to channel it. Abuela says not to worry, though. He'll find it when he needs it most.

Unlike me. I'm still stuck with the basics, able to read other people's emotions but not able to change them.

Clau casts an overdramatic glance in Abuela's direction. "While I've been *grounded*, I've been doing a lot of thinking...."

Clau has been housebound ever since she ruined the school talent show a few weeks ago. When she saw the pink boas, she couldn't help herself, throwing one over her shoulders as she shimmied under the spotlight. Of course, all everyone else saw was the boa, seemingly possessed by a ghost. They had the ghost part right.

My godmother, Soona, who is also our second cousin, our school librarian, and the oldest person in our town (even though she barely looks thirty) had to spike the punch with a fast acting potion to erase the event from everyone's memories. Everyone except Abuela's. She's been making Clau do chores, which takes a lot of energy for a ghost. But not enough energy for Clau to stop scheming completely.

I raise an eyebrow, waiting for her big reveal. "You've been thinking...?"

"Yes." Clau wriggles her eyebrows in response. "I've been thinking...about our Halloween costumes!"

Carlitos and I exchange a look.

Clau is constantly trying to pretend like she's one of the living. It's why she hasn't crossed over to the other side yet (and also why she's always ruining talent shows and getting into similar kinds of trouble). I know she can feel its pull, trying to sing her over the threshold. But her heart sings a different song. Most young ghosts have a hard time making the transition. Clau downright refuses.

"What do you guys think of"—she waves her hands around, trying to paint a picture—"discotheque vampires." She grins. "We'll wear giant seventies Afros and platform shoes with glitter fangs and—"

Carlitos wrinkles his nose.

"What's wrong?" Clau says.

When Clau goes off the rails with her whole pretending to be living schtick, neither one of us ever has the heart to tell her that she's wrong or ridiculous or dead. Even though she is, which means that she won't be wearing a costume or going trick-or-treating or gorging on candy all night.

She'll be following us around, the sadness slowly creeping in with every person who ignores her and every piece of candy that falls right through her hands.

Then she'll spend the next couple of days crying to herself in the attic until Abuela talks her out of her despair. When she hears about the fall dance or the Thanksgiving Day parade, the cycle will start all over, and Clau will be reminded again that she doesn't belong. But she still won't cross over.

When no one says anything, Clau just shrugs. "Well, I thought it was a good idea."

"It's a great idea," Carlitos finally says.

"Yeah," I add, "maybe we can do some more brainstorming about it tonight."

Clau knows we're lying, but she's as good at pretending that we're fooled by her little game of make-believe as we are at pretending that it isn't a game at all.

"Not tonight." Mami appears from the kitchen, hands stained red from the *Salvia elegans* she's been crushing up and adding to her beeswax. She smells like pineapple. "You're helping me make deliveries, remember?" She starts stacking an old milk crate with the finished veladoras, glass clinking.

At the supermarket the tall prayer candles are usually painted with the unusually pale face of Christ or the Virgin Mary floating over a bed of roses. The vendedoras at la pulga like to get all fancy with it and bedazzle them with jewels. But no matter how many rhinestones they glue to Jesus's crown of thorns, their candles still don't answer prayers quite like Mami's can.

Pineapple sage for healing, honeysuckle for joy, marigolds for getting through grief, chocolate cosmos for beauty, poppies for a better night's sleep, yucca for protection, and morning glories for healing a broken heart.

Everything that grows has a purpose. And a price.

"Now, no more IOUs. These are ten bucks each, and

Señor Jimenez owes us double for the veladora we delivered last week." Mami hands me the milk crate and the weight sinks it straight down to the floor.

I groan. "Help me with this, will you?"

"You can't send us back out there," Carlitos says. "Not with Abby still on patrol."

Mami sighs. "Abby…pobrecita."

"Poor girl?" Carlitos snaps. "Poor us! She's evil!"

"She's lonely," Mami corrects him.

I cross my arms. "Well, then she shouldn't have turned on her only friends."

"Well, maybe those friends should remember what changed her in the first place." Mami shakes her head, scrubbing some dry wax from the kitchen counter. "It was only six months ago that Abby lost her mom. I can't imagine what it must be like for that family, and for her especially."

I know what Mami means. Abby's brothers are rotten and were always tormenting her. Well, all of them except her twin brother, Aiden, because he's actually decent and kind and has nice dimples and an even nicer smile…but that's besides the point. After Abby's mom died, things got even worse, which is why she slept over so often right after it happened. She said she felt safe here and it was the only time I saw her smile.

Mami tosses her hair back into a ponytail, igniting the scent of her lavender shampoo.

Another one of her home remedies that always makes her smell like safety. Like home. I think about what it would be like if something happened to her. If I could never eat her food again, hug her again, smell her again. Maybe Abby can't help but be a monster. I'd probably become one too.

"I'm sorry, but Abby's mom passing away isn't what made her a pathological liar. She was like that before," Carlitos says. "And now she's lying about Omega being some sort of cat killer."

Mami crosses her arms, concerned. "I heard the Villarreals' cat went missing."

"And Doña Maria's," Carlitos adds.

"Apparently, there are others and Abby thinks I'm the one responsible."

"My little pepita?" Abuela makes her way over and squeezes my cheeks. "She couldn't hurt a fly."

Mami raises an eyebrow. "I wouldn't call her a cat killer, but innocent she is not." She looks toward the hallway leading to my bedroom. My very *messy* bedroom. "How many times have I told you to clean your room this week? You know company's coming."

"Yeah, but we don't know who or when."

Abuelo had another one of his prophetic dreams—this time about a mysterious visitor.

"It doesn't matter. They're coming." She pushes the milk

crate toward me again; Carlitos and I each take one of the handles. "And you're going. Remember, no IOUs." She kisses me on the cheek. "Gracias."

Abuela walks us out. When she opens the door, the sky is a few shades darker.

Storm clouds.

"They'll pass," I say, because they always do. It's one of the perks of living in a desert Bermuda Triangle. We always see the storm coming, but it never cracks over our plains.

But Abuela isn't looking at them like something that'll pass. It's just a flicker, just for half a second, but suddenly she looks afraid. I wonder if it has something to do with the visitor Abuelo's been dreaming about. Or maybe there really is a cat killer on the loose.

A shiver races down my spine, but when I turn, it isn't Clau.

"Abuela…?" Carlitos says.

She pushes us down the steps, still glancing up at the sky. "You two better hurry. No messin' around. I want you back here in an hour. ¿Entienden?"

"Sí, 'buela," Carlitos says. "We'll hurry."

We carry the milk crate toward the road, the breeze luke-warm and sliding over me like a stranger. The wind picks up a bit, and Carlitos and I exchange a look. Behind us, Abuela makes the sign of the cross.

CHAPTER 2

CLAU SHAKES HER HEAD. "IT'S HER TELENOVELAS. This week Esmeralda got into a car accident during a rainstorm and lost her memory."

"How many times has that woman lost her memory?"

"At least four." Carlitos snaps, "If they don't come up with another plot device, I'm going to start hiding the remote!"

"Right. Because Abuela won't be able to use her empathic abilities to sense its precise location just by looking at you."

"In case you haven't noticed, my own empathic abilities are almost fifty-fifty these days. My magic's getting stronger." He smiles to himself.

There's a twinge in my chest. "Well, at least that makes one of us."

"Maybe it just takes longer for mixed people," Carlitos offers. "Like the magic's not all there yet."

I always hate it when the magic side of my family says things like that. Like it's Papi's fault that my magic doesn't work. Because he's human and "ordinary," even though he's the most special person I know. I especially hate it when they blame him because I know the truth. Deep down in my gut I can *feel* it. My magic isn't broken because of him. It's broken because of me. There's something *wrong* with *me*.

As Clau floats to the end of the next gravel driveway, Carlitos and I follow behind, huffing and puffing until we reach Señor Jimenez's house.

"Speaking of not being all there...," Carlitos says.

"Be nice," I say. "Señor Jimenez isn't *that* old."

"Old enough to think handing out cabbage on Halloween isn't the most horrible thing a person could possibly do to a child."

"So just give them to Pega. Rabbits eat anything, don't they?"

Carlitos rolls his eyes. "Thank God your mom never let you get a pet."

I smirk, patting him on the top of the head. "You're my pet."

Clau crosses her arms. "Then what does that make me?"

"Fine," I groan, "you're both my pets."

"Woof, woof!" Clau barks in amusement.

"Now, go let Señor Jimenez know we're here."

"Will do." Clau gets fuzzy at the seams again, making herself less solid so she can fly through the wind chimes lining the porch.

As we approach, the front steps bend like jagged teeth, the porch columns creating an arched smile against the front of the house. The windows sink inward, matching the narrow set of Señor Jimenez's eyes, every inch of the house twisting to mimic his wrinkled face.

To a normal person, it's just a house. Just a plain front door and dusty windows. But an empath sees something different. Because a home *is* something different, holding the shape of the people inside, those heartbeats giving it life too.

It's the same reason why some people look like their dogs. When you exchange energy with something, it becomes a part of you and vice versa. That's why Mami says you shouldn't just put out good energy but surround yourself with it too.

Señor Jimenez may be old and his house may be the worst to stop at on Halloween, but he is also kind. It radiates from every inch of this place, the wind chimes mingled with his laugh as he opens the front door, a big smile on his face.

"¿Para mí?" he asks, pointing to the milk crate.

I take out the bright red veladora, pocks of orange poppy petals suspended in the wax.

He hands me two ten-dollar bills. "Tell your mother last week's worked like a charm." He takes the candle, back cracking as he stands up straight. "I've almost fixed this aching back."

"Gracias, señor."

The screen door creaks closed as he waves over his shoulder. The wind chimes are still laughing as we walk to the next house.

We drop off bitter melon and sunflowers for Mrs. Murillo's migraines, hopbush for Señor Rivas's gout, chigüisa for Señora Salas's asthma, and pongolote and pepper leaf for Mr. Huerta's unknown medical condition, which despite being invisible to the naked eye, seems to be incredibly urgent.

"Tell your mom she's a lifesaver," he says before rushing inside and slamming the door.

As we approach the next row of homes, all the kindness and gratitude still clinging to us from the last few deliveries slowly begins to vanish. Mrs. Statham, former president of the neighborhood watch group, practices her *watching* skills on us through her kitchen window. The glass tints and fills with spiderweb cracks to match her glare.

As long as I can remember, no one's dared to run against her. Until this year, when Abby's dad threw his hat in the ring and actually won. Now Mr. Montgomery and his buddies patrol the streets in his beat-up pickup truck looking for overgrown lawns and people playing their music too loud.

At the next house over, Mr. Fisher waters his roses. To him, they're probably blooming and vibrant. To me, they're black just like his stare. He looks from las velas back to our faces. Then he spits, the white mess almost landing on Carlitos's shoes.

Carlitos scowls at him. "I don't care what Soona says. Someday I'm going to learn how to cast a curse."

"Only an idiot would cast a curse," I say. "All it does is bind you to that person forever. You want to be spiritually handcuffed to Mr. Fisher for all eternity?"

"No." Carlitos groans. "I just want to sew his lips together so he can never spit at us again."

"I would make him water his roses under the hot sun for the rest of his life." Clau purses her lips, thinking. "Then I would make those roses grow thorns and s—"

"Okay," I say, "we got it."

Carlitos stops walking, eyeing Clau.

I shake my head. "Besides, it still wouldn't change the fact that he *wants* to spit at us."

"We could change that too!" Carlitos says.

"You mean if Abuela would let us use magic on the very people who are afraid of it the most?"

"That's exactly who we *should* be using our magic on. How else are we going to get rid of all the evil in the world?"

"And what do you think happens to all that evil? It doesn't suddenly disappear."

"Well then, what happens to it?"

I shrug, annoyed. "I don't know. But obviously something bad or else this town wouldn't be split in two. Abuela and Soona would have put it back together already."

"So you don't think evil can be destroyed?"

"It's energy," I say. "So no."

"Yeah." Clau rolls her eyes. "Haven't you taken physics? It's like the first law or something."

Carlitos wrinkles his nose. "I'm in sixth grade."

He kicks at a rock in the road and it tumbles end over end before landing in the middle of the town square, which should really be called the town oval. Or maybe the town blob?

There's a fountain in the center with no running water, and the old city hall building is bookended by a bingo hall and a dance hall on one side, and on the other, a dining hall and a meeting hall that leads to the post office.

I've seen old photos of this place lit up by twinkle lights while kids splashed their bare feet at the fountain's edge. They used to have weddings here and a band would play in the alcove, the acoustics carrying the sound far into the desert. Or, at least, that's what Abuela says. But then people started to leave, moving to bigger cities, and every time they did, they took a bit of the magic with them.

Then a stranger bought the town and started carving it into pieces, looking for oil. When they found some, people started coming looking for jobs. And that's how Noche Buena was cracked in two. First the earth was split and then the town.

From this spot, I can see how the two versions of Noche Buena sit like mirror images. The past and the present in a staring contest that's been going on so long, neither side can even produce tears, everything dried up and near dead.

But if I close my eyes I can still *feel* the magic. I can still feel the love that used to give it life. I can still feel where our family is rooted to this spot under this endless sky that will never be torn in two.

"Oh no," Carlitos hisses, "it's Mrs. Villarreal."

Down the street, Mrs. Villarreal is taping something to a lamppost. She presses her hand to the paper, smoothing out the edges before wiping her eyes.

"Ugh," Carlitos groans, "and she's crying too."

"Maybe because her cat just went missing," I snap.

"So? I'm sure it'll turn up eventually. Let's just take the long way."

He takes a step in the opposite direction and I snatch him

by the shirt, yanking him back. "We don't have time to take the long way. Abuela told us to hurry, remember?" I let go. "I'm surprised your Spidey-senses aren't tingling too."

"Oh, they're tingling and they're telling me that Mrs. Villarreal should be avoided at all costs."

"Come on." This time Clau nudges him forward with a cold touch that makes him jump. "It's not like she's going to use you as a human Kleenex."

"Yeah, just be nice."

He relents. "I'm always nice."

When Mrs. Villarreal spots us, her face scrunches up like she'd been saving her tears, waiting for an audience. Her lip quivers as she turns back to the missing poster, her

cat, Oscar, sitting up tall and staring into the camera, a white stripe down the center of his black belly.

She pets the photo lovingly. "Oscar never liked being the center of attention. He preferred the spotlight to be on me." She meets my eyes. "But it seems now I have no choice. I have to get the word out that he's missing."

Carlitos coughs into his hand. "Creepy."

Mrs. Villarreal blinks. "What's that, dear?"

"Nothing," I butt in. "He's just thirsty."

"Yeah," Carlitos says, "we've been walking around in this heat making deliveries for nearly an hour."

Mrs. Villarreal nods, closing her eyes slowly. "I walked for hours when Oscar first went missing." She opens them wide, tears welling up again. "I visited all his favorite haunts. The dumpster behind the Allsup's. The dumpster behind the church. The dumpster behind the school cafeteria."

Carlitos wrinkles his nose. "He sure liked dumpsters, huh?"

I elbow Carlitos in the side.

"It was like he just...vanished."

"Has he run off before?"

"Never for this long." She chokes back more tears. "He never would have left me...."

Carlitos narrows his eyes. "We're still talking about the cat, right?"

I elbow him again, the spot tender this time.

"Ow!"

Mrs. Villarreal sniffles. "Come again?"

"Uh, he said...ow...how can we help you?"

She exhales. "Oh, thank goodness." Then she slams a stack of missing posters into my chest. "Put these up anywhere you can find a flat surface." She lowers her voice. "I have a feeling someone around here knows more than they're telling."

"Why do you say that?" I ask.

She cuts her eyes to the empty road, then back to us. "This." She pulls a sparkly pink collar from her purse. "Oscar was practically human, but he certainly didn't have thumbs. Someone took his collar off and tried to hide it in the bushes."

Carlitos raises an eyebrow. "So you think he was kidnapped?"

"I think you mean catnapped," Clau corrects him.

"Of course he was!" Mrs. Villarreal's lip quivers again. "But I'm going to find out who took him. I'm going to find out if it's the last thing I do!"

I swallow, wondering if she's heard the rumor Abby's been spreading about me. Especially if Mr. Montgomery's been spreading it too. Maybe it just hasn't gotten around to her yet. Maybe this is my chance to prove it's not true before it does.

I hold up the stack, smiling. "And we'll do whatever we can to help. Starting with hanging these flyers."

"Thank you, dear." She cups my face before walking to the end of the street.

"Great," Carlitos says. "Now it'll be dark by the time we get home."

I hand him half the stack. "We'll make the last delivery and put some of these up on the way. It'll be fine."

"And it's good karma," Clau adds.

"What do you need good karma for?" Carlitos snaps, only because he's irritated. And because Clau's dead. Actually, it's sort of a fair question.

"None of your business," Clau snaps back.

On our way to the last house, we pass by Oscar's beloved Allsup's. Carlitos slips around the back and tosses his stack of flyers in the dumpster.

I kick the metal siding and he jumps. "What do you think you're doing?"

He shrugs. "She said he loves dumpsters. Maybe he'll see the posters and decide to go home."

"Or"—Clau points—"maybe he can't."

Back in the direction we came from, Mrs. Villarreal stands on her tiptoes, taping a flyer to the back of a bread truck. Between her legs, Oscar winds back and forth like he's made of fog.

"Well, that's not good," Carlitos says.

When someone dies, they're no longer made up of flesh and bone but of that last breath of life. That's why some people claim to feel the brush of a hand at a funeral or a soft kiss on the cheek when visiting a loved one's grave. Ghosts are literal whispers from the past. Like the smudged reflection in a dusty mirror. A shadow behind a cloud of smoke.

Only empaths can see them fully and that's only if they *want* to be seen. That's why Clau looks almost human. Because she trusts us.

But Oscar's just a shadow, his edges wispy like a low-hanging cloud. And his soul...it doesn't burn white like it should. It doesn't burn at all.

"Do you think we should tell her?" Clau asks.

Carlitos grins obnoxiously. "Uh, hi again, Mrs. Villarreal. Remember when you were telling us that Oscar adored you and never would have run away. Well, it turns out you were right because his ghost is currently licking up your toe jam."

Clau rolls her eyes. "You're so dramatic."

"Takes one to know one."

"Guys..."

They're still arguing.

"Guys!"

They both turn to look at me.

"What if...?" I swallow sand, feeling another shiver like when we first left the house. "What if Abby was right?"

"You think you've been unconsciously moonlighting as a catnapper? Stop letting her get in your head, Omega."

"Not me. But...*someone*..."

Carlitos crosses his arms. "Someone..."

Clau slides her cold body between us. "Or *something*."

We all exchange a look just as the sky darkens another shade.

"It feels heavy," Carlitos says.

And dangerous, I want to add, but my throat's dried shut.

Something jostles inside the dumpster, the metal lid slamming down hard, and then all three of us let out a scream, Carlitos clutching my arm while Clau slips back into her more invisible skin.

We're still shaking when the lid pops back up, just a few inches, a pair of yellow eyes peering out. They blink and then we hear the softest, "Meow."

I clutch my chest, heart racing. "It's okay. It was just a cat."

It slides out like a fish, landing on all fours. Pale as moonlight. Another shadow.

Another ghost.

Clau crouches, making herself small. She holds out a hand to the cat, and as it sniffs at her, she checks the collar. "KitKat." She flips over the tag. "Belongs to Doña Maria."

My heart starts racing again.

"At least this one died with its collar," Carlitos says. "M-maybe that means it wasn't kidnapped."

"Unless," Clau says as she scratches behind the cat's ears, "the person took it off *after* they murdered him."

I freeze at the word and something tells me Clau's not just

being her overly morbid overdramatic self. *Something* tells me that... *something's* wrong.

"Well..." Carlitos nods to the stack of flyers I'm still holding. "I guess you won't be needing those anymore."

"Yeah." I drop them in the dumpster next to the others before slowly backing away. "I guess not."

Carlitos backs up too. "Should we run?"

I nod. "We should run."

We approach the final house to deliver the last of Mami's veladoras, the exterior shaded the color of the sky, the clouds now churning almost green. Like something sick. I look down at the last candle, wondering if Señora Avila is just as sick. If that's why the windows are sunken in and almost black, the roof jutting up at odd angles like the house is covered in thorns.

My knees wobble as we approach, the same energy that's rotted the house from the inside out reaching for me with a cold grip.

"Okay," Carlitos breathes. "My Spidey-senses are definitely tingling now."

"Yeah," I agree. "Whatever Señora Avila needs this veladora for, I just hope Mami made it strong enough."

"Even without empathic abilities something about this house is definitely giving me the heebie-jeebies." Clau hangs back, shivering too, even though she's practically made of ice.

"Lighting one of those stupid candles is what started all of this in the first place."

I snap to one of the birdbaths in Señora Avila's front yard. "Excuse me? What did you say?"

Suddenly, every birdbath in the yard starts talking at once, spitting up algae water all over my shoes.

"If it rains, it'll definitely come back."

"And then it'll drink."

"What if it lands on me this time? What if it cracks me in half?"

"What are they talking about?" Carlitos asks.

"I don't know, but they sound afraid."

Like the trees.

"I think the Morales girl is talking about us to the pudgy one...."

"The name's Carlitos," he shoots back. "And I'm not pudgy. It's called big-boned."

"It was you...." The tallest fountain in the yard speaks up. The vines around it twist, jabbing in my direction like a pointed finger. "It was you and your strange family that summoned it, didn't you?"

"Summoned what?" I ask.

They all start talking in unison again. "The devil…"

"The biggest vulture you've ever seen."

"It wasn't a bird. It was a storm cloud!"

"A tornado!"

The fancy tall fountain says, "Enough! There's only one of us who actually got a good look at it." The vines slither out again, pointing to cracked cement blocks strewn across the far end of the yard.

"It was a monster," the broken pieces murmur.

Clau peers over my shoulder, the cold wafting from her raking down my back. "What *kind* of monster?"

It whines, remembering something terrible.

"Can you tell me exactly what you saw last night?" I ask. "Every detail."

"The storm clouds rolled in fast. It rode in with them before landing in the yard. I thought the clouds themselves had grown legs. But out of the mist, there were so many sharp points. Wings like razor blades. A beak as thick and broad as a sword. And then behind it…a row of teeth so sharp they glistened in the blackness."

Carlitos grimaces. "What kind of a bird has a beak *and* sharp teeth?"

"It wasn't a bird. It was an animal, yes. But also human. Darkness and light all mixed up and wrong…wrong… wrong."

"Why did it come?" I ask.

"It came...because it was called. But for what, I'm not sure. For a long time it just watched. Waiting. Staring into the night as if there was something out there...staring back. Then it spread its wings, black and glistening. When it took off, it sent out a gust of wind that knocked me over, filling me with cracks."

"Omega? Carlitos?" Señora Avila steps out onto the front porch. She comes down when she sees the broken fountain. "Ay Dios. Wind must have knocked it over last night."

Carlitos nudges me. "I didn't hear any wind last night."

"Because there wasn't any," Clau hisses. And she would know since ghosts don't exactly sleep.

"I'm sorry, señora."

She waves a hand. "It's nothing." She reaches for the candle I'm holding. "But you two are probably in a hurry. No need to worry about this mess." She shoos us away. "No need to worry."

"Let us know if you and Señor Avila need anything else."

She stiffens, face darkened for a moment. Then she shakes her head. "We will. We will." She hands me a ten-dollar bill, trembling hands almost dropping the cash. "Gracias, mija."

I scoop it up and it stings. Like the bill is on fire, angry and burning...with *hate*. "Gracias, señora."

Then she rushes inside before slamming the door. It ignites a gust of wind that pushes us back.

"Well, *someone's* in a bad mood." Carlitos wipes a bead of cold sweat from his brow.

I feel it too as I stuff the bill into my pocket, dizzy and almost feverish.

But as we turn to head down the porch steps, something dark falls from the rafters. It glides from side to side, catching the light before finally landing at my feet.

The single feather is as long as my forearm, the quill so thick it looks more like bone. The barbs are thick too, stuck together with something like mud. The light strikes it, catching hints of red and purple. It's unlike any feather I've ever seen before.

As I reach for it, I smell rain. Like heavy storm clouds ready to burst. And the feeling is electric. Like I'm standing in the middle of the desert, watching those clouds roll in, watching the lightning strikes inch closer.

Suddenly the feather feels heavy in my hand, like I'm holding some sort a weapon, like I'm sinking into a bad dream. Chalk fills the back of my throat, a stomach-turning drowsiness trying to drag me to the floor.

But beneath all that, there's something sharp. A feeling I can just barely name. *Grief? Longing?* So tight around my lungs that I feel like I'm about to take my last breath.

And then beneath the longing is something else. Something wild. Like an animal on the hunt.

I let go of the feather before the feeling takes hold, quickly reaching for the moonstone in my pocket. I squeeze it and count back from ten.

"What is it?" Clau asks, hovering over it to get a closer look.

"I don't know." I shake my head. "But…I think it's… *hungry.*"

Carlitos picks it up next, noticing the strangeness too. "Well," he says, holding it out like something dead, "I guess now we know what's been stealing people's cats."

CHAPTER 3

FACES CROWD IN THE WINDOW WHEN WE get home. Through the glass I see Tío Juan, Carlitos's dad, sitting on the couch while Carlitos's little brother, Chale, crawls all over him. Tía Tita is crouched next to Abuela, a safety pin in her teeth as she folds up the hem of Abuela's dress.

Abuelo's still in his favorite chair, snoring, while Mami's in the kitchen feeding Papi something from a spoon. He grins, savoring it, before kissing her on the cheek.

I imagine what Mr. Fisher or Mrs. Statham might see if they were staring through our kitchen window. A family that takes up space. Too big and too loud.

But I don't care what they *think* they see. I don't care what they think at all.

I look at my strange, magical family, at our skin the color

of the land, at our language and rituals and touchstones to the past, and I see *love*. Big and loud and taking up every inch of space. Love like the light from a thousand of Mami's veladoras. Love like butter folded into a warm tortilla. Love like the smell of onions and poblano peppers cooking on the stove.

Love that wraps you up and holds on tight, never letting go.

Finally, the smell of Mami's food is just too strong and it yanks us up the steps, Carlitos and I taking them two at a time as my mouth begins to water.

Just as we crash through the screen door, Abuelo heaves himself out of his chair and everyone watches and waits. For another prophecy. For our mysterious visitor to arrive.

"Papá?" Mami says.

We all hold our breath.

But instead of heading for the door, he makes his way over to one of the pots whistling on the stove. He lifts the lid just before the water boils over. He gives my mother a wink before lifting a hand at Carlitos, Clau, and me. Then he makes his way back to his favorite chair and dozes off again.

Out of all of us, Abuelo's empathic abilities are definitely the strangest. Once, one of Mami's veladoras tipped over and set one of the curtains on fire, and Abuelo leapt from his slumber to stomp it out. Another time I escaped my high chair and was about to nose-dive straight into the hardwood when suddenly he snatched me up by the pant loop.

Even the story of Abuela and Abuelo falling in love is told through a series of mishaps that he magically fixed. According to Abuela, it was the summer of her fifteenth birthday, and while at a dance with friends, she was walking past the refreshments table when she slipped in a puddle of spilled punch, and just before she hit the ground, Abuelo miraculously appeared and scooped her up.

He then proceeded to twirl her across the dance floor all night, and when it started to rain on their long walk home, he popped open an umbrella just in time to save her curls from being drenched.

It didn't take long for Abuela to realize that Abuelo was special. He knew she was from the moment he saw her. And when their marriage bonded the two families, every magical corner of Noche Buena came out to celebrate.

Mami takes the empty crate from me and asks, "How did it go with the deliveries?"

I count out the bills into her open hand.

"Did you two rob a bank?" Papi kisses me hard on the cheek, his scruff scratching my face. He musses Carlitos's hair. "What were you? The getaway driver?"

"They didn't rob a bank, Tomás." Mami slaps his shoulder with the fanned bills. "These are satisfied customers."

I hand Mami a slip of paper. "Some people placed more orders while we were out."

She looks to my father. "See?"

"Yo lo veo, mi amor. You're the best velera in all of Noche Buena."

"After me," Abuela cuts in.

Papi kisses her on the cheek too. "Of course. Por supuesto."

"Ah-huh." Mami rolls her eyes as she carries plates and silverware to the kitchen table. "Vamos, everyone. Está lista. Dinner's ready."

We circle around the table, Papi at one end, Abuelo, still half-asleep, at the other.

Everyone joins hands, Mami flashing me a look when I hesitate. I'm always the last link in the chain because blocking out their emotions is even harder than blocking out the emotions of strangers, which I also can't do.

I know as soon as I reach for the hands next to me, I'll be able to feel what they're feeling. Like a strong tide rolling in before crashing over me. Sometimes it's powerful enough to knock me off my feet. A few times I've woken up in bed, surrounded by lit candles, their tiny flames crackling as Abuela asked the spirits to keep me safe.

"It's just like flipping off a light switch," Carlitos whispers next to me.

Lightning doesn't have a switch, I want to snap back. Instead, I brace myself for the flood and then I close the chain.

As Abuela blesses the food, the prayer seeps into my skin and I feel Tía Tita's recent nightmares like a sour stomach. I feel Papi's worries about money like a clenched fist around my insides. I feel the warmth of Mami's gratitude for all the customers we made happy today. But overpowering them all is Carlitos.

Carlitos's hands are always sweaty, but right now they're even more sopping wet. I open one eye and realize he's staring out the window, at the clouds that are still too low. I squeeze his hand and he closes his eyes before anyone else sees. But I can still feel his fear like little shocks of electricity in the tips of my fingers.

"Amén," everyone says in unison, just before the tingling can climb any higher.

"Eat your frijoles, Omega." Abuela motions with her fork and I know there's magic in them.

A medicine she and Mami have been perfecting since my empathic abilities first showed up.

Those first few months, people's emotions used to overwhelm me and I got sick a lot. Sometimes they still do. But things got better after Mami and Abuela came up with a special remedy that helps me get the bad stuff out. Like sucking the poison from an opened wound except my body is the wound and feelings are the poison.

It's tricky, though. If they don't get the balance just right, the potion may not work or it may work too well, draining me of my emotions too. It's only happened once, but I was basically a walking zombie who only saw the world in shades of gray. I couldn't laugh or love or hate. I was just numb, which is the worst thing a person can be.

I scarf down my food until I don't feel so twisted up, the feather and the heaviness it left behind finally fading.

"Why aren't you eating?" Abuela asks Carlitos after my plate is almost clean, and I wonder if she can sense what I can—that Carlitos is afraid.

Usually, we'd talk about things like this at dinner and each of the adults would take turns telling us why we don't need to worry. For some reason, Carlitos isn't saying a word. Maybe I shouldn't either. Maybe what's going on inside Señora Avila's house is none of our business.

Who knows if it's actually a giant bird that's been taking people's cats? Maybe that feather has been there for years.

But it was the size of your arm, Omega.

"Sorry," Carlitos breaks the silence, "I was thinking about some homework that's due tomorrow."

I give him a soft kick under the table. *Why are you lying?*

He ignores me, taking a big bite of his asado de puerco.

"Why do they give you so much homework at that school?" Abuela asks. "Life's not in those books. It's out here. With your family."

Tío Juan gets up from the table, taking a few of the empty plates. "If he wants to get out of this small town, then he's going to have to do his homework."

"Get out and go where?" Abuela says. "Carlitos doesn't want to leave his family."

"He's twelve," Abuelo cuts in, his voice deep and gruff. Which is why he only uses it when it's important. "You've got him for six more years. Then the boy can do whatever he wants." He winks at Carlitos and it's full of knowing.

I wonder what prophetic dreams he's had about Carlitos's future. Maybe Carlitos will go to a big fancy college somewhere and become a doctor. He's always been great at science. Maybe he'll be an astronaut or do something with computers.

Either way, Carlitos has the kind of brain that makes people rich. I know that's what Tío Juan is banking on. He doesn't just go on and on about Carlitos getting out of Noche Buena because he wants him to have a better life. He goes on and on about it because he wants to get out of Noche Buena too.

Abuelo looks to me, gives another wink, and I wonder

what prophetic dreams he's had about me. About *my* future. I wish he'd tell me because I have no idea what I want to do when I get older and sometimes I lie awake at night wondering if I'll ever know.

After dinner, Carlitos and I stand at the kitchen sink, washing dishes while the adults talk on the porch.

The clouds outside haven't broken yet, Carlitos is still watching them.

"Are you going to tell me what's wrong?" I ask.

"Huh?" Carlitos isn't even listening.

"I said, what's wrong?"

"Yeah, you're acting weird." Clau floats above the kitchen counter like she's sitting in a chair, legs swinging back and forth.

Carlitos sets the last dish down to dry on the rack. "I just have a bad feeling."

There's a pinch deep at the base of my gut. "Yeah, something's definitely off."

"Maybe that giant feather was cursed or something." Clau raises an eyebrow. "Or maybe Señora Avila gave you ojo." She ruffles Carlitos's hair with her icy fingers.

"Hey, stop that!" He swats at her, blushing.

"I'm just checking you for bald spots."

I roll my eyes. "Señora Avila didn't give you mal de ojo."

"Well"—he glances from the window to the pantry—"there's one way we can know for sure."

Carlitos's rituals aren't foolproof, but if there was ever a time when we needed a sign from the spirit world, this would probably be it.

I sigh, "Okay," and push him toward the pantry. "But make it quick."

He slips inside, rummaging through last year's Halloween candy. Mami only ever lets us eat some of what we collect. Then she stores the rest to give out the following year. This way my parents never have to spend money on candy and the kids never catch on. At the end of the night when they're digging through their spoils and sorting them into good, bad, and downright insulting, they have no way of knowing exactly where the stale candy came from.

Carlitos comes out with a shiny orange Reese's Peanut Butter Cup. When he was first starting to learn how  to control his abilities, he used something called the Reese's test to channel outside energy—see if anything was off. If he peels back the brown wrapper and the candy comes out clean, all is right with the world. If he peels back the wrapper and some of the chocolate has stuck to it, then there's definitely something wrong.

"Stop squeezing it so hard," I say. "It's going to melt and mess with the results."

He takes a deep breath. "Okay, here we go." Then he peels back the wrapper.

At first it's clean, edges coming out smooth.

"Gentle. Gentle…," Clau whispers.

"I know what I'm doing," he says.

All the edges are free. Now it's time for the bottom of the peanut butter cup.

The three of us stare, unblinking.

There's a drop of sweat on Carlitos's forehead.

"Now," I say, and he pulls the rest of the wrapper off.

A giant chunk of chocolate comes with it.

Carlitos has the peanut butter cup in one hand, melting against his sweaty palm, and the chocolate-stained wrapper in the other. We stare at it.

"Wait a second." He gulps. "Doesn't that look like…?"

I squint. "Like what?"

Clau squeezes between us and breathes, "An owl."

Carlitos holds out the wrapper like something rotten.

I take a step back too. Because Clau's right. Within the melted chocolate is a small rectangular head, two pointed ears, and two round eyes.

"I remember something...." Clau pinches her eyes shut. "Pavita Mortera. That's what they call it in Venezuela. They're bad luck."

The hairs on my arms stand up. "There was a white barn owl that used to sit in one of the trees out back. When Abuela would see it there, she'd make me stay inside, both of us watching it from the window."

"I remember," Carlitos says. "What did she used to call it?"

I shake my head. "I'm not sure."

Clau makes a face, eyes wide. "Um, I think you guys should follow me."

Carlitos and I exchange a look before following her upstairs. Clau leads us to the attic. I push the door open and dust swirls in the moonlight spilling between the cracks in the roof. Carlitos sneezes, bumping into boxes while Clau carefully floats to the far corner of the room.

Carlitos and I used to dare each other to stay up here alone. Whoever lasted the longest got to take the other person's Creamsicle during our afternoon snack. We'd take turns holding the door closed, trapping the other person inside until they screamed or cried. Sometimes when it was my turn, I would get really quiet, waiting for Carlitos to start worrying and peek inside. Then I'd pop him in the nose and declare victory.

But then Carlitos got a PlayStation and we started to realize how hot it was up here without any air-conditioning and video games were just more fun. I asked Clau once why she likes to hang out up here and she seemed a little sensitive about it. It must just be a ghost thing.

Carlitos shivers. "You two aren't conspiring to lock me in here, are you?"

Clau rolls her eyes. "If we were, we wouldn't tell you."

"Come on," I say, "this place doesn't still give you the creeps, does it?"

It should, considering there is now an *actual* ghost up here. But somehow Clau only makes the place less scary. Until I see what's in the box next to her.

She points. "Look familiar?"

Carlitos and I huddle around the box. It's full of old books, like the kinds my abuelos probably read to Mami and Tía Tita when they were kids. Covers faded, spines cracked, pages torn.

Clau takes a deep breath and then blows a stream of ice-cold air across the cover of the book on top of the stack. The dust parts, making Carlitos sneeze again. And there, faded from the brush of fingertips, is the black outline of an owl. I reach for the book, the pages falling open and making a garbled sound. I drop it, the three of us jumping back.

Carlitos pants. "Is that thing possessed?"

Clau raises a hand, fingers flexed over the book. There's a static sound and that's when I notice the small speaker stuck to the front flap. She taps into the battery the same way she does the TV remote when we're too lazy to reach for it to change the channel. (Even her poltergeist skills are sharpening faster than my powers.) Then, on Clau's command, the music begins to play, tinkling bells accompanying the voices of children singing.

"La Lechuza, La Lechuza, dice shh. Dice shh. Estamos en silencio, como La Lechuza, que dice shh. Dice shh."

Clau lets go, the song stopping abruptly.

My insides go cold.

Carlitos takes a small step behind me, as if the book might reach out and grab him. "My mom used to sing that song before bed. She said if I didn't be quiet and go to sleep, La Lechuza would make me."

"Abuela used to sing it to me too. But it's just an old nursery rhyme. La Lechuza isn't real." I turn to Carlitos, then Clau. "Is she?"

CHAPTER 4

"Carlitos?" Tía Tita calls from the bottom of the stairs. "¿Dónde estás?"

"Coming, Mom."

"Vamos. Get your backpack."

"I…" He fumbles for words. "I'll see you tomorrow at school?"

Clau looks between us. "If you two survive the night…" Then she disappears.

"I'm getting a little sick of her morbid sense of humor," Carlitos says.

I cross my arms. "Same."

"Carlitos!" Tía Tita's halfway up the stairs. He hesitates.

"Don't worry." I push him toward the door. "Like I said, it's just an old nursery rhyme."

And yet, as soon as he disappears down the stairs, I find myself turning back to the book, my hands reaching for it. Unsure...

"Omega, that means you too," Abuela calls. "This kitchen isn't going to clean itself."

The song is still playing in my head as I finish cleaning the kitchen. As I go to toss some onion skin in the trash, I'm stopped by the sight of the wrapper where it sits at the top of the pile. I stare at it, trying to convince myself that the chocolate isn't shaped like an owl. That it isn't an omen. But the longer I stare, the more energy starts to waft from it like a bad smell.

I slam the lid closed.

"You all right, mija?" Mami takes the towel I used to wipe down the counter. "You and Carlitos were a little quiet at dinner."

I know Carlitos lied earlier when Abuela asked him the same question, but families aren't supposed to keep secrets from one another. It's why Carlitos and I know the real reason people like the Fishers and the Stathams don't want us around and why Soona and my other godmother Luisa get stares when they hold hands in public and why people in pain can be so cruel.

Every time the truth was hard, every time the truth was

scary, they told us anyway. So that we would see the world the way our empathic abilities allow us to see every single thing and person in it. Whole. *Honest.*

So even if I wanted to keep a secret from Mami, I don't think I actually could. But I don't.

Because I'm scared. Because I want someone to tell me that La Lechuza isn't real and that everything is going to be okay.

"Díme, Mega." She nudges me with her hip. "What's wrong?"

"Is La Lechuza just a story?" I ask.

Mami quirks her head, her eyes widening in surprise, and with our hips still touching, I can sense that it's not the good kind. She's not just caught off guard. She's...She backs away, takes a breath before I can figure out the feeling that's making her flush.

Then Mami looks down and shakes her head. She fixes a smile to her face. "Has Clau been scaring you with stories again?" She rolls her eyes. "I swear, that girl..."

"No, it's just...the trees. They think they saw something the other night. The birdbaths in Señora Avila's yard said the same thing. They all seemed pretty freaked out."

"Mm-hmm." She goes back to cleaning.

"You don't think it could have been her, do you?"

She hesitates, eyes down.

"Mami?" I want to reach for her again, to try to sense what she's thinking.

She swivels out of reach before glancing over her shoulder as Abuelo and Abuela head off to bed. Then she lowers her voice as she says, "I think your abuelos come from a generation that used fear to raise well-behaved children. All those stories—La Lechuza, El Cucuy—they're meant to scare children into being good and following the rules."

"So they're just stories?"

"Probably."

I furrow my brow. "Probably? So you're not sure…?"

She sighs. "I'm sure I've never seen them. And if you haven't noticed, we're not exactly what you'd call normal. If there were some supernatural beings out there that could snatch naughty children from their beds, I think we would have run into them by now."

"What about the cats?" I ask. "When we were making deliveries, we found Mrs. Villarreal's cat, Oscar. Doña Maria's cat, KitKat, too. They were both dead."

Mami straightens, examining me more closely. "That's terrible."

"I know! And it can't just be a coincidence, can it?"

Her skin flushes again. "Those poor women." She shakes her head. "Your abuela and I will see them first thing. Were there…others?"

"Other cats?"

She meets my eyes, serious. "Other ghosts."

"Not that I saw."

She exhales. "Good."

"Good? So you *do* think La Lechuza could have"—I swallow—"killed them?"

She sighs. "It's all very strange, yes." Then she squeezes my shoulder. "But that doesn't mean it was La Lechuza." This time when she touches me, I feel her calm. I feel it washing over me until my thoughts aren't racing anymore.

"But if it wasn't some kind of monster, then who would do that?"

She wraps an arm around me, the other hand tucking a curl out of my face. "I didn't say it wasn't a monster." She looks me in my eyes. "Never forget, people can be monsters too, Omega." She kisses me good night, and for the first time since seeing the ghosts of Mrs. Villarreal's and Doña Maria's cats, I feel safe. "Que sueñes con los angelitos."

When I reach my bedroom door, I hear something running across the carpet. For a second, I worry the mess I still haven't cleaned has suddenly grown legs. But then I push the door open and Clau is on her hands and knees, ducking under the bed.

"Ven aquí, gatitos." She squeezes farther under the bed. "No te voy a hacer daño."

"What are you doing?" I kneel next to her.

"They won't come out," she says.

"Who's *they?*" I lie on my stomach and there, pressed to the wall, are two cats curled around each other, watching with wide eyes.

"How did they get in here?"

I try to wedge myself deeper, reaching for the calico. The black cat next to it hisses, but there's something strange about its fangs. They're not shiny and sharp like most cats'. I reach for a flashlight, angling the beam over their soft faces. Then I see what's wrong. Their bodies are translucent, the light shining right through them.

"Oh my God!" I drop the flashlight, getting to my feet. "Abby...she said there were more. These must be the other cats that went missing. But how did they get here?"

"They could be strays," Clau says. "You know your house is kind of a hot spot."

Clau's right. Our strange magic that Mami mentioned earlier has a tendency to attract other strange things too. So far it's the only explanation Mami's been able to come up with for Clau's sudden appearance. Maybe these ghosts were drawn here for the same reason.

"They might have been trying to cross over and got lost," Clau adds.

"Yeah...I guess it could just be a coincidence." *But it's*

a really freaky coincidence. The calico leaps out from under the bed, the black cat chasing it behind my nightstand. Clau laughs. "Look, now they're playing."

The calico jumps over Clau's knees before stopping to rub against her side. It purrs.

I change into my pajamas before sitting cross-legged on the edge of my bed. Both cats are climbing Clau and licking her arms. She giggles.

"Didn't your mother ever tell you stray cats have worms?" The tall antique lampshade in the corner of my bedroom shakes its tassels.

"They're dead," I say.

"Exactly. And so's the girl. All three of you should be stepping into the bright light of eternity instead of playing around—"

"Ay Dios." The Virgin Mary sculpture on my nightstand rolls her eyes at the lamp. "Leave her alone."

"She's so young." The Selena Quintanilla poster above my bed frowns. "She'll cross over when she's ready."

Clau crosses her arms instead. "Will you tell your stuff to stop talking about me like I'm not here?"

I wish I could tell my stuff to stop talking period. But they have a mind of their own. Well, not really a mind of their own. More like the mind of the previous owner.

The lamp belonged to my great-great-aunt Teresa who used to live in New Mexico. She never left her house and insulted every person who dared to enter it. That's why most of her children moved to Texas. When she died, all my father got was this lamp.

The statue of La Virgen belonged to Abuelo's older sister, Kitty. After her first love ran off with another woman, she became a nun. Then she was kicked out of the convent for starting a garage band with the other nuns.

The Selena poster used to hang in Mami and Tía Tita's room when they were teenagers, which is why she's always trying to talk to me about boys I like (even though there's only

one I like and I've already sworn to myself that no one will ever know) and singing the words wrong to her own songs.

Luckily, that version of Mami doesn't exist anymore. Those versions of all three women don't exist anymore except in this room, in the energy they left behind in these things.

In some ways, it's nice to still feel connected to my relatives. But just like living relatives, they can be extremely nosy and judgmental.

"It's time for bed, anyway," I say. "Now, quiet, all of you, so I can get some sleep."

"Fine..." The lamp dims.

I roll over, pulling the blankets over my head.

"Bonito gatito...ven...ven aquí."

I shoot up in bed. "Clau!"

She freezes. "Sorry, we'll be quiet."

My hand hangs off the bed, and one of the cats brushes against it. It's cold, like touching winter.

I pull the blankets tighter. It's finally quiet and when I peek out of the blankets, the cats are curled up on Clau's lap. They're not sleeping—ghosts don't sleep—but they are resting. Staying on this side of the veil takes a lot of energy, energy ghosts sometimes have to steal from the living. Clau does her best to draw energy from outlets and light sockets, but at night when all the lights have been switched off, she can't help but take a little from me while I sleep.

I yawn, hoping that maybe her and the cats' presence will help me nod off. Nothing knocks you out like a ghost siphoning your life force. Except my eyes are wide open. I'm exhausted from all those deliveries, and yet my mind's racing again, Mami's calm finally wearing off. I can't stop thinking about the trees and the birdbaths and the strange clouds.

But mostly I can't stop thinking about what Mami said about monsters. That some are human. And I can't help but wonder *how*. How does evil take control of a person? Does it hunt them down? Or do they chase after it themselves? Or maybe it's more like a seed, planted by hate or fear, and then the more you feed it those things, the more it grows.

Until it's alive inside you. Until it's just too strong.

It feels like another one of Mami's hard truths, another glimpse at a part of the world beyond Noche Buena. Unless one of those monsters is *here*. Unless...those monsters have been here all along.

But what the birdbath in Señora Avila's yard described sure didn't sound human. It sounded beastly and strange with a giant beak and razor-sharp teeth. Torn straight out of the pages of a storybook.

Except Mami said that's all La Lechuza is. *Just* a story. That if she was real, we would know about her the same way we know about all the magic folk in Noche Buena. Like the Nguyens, who carve enchanted staffs for sorcerers all over the world, and the Gallegos, who read migrating bat formations the same way some witches read tea leaves, and the Dubois that dream walk and only voice with other magic folk.

In the dark, I hear the cats softly purring. What if they saw the same creature the trees did?

What if that's why they're ... dead?

"It's almost midnight, Omega. Why are you tossing and turning?" I lift the blankets and the lamp light brightens a few shades.

La Virgen looks down at me. "Are you having trouble sleeping?"

I glance at the clock on my nightstand. It flashes 11:36 PM. "I guess so."

"Are you worried about something?" Selena asks.

"I was just joking around earlier," Clau says. "I don't actually think you and Carlitos are in danger."

"Danger?" La Virgen gasps. "¡Ay Dios! What kind of danger?"

"La Lechuza," Clau says.

Another collective gasp.

Clau's brow furrows. "¡Ay caramba! She can't be that bad if she was on the cover of a children's book."

La Virgen shivers. "She's a witch."

"A giant bird," Selena adds.

"A freak show attraction." The lamp flips its tassels again.

"What do you mean?" I ask.

"I mean, I've seen her get into costume. I used to be in one of the changing tents of a traveling carnival in the forties. The only thing paranormal about that woman was her willingness to glue hundreds of feathers to herself. And for pennies. I'm telling you, she was the least visited attraction every town we rolled into."

"See?" Clau says. "She's not even real. Or bad. Just a little...odd, that's all."

"You're lying," La Virgen says. "The only place you've ever been is the back of a pickup truck."

The lamp shakes. "I'm sorry, but I believe you were in the back of that same pickup truck. At least I wasn't tied down with ropes like some kind of animal. They literally tried to strangle you."

"And by the grace of God I survived. And it seems for the purpose of correcting your lies."

"I think we're getting a little off track." I exhale, turning to Clau. "What do they say about her in Venezuela?"

She shakes her head. "I don't remember exactly." She looks down. "There was some kind of riddle, I think? Again, silly kids' stuff."

I didn't know much about Venezuela before I met Clau. I don't even know how long she really lived there before her family came to the United States. What I've learned, though, is that Venezuelans love life. They love to eat it and drink it and summon it with dancing bodies. They love to wake it up in you if you're sleepwalking through life—challenging you to speak louder and faster, to paint stories with your hands. Clau's excitement is how she shows us love. It's how she shows gratitude for this life she is technically no longer living.

That's the thing—she loves life so much she's *refused* to stop living it.

I've never asked her to talk about what happened so I don't know how long her soul's been out of her body or even how it got out in the first place. All I know is that meeting Clau is the best thing that's ever happened to me.

"Oh, wait!" She jumps onto her knees. "I remember it now. It was something like, cuando el tecolote canta el hombre muere. No será cierto pero sucede."

I almost choke. "When the owl sings, the man dies? That doesn't sound like just silly kids' stuff, Clau!"

She rests her head on my blankets. "Hmm, yeah, it's definitely creepier than I remember. Almost as creepy as the song we heard up in the attic."

"The song…" I roll to the edge of the bed before reaching under my mattress. I feel the torn cover of the book and gently pull it free, careful not to rip any of the pages.

"You brought it down here?" Clau crawls over to get a closer look.

"Before Abuela stuck me on trash duty." I rest the book on the blankets. "We didn't listen to the whole song, remember?"

"That's right."

I lock eyes with Clau. "I'll flip while you press play?"

She nods, her hand open over the speaker. As soon as the song begins to play again, I flip to the first page. It's a drawing of an owl sitting on a tree branch outside of a child's bedroom window. Watching them sleep.

> *La Lechuza, La Lechuza*
> *Dice shh*
> *Dice shh*
> *Estamos en silencio*
> *Como La Lechuza*
> *Que Dice shh*
> *Dice shh*

In the next illustration, a strange wind winds its way from the owl's beak to the sleeping child, waking them, and luring them toward the window.

> *La Lechuza, La Lechuza*
> *Dice shh*
> *Dice shh*
> *Si escuchas silbar*

No mires por la ventana
Dice shh
Dice shh

Now the child is running while the owl flies overhead.

Si tu corres
Si tu corres
Rápido
Rápido
No mires arriba
No mires arriba
Escapa
Escapa

The next page is just La Lechuza's face, black and scarred and angry.

La Lechuza, La Lechuza
Dice shh
Dice shh
Si ella te encuentra
Di tus oraciones
Adiós
Adiós

I slam the book closed, my hands covered in sweat.

Clau breathes, "If you hear her whistle, don't look out the window."

I pull my knees in to my chest. "If you run, don't look up."

Clau gulps. "If she finds you, say your prayers...."

"If you two keep telling each other scary stories, you're going to be up all night scared," La Virgen warns.

"Mami says that's all she is...." I hug my knees tighter. "She wouldn't lie to me."

Would she?

I remember the way her face changed, how she pulled away. But when she reached for me again, she filled me with calm. Is that what she was really feeling? Or is that what she wanted *me* to feel?

"Oh, it's not just a story," Selena cuts in. "One night we were driving to Houston after a concert in San Antonio. A giant white barn owl landed on the front of our tour bus. The battery died instantly and we had to pull over."

Clau sits up straighter. "Wait a minute. And you think she's been seen in Noche Buena? Like she could be flying around outside this very minute?" She slowly turns toward the window.

We both stare at it for a long time until the darkness outside looks like it's breathing.

The cats leap up, hissing and boxing before scurrying under the bed again. Clau screams. I duck under the blankets.

"We reacted the same way," Selena goes on. "In fact, it was so terrifying I wrote a song about it—"

The lamp bangs itself against the wall. "No one wants to hear you sing about a broken-down tour bus."

"Actually, it's more about the owl. Its eyes were—"

"No one wants to hear you sing about a bird with bulging eyes."

"They weren't really bulging. They were actually flat like—"

"No one cares!" The lamp shuts off.

In the dark, Selena's voice starts as a whisper. "Late at night our bus broke down and then we saw the wings of a white owl...."

The light flashes on again. "¡Basta!"

Selena stops singing. The light flicks off.

"And I wait for the bird to fly down and hurt one of us...."

The light flashes on. "¡Ya!" Off.

"Because I'm screaming in fear tonight. Till tomorrow will we all be all right?"

This time Clau cuts her off, her voice quivering. "What did you do?" The light slowly comes up again. "How did you get away?"

"Breathe," La Virgen says.

"But I need to know," Clau growls.

"Why?" the lampshade shoots back. "You worried she

might kill you? You're a ghost. You should be the thing scaring misbehaving children, not the misbehaving child who gets scared."

"Stop it!" La Virgen says. "You've picked on Clau enough tonight." But Clau isn't paying attention. She's staring out the window again.

"Eventually, the owl flew away and the engine started again," Selena says. "We kept on driving and everything was fine."

"So maybe it wasn't her," Clau says.

"Or maybe there is no her." I yawn, but my brain still isn't fuzzy enough for sleep.

"Well, there's no good in worrying about it right now," La Virgen says. "Omega has school tomorrow. We should all let her sleep."

The lampshade dims again. In the dark I can still see Clau staring out the window. This time the two cats have joined her. All just staring. *Waiting.*

I roll over onto my side, clutching my pillow. But I still can't get comfortable.

"Would you like me to sing you a lullaby?" Selena asks.

Clau answers for me. "Yes."

She begins to hum and the soft sound falls over me until every muscle is relaxed.

I close my eyes and take a few deep breaths. But in the

dark there is another sound. Selena's song has ended and all I can hear is a faint whistle.

It grows louder, making my ears itch. I pull the blankets down again. The lamplight is gone and so is Clau. Maybe she's trying to lead the cats to the other side. But then I notice the window is open, the curtains fluttering in the breeze.

Suddenly, the whistle is tighter and sharper. I slip out from under the blankets and take slow steps in the direction of the breeze. It brushes against me like fingers tracing my skin.

And then the whistling grows louder, a thick vibration that sends my heart into my throat.

Two bright yellow eyes appear in the darkness. They blink, saying hello. I take another step closer, my lips pursing, trying to form a whistle, to say hello back.

"Omega!"

I blink and Clau is in front of me. Her cold hands are gripping my shoulders, shaking me.

"Omega, wake up!"

I take a step back, woozy. "What's going on?"

"You were sleepwalking," she says. "I thought you were about to climb out the window or something."

I scrub my eyes, still trying to keep my balance. "I never sleepwalk...."

"Were you having a bad dream?" she asks. "Maybe La Virgen was right about scary stories being a bad idea before bed."

"Yeah, I guess. But it felt so..."

"Real?"

I nod, still staring out the window. The darkness has a gray tint, the sun just beginning to come up.

I turn back to my alarm clock. It's almost time to get ready for school. The cats pounce on my feet, tugging at my pajama pants.

"You haven't helped them cross over yet?" I ask.

Clau frowns. "But they're so happy."

"They'd be even happier if they were home." I almost say, *And you would be too*. But I don't.

Because even though I know Clau's soul would finally be at peace if she crossed over to the other side, mine wouldn't. I miss her just thinking about it.

"Fine," she sighs. "One more day and then I'll make them go."

"It's the right thing to do," I say.

She nods. "I know."

I can tell she means it. Maybe there's even a part of Clau that knows crossing over is the right thing for her too. But that doesn't mean it's easy. Nothing good or true ever is.

CHAPTER 5

THE LIGHTS IN THE LIBRARY AREN'T EVEN on yet—I got to school early since there was no point in trying to get any more sleep—but I can hear the tap-tap-tapping of Soona's long fingernails on her keyboard.

She looks down the nose of her glasses, still typing away. "Tell your mother she shouldn't have."

She's talking about the veladora Mami stayed up late last night making for her. She knows Mami stayed up late making it because just like the trees, Soona's soul has been around so long that it's planted roots, which means she's connected to things in a way other witches aren't.

If I want a little privacy, all I need to do is cross my fingers behind my back, locking away the thoughts. But sometimes

I forget and she overhears me complaining about Carlitos or one of my teachers.

Once she even heard me thinking about Aiden, which almost ruined my plan of keeping my feelings for him a secret until the day I die. Not just because if anyone knew I had a crush on him, my life would be over, but because I will never give Abby the chance to use him to humiliate me.

"So you didn't place an order?" I ask.

Soona takes the veladora, examining the strange color. "Not this time." She finds a match. "But if your mother thinks I need it, she's probably right."

Soona's own empathic abilities are basically as old as time. She's lived here all of her lives, even back when Noche Buena was just a pile of dirt that belonged to Mexico. Back when Noche Buena was a pile of dirt that belonged to no one.

I don't know how old she really is, but she's cast some enchantment on the other residents to keep them from realizing how long she's been around. Luckily, I get the goddaughter exemption.

"How's business been lately?" she asks.

"Same loyal customers. I know Mami wishes more people would give them a try, but my arms are sore just from the deliveries we made last night."

"So those flyers on the west side of town haven't gotten any bites?"

I shake my head. We used to make a few deliveries there a month, but then Mrs. Statham took over the PTA and suddenly people stopped calling.

"I overheard Mami tell Abuela that Mrs. Statham won't even let her set up a booth at the Fall Festival this year."

Soona sighs. "Mrs. Statham has been giving me grief too. She gave me a list of books she thinks are inappropriate and should be removed from the library." She rolls her eyes. "If I let her get her hands on them, she'd probably burn them."

"What did you do?"

"I burned her list instead." She rummages through her desk drawer. "Speaking of which, where are those matches?"

I lean against the desk and look out at the mostly empty library; the few kids in reading chairs are scrolling through their phones instead of actually, you know, reading. If only Mrs. Statham knew that the books she's so worried about keeping out of the hands of kids are probably just collecting dust.

"Noche Buena has survived far worse than Mrs. Statham, believe me," Soona goes on. "I remember when fearmongers like her were trying to burn people instead of books."

"That's horrible."

"Fear has a way of turning people into monsters. But the good news is that you can unlearn it." She pauses, remembering something. "You know, people used to be drawn to

Noche Buena *because* there was magic here. People who were sick, who were heartbroken. We took them all in, taught them all the old ways. Magic was shared and celebrated." She shakes her head. "But now, people don't like different."

"Why do you think things changed?"

"Things always change."

"So do you think they might change back? Do you think people might learn to embrace magic again?"

She smiles. "Things may change at a snail's pace, but I believe we'll eventually get there." She finally pulls out the matchbook. "Ah, here they are." She scrapes the match across the striker, igniting a spark. "Because fear is not sustainable. Remember that, Omega. People like Mrs. Statham and all of the other superstitious bigots in this town can't survive on hate forever."

"Why not?"

She tosses the match and tries another one. "Because hate needs to feed and if it's not feeding on others, it's feeding on you." The match finally lights. She holds up the flame. "Until you're completely consumed by it." Soona lights the candle, the flame taking on the same dark color as the wax. Then she puts out the match with a few shakes of her hand. "Until there's nothing left of you."

The flame dances as Soona takes a deep breath, inhaling the scent. Her eyes suddenly narrow, her brow scrunched. Then she quickly blows it out.

"What is it?" I ask.

The smoke twists, but instead of breaking apart, it tries to wrangle itself into a strange shape and I almost break Mami's rule of never invading her customers' privacy by leaning in to smell it.

Before I can, Soona slaps her hand over the mouth of the candle, trapping the smoke.

"Is everything okay?"

She straightens her skirt. "Oh, uh, just something for… Luisa. She's been having trouble sleeping."

I examine the veladora again. Yellow poppies are best for sleep. But this wax is a dark burgundy color. Like the clay earth after it rains. Like blood. Something rough like tree bark is suspended inside instead of flower petals. Actually, it's pretty ugly.

I examine Soona more closely, but when she meets my eyes, they're cool. Calm. The unease evaporating the same way it did last night when I was asking Mami about La Lechuza.

"Probably my fault, though," Soona goes on, pulling a heavy leather-bound book from her bag and placing it on the desk. "I've been up late every night working on my thesis."

"Aren't you always working on a thesis?"

Soona has fifty-six college degrees, thirty-four doctorates, a pilot's license, and has been shortlisted for a Nobel

Peace Prize under three different pseudonyms. She always says one of the perks of living forever is that you get to go to school forever. I'd call that a curse.

She laughs, but it's forced. "You sound just like Luisa...."

I think about Mami's look of concern last night when I brought up La Lechuza. I remember Abuela making the sign of the cross as Carlitos and I set off to make deliveries. Now Soona and the veladora, her nervous laugh as she tries to change the subject.

Why are all the adults around me acting so strange?

"What about you, Omega? Been staying up late reading any of those books you checked out?" She glances at her computer. "And that are now three weeks overdue."

I lean over her desk. "Finished one. Didn't like the ending."

She laughs. "Well, if you're so dissatisfied with the endings you've been reading lately, why don't you try writing a story of your own?"

"I'm not a writer." And I'm definitely not letting her trick me into doing *more* homework.

She raises an eyebrow. "You and Carlitos come in here every day during lunch and spend the entire thirty minutes telling me stories."

"Those aren't stories," I say. "They're facts."

"And the two aren't mutually exclusive. Stories are truth,

Omega. If you know how to tell the truth, you know how to tell a story."

I pick at the hem of my *Bob's Burgers* shirt. "Speaking of stories…"

She gives me a curious look.

"Have you ever heard of La Lechuza?"

She sits back, completely still. "Why do you ask?"

I start where it's safe. "I found an old children's book about her up in the attic. Then Clau remembered a riddle about her from Venezuela."

"A riddle?" She turns her attention back to the veladora, not making eye contact.

"Yeah. Something about her song bringing death. Can owls even sing?"

"They whistle," she says, unblinking.

I wait for her to continue, but it's like she's drifting, lost in one of her millions of memories. "Soona?" I wave a hand.

She clears her throat. "I…think we may have a book or two on the topic. Why don't we go have a look?" She gets up slowly, leading me to the stacks with a wag of her finger.

We wind through the rows of dusty wooden shelves, gum and amateur graffiti stuck to some of the endcaps: *A + M* equals a big Sharpie heart. Soona props up some fallen books, still taking slow steps as we near the threshold of section *O*. The *O* stands for "Otro Lado." *Other Side.*

Ahead of us is a glistening wall of beads. Beyond them, something lures us closer. A feeling like curiosity. Like a powerful thirst. The way learning is supposed to make you feel. Like you've stumbled upon buried treasure.

Soona glances back to her desk, making sure the coast is clear, and then she leads me across the threshold. The beads part like rain, revealing the section of the library that's older than Soona.

Students aren't allowed back here because it's technically *not* here. It's somewhere in the space between this world and the next, Soona's magic keeping the portal open. I've only been back here a few times—Soona is always wary of me or Carlitos spending too much time in the in-between, but I'm not sure why.

Maybe because the feeling it puts off, that thirst, that wonder, only intensifies, pulling you deeper and deeper into the infinite rows of shelves. Making you think the next book you pick up will be the one to answer your questions. But then it only leaves you with more. Which means more wandering. More searching. Until you're so deep in the stacks you can't find your way back out again.

Soona has read every book ever written, which is why she's the best guide in a place like this. She has very few unanswered questions about the past and present. Either she was there herself or she read about it already.

Above us, the space opens up and up and up. So far that I have to crane my neck to see where the stacks climb into a thick fog that swirls like a steaming bowl of soup. Winged creatures flit in and out of the fog, their screams making the hairs on my arms stand up.

"Just stay calm and they won't peck your eyes out." Soona smiles, mischievous.

Soona's enchantments aren't the only thing keeping the portal hidden. The winged alebrijes flying in slow circles above our heads keep time in the in-between from moving forward. Every pass winds the clock back to where it started, which means we could stay here for hours and when we emerge, it would be the same time it was when we first entered.

"There's an entire section on owls alone," Soona says as she leads me down row after row of sleeping books.

That's the other difference between the school library and this one. The books here aren't objects. They're tomes—living, breathing records of the past.

Soona glances back at me. "Did you know some owls like the great horned have fringed wing feathers, also called fluting, that allows them to fly in complete silence? Great for hunting. They're also incredibly curious beings. If you imitate their hooting, they might just be inclined to come take a closer look."

"Don't hoot at them, got it."

"Not unless you want to see their eyes up close. They produce almost three times as much light as the human eye and can see three times as far too." She looks over her shoulder. "But they're not quite as keen as a cat's. Just another thing feeding into the cats' sense of superiority."

"Or more evidence that they're demons like the trees keep going on about."

Abby used to have a cat, which was one of the many reasons why I never slept over at her house. Allergies are the one thing Mami's remedies can't fix. Which is fine with me, considering cats are total jerks.

"When you've been reincarnated as many times as they have, you'd be a little irritable and detached too. It takes a special person to make a connection with a cat."

"Yeah, well Clau's made a connection with two. But at least they're dead so I'm not itching and sneezing all over the place."

"Two of them? Dead?" Soona turns down one of the rows. "That's...interesting."

"You mean weird? That's kind of why I'm here. The trees think they saw some kind of winged monster the other night. The birdbaths in Señora Avila's yard said the same thing. And then four cats turned up dead. I just need to know if they're all connected. Otherwise, I won't be able to sleep. Again."

"Bad dreams?" Soona asks, brow furrowed in concern.

The memory of myself sleepwalking feels even fuzzier than it did this morning. But it still sends a chill down my spine. "Something like that."

"Well," Soona says, "I can't promise we'll find what you're looking for, but maybe we can bring you some peace of mind."

We stop in front of a row of shelves made of twigs and crooked branches, the books nestled like eggs in a bird's nest. With each exhale, the books softly coo, mimicking the sounds of an actual owl.

With a wave of her hand, Soona summons several leather-bound books from the shelves, the cooing louder and faster as the books begin to wake. They hover, waiting for her attention.

She points to one and the pages splay open. She takes a deep breath and then she blows, the words turning to dust and spreading into the air.

The pages turn fast, until the entire thing is blank, the dust forming the wings of a bird, then its large round body, and finally its head, speckled white with a sharp beak and pointy ears. It coos, jerking its head nervously.

"Couldn't we have just read it?" I ask, the bird's wide unblinking eyes making my skin crawl.

"That's how mistakes are made. You want to know the true story? You ask the thing itself."

"The thing..." I take a step back, the bird still staring too deeply into my eyes. "This isn't her, is it?"

Soona snaps a finger at the owl. "Speak."

It coos, head twisting from side to side. Then it finds its voice.

> *Atop the branches*
> *Of celestial skies*
> *Two bright yellow moons*
> *You thought were eyes*
> *Older than time*
> *Too wise for lies*
> *Feathers and bones*
> *Just invisible binds*

It goes on, describing the sky before it held the earth. When it was just endless darkness, waiting for things to be born. First came the fire, then the smoke. The stars and the spaces in between. Magic forming in the cracks. And out of the magic came other things. Thread. Breath. Wings.

The owl remembers it all. How it was made. How we were all made.

And then the poetry ties itself into knots I can barely untangle—into knots my English teacher, Mrs. Machado, could probably barely untangle. The owl says something about time travel or maybe the rainforest and I'm completely lost. Finally, the last of its strange song trails off.

I roll my eyes. "I should have known it would speak in riddles." I gesture to the bird. "So what did all of that mean? That they're not birds? They're not even animals?"

"Depends on who you ask. To many, owls are simply messengers from the underworld. Sometimes they carry warnings about sickness or death. Sometimes they carry the souls of the living or those that used to be. In essence, owls are magic—every bone and every feather stitched with a supernatural thread."

"But magic doesn't necessarily mean bad. I guess I don't understand how La Lechuza became so...evil."

"People didn't start believing owls were bad omens because they're evil. They started believing it because they're wise. Because they're mirrors that show truth in a way most people aren't ready to see. La Lechuza was created to scare children away from that truth, from seeking it out."

"So, she *is* just a story...."

"*She's* just a story." Soona puts a hand on my shoulder and something flows between us, slipping from her skin to mine. *Knowing. Regret.* She quickly pulls her hand away, trying to erase the feeling with a smile.

I smile back, pretending I never felt it either.

Even though I did.

Even though now I know...that she's lying to me. What I don't know is why.

Soona turns on her heel before leading me back through the wall of beads, a strange tingle racing down my spine as time starts ticking forward again.

"Look, I don't want you to worry, Omega. You know how the trees like to overexaggerate. It's a symptom of being stuck in one spot for their entire lives. Sometimes they make up stories to entertain themselves."

"But I thought you said all stories are truth."

She smiles. "Touché. I'm not saying the trees didn't see anything. I'm saying they could be wrong about what they saw."

"And the birdbaths in Señora Avila's yard?"

"They could be wrong too."

"What about the dream I had last night?"

She places the back of her hand against my forehead, her

touch filtered this time, the energy only flowing one way. She closes her eyes, exhales. "You were feeling afraid."

"So that's all it was? My own fears?"

"They were strong last night. You're still warm with them."

She leads me to the exit, the squeak of sneakers on linoleum on the other side of the library doors signaling that the first bell is close.

"But what if I'm feeling afraid because there's something to be afraid of?"

She sighs. "I'll have a talk with the trees. Maybe the birds and squirrels too."

"Thank you."

"No problem. Now go kick butt on that math quiz."

I spin around. "Quiz?"

She presses a hand to her mouth. "Oops."

CHAPTER 6

THE HALLWAY BEFORE SCHOOL IS A MINEFIELD of emotions. I'm usually sitting at my desk by now, my classmates trickling into the room making all the things they're feeling easier to digest. Excitement about the start of a new day. Anxiety about the homework they didn't do. Embarrassment about their growling stomachs or the clothes they're wearing. Each one a mild zap to my insides like they're all a bunch of moths and I'm the flame.

But the halls between passing periods are different, the students racing to class or huddled in groups. It feels like walking through a hailstorm, the moonstone in my pocket the only thing I have that's even close to an umbrella.

I squeeze it, concentrating on the cold, on counting to five. *One.*

I pass the wannabe micro-influencers, snapping selfies in the sunlight filtering in from the big windows marking the science wing. Their jealousy makes me itch, insecurity bubbling at the base of my stomach.

Two.

On the other side of the glass are the kids in Future Farmers of America kicking the mud off their boots from their morning at the stockyards. I can practically see the heart eyes on the guy and the girl shyly holding hands behind everyone else. Their crush like Pop Rocks fizzing behind my teeth.

Three.

Then there's the dance team all sprawled out on the linoleum floor in front of the cafeteria in their short shorts and tank tops, popping bubble gum and doing one another's makeup. Beneath their laughter, someone's anger feels like tiny burns. I notice a girl hugging her knees, her sadness at being left out forming a lump in my own throat.

Four.

I pass the robotics team and the baking club and the theater kids.

Feeling their excitement and their anxiety and their impatience.

Five.

I try to swat the emotions away like flies, but they're everywhere—sticking to my skin, tangled in my hair.

I find the nearest wall and press against it. Then I just look. Gripping the moonstone and trying not to explode while everyone else rushes to class, putting one foot in front of the other like it's nothing.

And it feels like a movie. Like I'm watching them all from behind a screen: a day in the life of a normal kid with friends and inside jokes and things to look forward to after the final bell. I feel their giddiness and their belonging and I try to imagine what it would be like to sit with the dance team while someone braids my hair or to snap fierce photos with the wannabe micro-influencers, who think everything they do is worth remembering.

Then I remember too.

The dream I had last night, how I almost sleepwalked right out of my own window, how the nightmare isn't even the strangest thing about me. How Abby rejected me the moment she found out what else I was hiding.

There are more people in Noche Buena like her than there are like me. Like Mrs. Statham and Mr. Fisher. So I can't be on the dance team. I can't join the bass fishing club or the school newspaper. I can't have real friends.

Not if it feels like *this* once those friendships finally end.

Not if it means people might be so afraid of me that they want to burn me at the stake.

"You okay?"

I look up at the sound of Carlitos's voice.

"Yeah..." I massage my temple. "Just a little loud out here, that's all."

And lonely, I think. But I don't tell him that.

"Your moonstone still working?"

I squeeze it tighter. "Sort of? I don't know. Maybe people are just feeling big things today."

Or maybe I'm the one with the big feelings.

Carlitos turns his attention back to his locker and starts changing the batteries on the neon string lights he taped to the inside. It's decorated with black-and-white panels from his favorite Webtoon. There's also a magnetic pencil holder shaped like the head of Albert Einstein stuck to the back, but instead of pencils it's full of Rebanaditas—chili-watermelon lollipops. I snatch one for later.

"Did you have any weird dreams last night?" I ask him.

Carlitos stops. "What do you mean *weird* dreams?"

"Weird like something was trying to lure you outside. Weird like you were sleepwalking and woke up before the monster could show its face."

He bristles. "You were sleepwalking? You never sleepwalk."

"I know. Clau woke me up before I crawled through the window."

"*Crawled* through the window?" He lowers his voice. "What do you think was out there?"

I lower mine too. "I don't know. I went to talk to Soona about it. She said she'd look into it, but that I shouldn't worry. I was probably just freaked out about all of this La Lechuza stuff."

"Did you tell her about the Reese's test? Once that thing has spoken it's usually never wrong."

"She was sort of adamant about it." I shrug, still just as confused as I was when we found Doña Maria's cat. "Maybe last night's nightmare was a one-time thing."

He frowns. "Well, I guess you'll find out tonight."

"Yeah." I swallow and it feels like sand. "I guess I will." I try to shake off the nerves, but they're stuck to me like everything else. "But I don't really have time to think about that right now considering we have a pop quiz in math today."

"What?" Carlitos slams his locker closed. "That sucks. How'd you find out?"

"Soona let it slip."

He groans. "Ugh, then you know it's true."

"Join the search party this weekend. All animal lovers are invited." Abby's at the end of the hall, handing out flyers with photos of the missing cats on them. "There will be snacks and refreshments. Everyone's going to be there."

We try to squeeze past her on our way to class, but she spots us immediately.

"Unfortunately, suspects can't be part of the search party. I guess you two will just have to spend your Friday night doing whatever it is you normally do—nothing."

"We don't want to be a part of your stupid search party anyway," Carlitos snaps back.

"Why?" She crosses her arms. "Because you already know where they are?"

Anger oozes from her, my body soaking it up like a sponge. But it's not the only reason my face is turning red. My cheeks burn because she's right. I *do* know where they are.

She stares into my eyes and then her own widen, like she's seeing their ghosts in my memories. And I *know* that she knows.

"Maybe we'll start with the woods behind your house." She grins.

"Abby, leave Omega alone." Behind her, Aiden pulls on the strap of her backpack and my face gets hot for yet another reason. Because Aiden Montgomery, with the most perfectly swooped bangs and big brown eyes, is looking right at me. Because Aiden Montgomery is *standing up* for me. "Seriously," he lowers his voice, "you're acting just like Brian and Caleb."

Aiden comparing her to their brothers, notorious bullies

(both at school and in their own home) makes her pause and bite her lip. Then Aiden brushes past her, heading to class.

We follow, slipping into math class right before the bell rings. Everyone else is already in their seats, kids chatting about the weekend and trying to finish the homework last minute.

I spot Aiden at the back of the room, talking to Naomi Davis about the search party this Friday. I know Abby must have told him all about her theory that I'm some sort of sicko building my own pet cemetery. But if he told her to leave me alone, maybe that means he doesn't believe her. Or maybe he does and he wanted her to back off for her own safety.

When he looks up at me, my cheeks burn again and I bury my face in my hands.

When Ms. Schulz steps to the front of the room, everyone falls silent. Usually, there's a ten-minute warm-up. But today there isn't and Carlitos and I are the only ones who know why.

"Good morning, class. Today we are going to have a pop quiz...."

There's a collective groan and then panic. My skin itches, sensing the spike in anxiety. Ms. Schulz's pop quizzes are notoriously killer, and it's the last week of the grading period, which means some kid's future freedom will depend on how they do on this one assignment.

Carlitos nudges me. "Mega, you okay?" His voice sounds

like it's underwater. "Just concentrate," he whispers, sensing the shift in energy too. "Like turning off a light switch."

Again, with that stupid metaphor.

I try, taking deep breaths, imagining the emotions like a wave moving farther and farther from shore. But no matter how loud my brain screams, my body just won't listen.

As kids get out of their seats to grab a copy of the quiz or sharpen their pencils, a few brush past me, touching my skin. Now I'm not just itching. I'm…I'm…

"Omega…?"

I tear out of my desk, running for the door. But I don't make it. I catch myself on the wall, hurling into the trash can.

There's a collective "Ewww."

From the corner of my eye, I see Aiden, his eyes wide, and in that moment I wish La Lechuza was real. That she would swoop down and strike me dead.

Carlitos grabs me by the arm, holding me up. "It's okay, Omega. I'll take you to the nurse."

I nod, noticing my backpack already hanging over his shoulder. We hobble to the nurse's office, my stomach still knotted and sour, even though we're almost to the other side of the school building.

"Do you think you're going to be sick again?"

I nod slowly, afraid that opening my mouth will let something else out.

He tightens his grip on my arm and I know he's trying to soothe me the way he does Chale. But it's weak, not quite reaching me.

"It's not working," I croak.

"I'm sorry, Omega." He shakes his head, confused. "We're almost there."

We round the corner and the nurse looks up from her desk.

"Oh, poor thing. Get her inside." Ms. Zapata helps me to the bed. "Were you feeling sick this morning?" she asks.

I shake my head, clutching my stomach.

"It sort of came on all of a sudden." Carlitos speaks for me.

Ms. Zapata pours something fizzy into a plastic cup. "Here, sip on this."

I taste it and something about the sound of the bubbles popping helps me relax.

"Thanks for bringing her in, Carlitos. You can go back to class now."

He gives me a thumbs-up, but it's more of a question.

I nod. "Thanks."

"I'll see you after school."

Ms. Zapata takes my temperature. "You're burning up." She wets a washcloth and tells me to hold it to my forehead. "It could be this nasty flu that's been going around." She helps me lean back on the plastic mattress. "Just rest here while I give your mom a call."

Mami shows up five minutes later, crushed flower stains on her clothes. When she's not using the plants from her garden to make veladoras, she's arranging them into bouquets and dramatic archways and table decorations for weddings and baby showers and quinceañeras. Today, she's getting flowers ready for Marisol Montoya's quinceañera this weekend. The Montoyas hardly ever go to church, but they're still throwing her a big fancy party anyway.

When she sees me, she immediately presses her hands to my face, squishing and kneading me as if I'm dough. "How are you feeling?"

Usually, I'd be feeling better by now, the poison of other people's feelings out of my body the moment I puke. But for some reason I still feel just as jittery as I did in the middle of that classroom.

"Can you make it to the car?" Mami asks.

"I think so."

Mami waves to Ms. Zapata as we head out the door. "Gracias, señora."

"De nada. Espero que te sientas mejor, Omega."

I hobble to the car, the bright sun making me even dizzier. Mami starts the engine and turns the AC to full blast. She never lets us use the AC. Usually, if it's hot out, which is always, she makes us roll the windows down to stay cool.

"You're still burning up," she says. "Did something happen?"

"Pop quiz in math today. Everyone freaked out."

She sighs, relieved. "A couple of rituals and you'll be back to normal. But it has been a while since you got sick at school. I thought the moonstone was helping."

I shrug. "It was."

"Your classmates must have really been on edge today." She reaches for my hand, every part of me clammy. "Don't worry, we're almost home."

The first thing she does is run a bath. I sit on the edge of the tub, letting the steam hit me, making me sweat even more. Mami carries in some glass bottles from the pantry and begins dressing the bath with salts and oils and wild things from her garden.

The water is a murky mess by the time I get in, but I let myself sink, waiting for her potion to soak into my skin. I breathe deep, letting it fill my lungs, before rubbing some of it on my face. Mami knots my thick curls on top of my head, rubbing something warm into my shoulders.

"What's wrong with Omega?" Clau floats in the doorway.

Abuela comes up behind her, handing Mami some more herbs. "Just a small attack."

"What happened?"

"Pop quiz in math," I croak out.

Clau kneels next to the tub. "That must be one scary math teacher." The calico comes around the corner, hopping onto the toilet seat. "Well, don't worry. Romeo and Julieta will keep you company."

"You named them?" Abuela huffs.

Mami eyes Clau too. "I thought you were going to help them cross over."

"And…" She looks away. "I will. But first, we'll spend the day keeping Omega entertained. Do you want to see them do a trick?" She claps. "I taught them how to say hello." She waves her hand. "Di 'hi.'" They ignore her. "Vamos. Di 'hi.'"

"Cats can't be trained," Abuela says. "It's part of their creed."

"Cats have a creed?" Clau asks.

"Every living thing has a creed," Abuela says. "And a cat's creed is to never be ruled by another living thing, which means that every time they refuse to do what you ask, their soul is fortified."

"Is that how they get their nine lives?"

"It's not just nine. The more stubborn a cat is, the longer it lives."

"Hmm." Mami rubs some more oil on my face, not making eye contact with Abuela. "Sounds like someone I know."

Clau and I both laugh.

Abuela swats at Mami with a dry washcloth. "You're going to miss me when I'm gone." She points at me and Clau. "All of you." She saunters back to the kitchen, annoyed. "I'll start the broth."

"All right," Mami calls back, "but let me season it."

"I know how to season the broth. Who do you think taught you how to do it?"

"And who do you think perfected it because you always add too much salt?" Mami says that part under her breath.

Clau laughs again, but the heat from the bath is starting to make me feel light-headed.

"Too much?" Mami asks. "Clau…" She snaps a finger, calling her closer.

Clau sticks both hands into the bath, steam rising from her ice-cold skin. The temperature of the water drops a bit. I lean back.

"Now, get comfortable and just try to relax. I'll check on you in a few minutes."

After Mami leaves, Clau turns to me, brow furrowed. "This is a bad one." She presses a finger to my cheek, igniting more steam.

I can't help but wonder if Clau is right. I'm miles from school. My classmates' anxiety was just about a pop quiz. It's not like someone died. But there's this fire in my belly, this darkness in the pit of my stomach that makes me feel like someone has. Or maybe it's me. Is this what dying feels like?

I wake up in my bed in my fuzzy bathrobe. Abuela comes in carrying an egg from the chicken coop out back. She murmurs to herself, her prayers a half whisper as she breathes them over me. She traces me with the egg, hovering the delicate shell an inch over my skin. I try to feel it sucking the poison out—the ojo Carlitos was so worried that Señora Avila had cursed him with—but all I can feel is the room, spinning again.

I fall over the side of the bed, dry heaving into the trash. There's a splat, but when I open my eyes, it's the egg that's all over the floor.

"¡Ay Dios!" Abuela runs for the kitchen. "She let it escape!"

I blink and the sun is lower outside my window.

"You need to eat something." Abuela dips a spoon into a cup of broth before leading it to my mouth. I swallow some, but I still feel dizzy. I take a few more sips and then it all comes up again, staining my bedspread.

"We've tried everything." I can hear Mami whispering in the hallway.

"Then maybe it's time to take her to the doctor." Papi's home. "I'll help you get her into the car. We should go before it starts to rain."

"It's looked like that since yesterday. I don't think it's going to break any time soon."

"You never know. Better safe than sorry."

The bright lights of the supermarket burn my eyes. In movies and TV shows people go to fancy doctor's offices where there are giant fish tanks in the waiting room and televisions on the walls. The doctor's office we go to is in the Amigo's supermarket two towns over, sandwiched between the adult diapers and the candy aisle. It's already decorated for Halloween, but the sugar still doesn't mask the smell of old plastic and grape-flavored cough syrup.

There's a line to be seen—two little boys with snotty noses, an old man with a hand pressed to his chest, a woman with a crying baby. I spot a girl from my school, a grade above me. She looks pale, almost green. Maybe there is a flu going around. Maybe I've got it too.

I lean my head against Mami's shoulder and when I open my eyes again, she's pulling me back behind the curtain to see the doctor. He shines a light in my eyes, then in my nose and throat.

"We can do a diagnostic test to be more certain...."

"But you think it's the flu."

"Almost certain. But the test—"

"No." Mami's voice becomes small. "We don't have health insurance."

The doctor nods. "Well, there's a few things we can

prescribe, but for the most part a flu like this just needs to run its course. In the meantime, make sure she's getting plenty of fluids and lots of sleep."

"Yes, thank you, doctor."

A single drop of rain lands against the windshield. Then another.

"Well, would you look at that..."

"I guess the clouds weren't teasing us this time."

"What did the doctor say?" I hear Papi ask.

"Sleep and fluids. He thinks it's the flu."

I rest my head on the window, barely able to open my eyes.

"Well, she's got the sleep part down," Papi whispers.

I want to say I'm still awake, but I'm too tired to open my mouth. Also, I'm not sure that's entirely true, my brain foggy like I'm halfway dreaming.

Rain splatters against the windows, the windshield wipers squeaking across the glass.

"Farmers will be glad for the rain," I hear Papi say.

"I'm glad the clouds finally popped," Mami says. "Mamá was going on and on about the sky being some kind of bad omen. Now that we know it was actually just an end to this terrible drought, maybe she'll finally let it go."

"She will once she sees how happy her petunias are."

Rain pounds the windows, so hard it sounds like we're going through a car wash.

The car slows and I glance out the window. The storm still looks like a bruise, so dark all I can see are the veins of lightning crawling across the sky. They stretch, almost mirror images. Like the bones in a bird's wing. A few seconds later, the boom of thunder rattles the car.

Papi looks back at me. "We're almost home, Omega."

I just moan, my eyes trying to fall closed again.

"Tomás, look out!"

The car swerves and I accidentally bite my tongue.

The tires skid across the wet road, Papi groaning as he yanks the wheel.

We jerk to a stop, the car sideways, windshield wipers still thumping against the glass.

Just on the other side, something moves in the downpour. Giant and black, so dark I can barely make out its shape beneath the rain. All I know is that it's coming closer.

Closer.

The windshield wipers stick to the glass. The lights on the dash go black.

Papi turns the key. The headlights flicker, but the car doesn't start.

"Is it the battery?" Mami asks.

"Come on…" Papi turns the key while the engine squeals. "Come on…"

Darkness swallows the car and then all of the sudden the lights snap back on, and I can finally see that it's not a shadow or a hitchhiker trying to get out of the rain. It's a bird, wings spreading wide until they're a mile in each direction.

They stretch, moving up and down, slowly gathering strength. And then the darkness leaps into the sky, blocking the rain for a few seconds as my heart pounds in the silence.

CHAPTER 7

I WAKE UP TANGLED IN BEDSHEETS, COMPLETELY DRY. Beneath my nightgown, my heart is still pounding like I ran all the way home. How *did* I get home? I try to remember the car finally starting, pulling up to the house, getting into bed. But there's just a blank space. A black hole.

A black hole.

That's what it looked like at first. And then it grew wings.

"Earth to Omega." Clau waves a hand in front of my face. "You still feeling crummy?"

On the other side of my bedroom door, I can hear the quiet clink of forks on plates as everyone else eats dinner without me. I must have been asleep for hours. Dreaming. Maybe that's all it was.

"Now that they know you're contagious they sent me in

here to look after you." Clau sits on the floor, Julieta nuzzled against her side while Romeo sits on his haunches, peering out the window. It's pitch black, sending a shiver down my spine.

"I don't want to sleep." I try to sit up.

"But the doctor said you have the flu. You need to rest. You know, my little sister had the flu once. She puked all over her toys. Then she slept for three days straight. I think those were the best three days of my life." She grows quiet and I can't tell if she really means what she just said about her sister. Maybe she did when she was alive. But the look on her face now is more like regret.

"You never really talk about your family...."

Clau gets up and goes to the window. She stares into the darkness.

"Clau?"

"I don't talk about them because...well"—she gives me a weak smile—"you're my family now."

"But if you miss them...if you want to talk about them... you can."

Clau snatches the pink fuzzy boa from my nightstand in an effort to change the subject and drapes it over her shoulders. "Hey, do you think I look like an owl in this?" She twists it around her arms, flapping them. "Or more like a chicken?" She squawks, pecking at the air.

"No, Clau..." I clutch my chest. "It hurts to laugh."

"But laughter is the best medicine."

She flaps her arms faster, squawking and snorting with laughter.

Suddenly, Clau is a flash of white, lightning striking outside the window. But she's not alone.

For half a second, there's a face, long and gray and hideous. It stares at me with eyes like giant flames. Bright and burning and then... gone.

The cats shriek, racing into the closet. Clau screams too, jumping into the air.

"What's going on in here?" Mami flips on the light, Papi right behind her.

Clau rips off the boa, floating back down to the ground. "Uh, nothing."

I use all of the strength I have left to point to the window. "Something... there was something out there."

"¿Qué está pasando?" Abuela barrels in next.

Mami presses her hand to my forehead. "You feel even hotter than before."

Abuela gives Clau a look. "Probably because she hasn't been sleeping like she was supposed to be."

I'm still pointing, my arm shaking. "But there's something outside."

Mami looks from me to Papi before pulling the curtains

closed. "Omega, there's nothing out there. This fever's giving you nightmares, that's all."

"But I'm wide awake."

She's quiet, looking from me to Papi again.

"And what about after we left the doctor? There was something in the road. Was that just a dream too?"

Mami brushes my cheek. "You snored the entire way home."

"I don't understand." I pinch my eyes shut, trying to remember. "It felt so real."

Mami looks down at me, her eyes full of concern.

"Let me talk to her." Papi leads Mami and Abuela to the doorway. "You two finish eating dinner. I'll take care of this." After they leave, he comes to sit next to me on the bed. "I know it's been a long time since you were this sick," he says. "So long you might have almost forgotten that you're half human. Like me." He smiles, teasingly.

"I haven't forgotten," I say, more annoyed than I meant it.

Papi looks down like the words have stung him. Like *he's* to blame. For the parts of me that are missing. The parts of me that make me strange in a family that's already as strange as it gets. That keep me in bed with a flu that Mami would have been able to zap from herself within hours, that Abuela would have prayed away by now. Even Carlitos barely gets sick anymore. And Chale, who literally eats bugs, has never had a stomachache in his four years of life.

Because they are entirely made of magic and I'm made of something else.

"Well"—Papi clears his throat—"as the only full human in this house, let me remind you—magic can't fix this. Your body has to fight it on its own and it can only do that if you rest."

"But it can't just be the fever that's making me see things." I try to sit up, motioning to Clau. "Clau saw it too."

Papi can't see Clau, but he turns in her direction, probably sensing the cold she gives off. "Clau saw it too?"

"Saw what?" Clau says, looking confused.

I narrow my eyes at her. "You screamed. Didn't you see La Lechuza? She was right outside the window."

Clau creeps closer, looking as concerned as Papi. "I only saw the lightning, Omega."

I turn to my Selena poster. It faces the window. There's no way she could have missed it. "You saw her, though, didn't you?" I ask.

She frowns. "Just the lightning."

"But it was very bright and very scary," La Virgen adds.

I sink into the mattress, confused.

"It's your fever, mija." Papi presses his scruff to my forehead.

He feels almost as cool as Clau. Maybe I really am still burning up.

He tucks me in tighter. "Just try to get some sleep. We're all right there in the next room. You're safe, I promise."

I nod and he disappears into the hallway, pulling the door closed until only a sliver of light shines through.

I can feel myself drifting, but what if I see her again? Maybe she wasn't really outside my window. Or standing in the middle of the road. Maybe it was the fever making me see things. But what if she finds me anyway? What if she finds me... and I can't wake up?

"It's all right, Omega," Clau whispers. "We won't leave you alone."

She curls up beside me and I sigh, leaning into the cold. The cats jump onto the bed, snuggling up against me too. My eyes flutter, fighting to fall closed, and I finally let them. In Clau's and the cats' cool embrace, I fall fast asleep.

The smell of onions tugs my eyes open. A knife chops as footsteps shuffle around the kitchen. I lie still for a few seconds, trying to feel my fever. But I'm not sweating anymore. I loosen the blankets and my arms and legs don't feel so sore. I sit up, waiting for the world to start spinning again. But everything is perfectly still.

When I finally get out of bed and step into the kitchen,

Mami and Abuela both look over. Abuelo puts his newspaper down.

"Mija, why are you up?" Abuela rushes over, touching my face.

"I'm fine, Abuela. I feel much better."

Mami comes over next. "No fever..."

"It must have broken last night while I was sleeping."

"It was the broth." Abuela nods, satisfied. "I added a little extra cinnamon bark. That must have been the trick."

"So that's why it was so bitter...," Mami says.

Abuela's not listening. She's too busy looking me up and down, suspicious. But then my stomach growls and she perks up. "Come sit. Have some menudo." She pours me a bowl before squeezing the juice of a couple lemon wedges into it.

I swallow it in giant mouthfuls, every bite reminding my body how many hours it's been since I last ate. I drink the last of the broth and Abuela pours me another bowl.

"Take it slow," Mami says. "I know you feel better, but I don't want you upsetting your stomach again."

I take slower bites...until she leaves the room. Then I scarf down the rest, my belly a big round balloon. It isn't until I put my bowl in the sink that I realize I haven't seen Clau, or more importantly, heard her, since I woke up this morning.

"Where's Clau?" I ask Abuela.

She waves a hand toward the back door. "With the chickens. She's been out there all morning."

I find Clau by the chicken coop, watching them through the wire enclosure. "What are you doing out here?"

She scrubs at her face. She's been crying.

"What's wrong, Clau?"

She turns her back to me, and suddenly, I wish I hadn't asked about her family last night. If I bring it up now, she might disappear for days.

She's done it before, hidden up in the attic until Abuela convinced her to come back down. No broth or magic touch. Empaths can't manipulate the emotions of supernatural beings so Abuela had to help her the old-fashioned way. Talking. Lots of hugs if Clau felt like making herself solid enough to receive them.

That's all I can do too, wrapping my arms around her just to let her know I'm there.

Part of me feels selfish for keeping quiet. But with all these nightmares I keep having, I don't want to be alone. So even though I can still see her shoulders bobbing up and down, the tears silent but still coming, I don't ask her again if she misses them.

"I made Romeo and Julieta cross over," she finally says.

"I'm so sorry, Clau." I'm relieved it wasn't me that upset her, but I still feel bad about Clau having to say goodbye to them. "I know how much you loved having them around."

She rests her head on my shoulder. Without a fever, Clau's skin feels like touching ice again. "Well," she sighs, "I love you more."

"What does that mean?"

She looks at me. "Last night when they were curled up next to you, I noticed you sweating through the blankets. You were tossing and turning and talking in your sleep."

"What was I saying?"

"You were begging." She pinches her eyes shut. "Like someone was hurting you and you wanted them to stop."

I search my memory for a nightmare—something that would have made me act as scared as Clau said I was. Seeing La Lechuza in my dreams the first time was almost enough to keep me from falling asleep at all last night. But I don't remember her. I don't remember anything.

"The cats started meowing like they were scared of something too. Julieta jumped down and hid under the bed again. The blankets were soaked where she'd been lying against you. I touched you and you were on fire. I shooed Romeo away and you were hot where he'd been lying too."

"I don't understand."

"I don't either." She shrugs. "But it seemed like they were making you worse...so I made them go."

"Clau..." I rest a hand on her shoulder, not sure what to say.

"It's okay," she says, trying to dry her eyes.

But it's not okay. Romeo and Julieta were Clau's only friends when I wasn't home and Carlitos wasn't around to bug her. And then I took them away. I know they belonged on the other side—I know Clau does too—but they made her

111

happy. As vibrant and silly as Clau can be, I know it's not always easy for her to generate that kind of energy. It's not always easy for her to keep pretending to be human.

Maybe it's better this way. Maybe helping the cats cross over means Clau's thinking more about what's real and what's not. I don't want Clau to go, but I also know that she doesn't belong here and that the longer she stays, the more often she'll have days like this. Sad and lonely. That's what happens when you've been away from home too long. You get lost in more ways than one.

I hear the screen door slam and we both look back to see Abuelo walking toward the old pecan tree next to the chicken coop. He stands under it, looking up. Then a few seconds later, something tumbles down from the branches, landing in his cupped hands.

We rush over to find a baby bird that's fallen out of its nest.

"I still don't get how he does that," Clau says.

"It's magic," I breathe, watching the tiny bird cock its head from side to side.

It's so small, so helpless, and it dawns on me that whether La Lechuza began as a woman or a bird, she was once this small and vulnerable too. The thought makes her a bit less scary.

"Clau, can you do the honors?" Abuelo holds up the baby bird.

Clau grins from ear to ear, borrowing some of our energy

to scoop up the bird and float it back up to its nest. "Go home, little bird," she coos. "You're safe now."

Mami lets me stay home from school, and Clau and I spend the day watching movies, and even though I'm not supposed to be eating junk food, Abuelo sneaks me some chicharrones anyway. Mami and Abuela are busy in the kitchen, still getting things ready for the quinceañera this weekend. They mostly argue, Clau and I peeking over the couch to laugh at all of their eye-rolling and passive-aggressive comments.

Papi gets home early, he and Tío Juan carrying in a couple boxes of pizza. Mami gives him a look—the *we can't afford this* look—but Papi just kisses her on the cheek and says, "You've been working nonstop. It's okay to take a break."

"I've been working on the alterations for Marisol's dress all day." Tía Tita sighs, tossing her purse on the couch before sitting down and kicking up her feet. "I told Juan he was on dinner duty tonight."

Tío Juan grins. "So I called Tomás and told him we were coming over." He slaps his knee, laughing.

"Please tell me there's pepperoni with mushrooms!" I flip the lid on the first box. It's anchovies and jalapeños. I gag. "I think I'm going to be sick again."

Carlitos grimaces. "That makes two of us."

Papi laughs. "Check the other box."

I open it and see six slices of plain cheese and six slices of pepperoni and mushrooms. Jackpot.

I'm stuffing a slice in my mouth with both hands when suddenly there's a knock on the screen door. When I turn, still in the pajamas I've been wearing for the past two days, hair in a mess on my head, with grease dripping down my chin, I see Aiden Montgomery, an awkward smile on his face.

"Uh, hi," he says on the other side of the screen. Abuela rushes over to greet him, but Carlitos beats her to it.

He kicks the door open. "What are *you* doing here?"

"¿Perdón?" Abuela pinches him hard on the hip. "Is that how we treat guests around here?" She tries to wave Aiden inside. "Are you hungry? Come on in, let me make you a plate."

"Oh, actually, I'm not here to stay." Aiden seems to suddenly remember the textbook he's carrying and holds it up. "I just came by to, uh, bring Omega her homework."

I set down my pizza, smooth my hair, and take a deep breath. "Excuse us." I avoid eye contact with the adults before meeting Aiden on the porch and closing the door behind me.

Carlitos follows. "I already brought Omega her homework."

"Oh." Aiden's face falls. "I…"

"What are you *actually* doing here, Aiden?" Carlitos scowls. "Did Abby send you?"

"No. No...I..." His cheeks go red. He tugs the bill of his baseball cap lower. "I just wanted to make sure you were okay," he finally says. "You weren't at school so..."

"Yeah, because she puked her guts out, remember?"

I elbow Carlitos in the side, then meet Aiden's eyes. "I'm fine."

"Oh, good." He exhales and suddenly the air between us is filled with relief.

Aiden Montgomery was worried about me?

"I also wanted to come here to say that...I'm sorry about Abby. I know she doesn't really believe you're responsible for the cats that have gone missing." He tries to smile. "I don't either."

"Gee, thanks," Carlitos spits.

"It's messed up what she's doing," Aiden says. "I know that."

Carlitos steps to him. "Then make her stop."

Aiden frowns, his big brown eyes sucking me right in. "She's going through a lot...and I can't change the reason why."

"It's okay," I tell him because his heartache is making me ache too.

There's an awkward silence, Carlitos just standing there, nostrils flaring, while Aiden chews on a scab on his bottom lip.

"Anyway..." He stuffs the textbook into his backpack. "The math homework yesterday was killer." He meets my eyes again. "If you need any help, maybe we could meet before school or something. You like to hang out in the library, right?"

I swallow. "I, uh, I mean, yes. I do. Like the library."

Clau squeals behind me. I glance at her, my eyes scream-ing, *Shush*.

Aiden smiles. "Tomorrow?"

I smile back. "Sounds great."

And then Aiden Montgomery, with his perfect dimples, walks down the porch steps, along the little dirt road that leads to our house, and back toward the west side of town.

Too many slices of pizza later I finally crash into bed, my makeup of yesterday's pop quiz looming in the distance. And also my study session with Aiden. My stomach flutters.

"I'm so glad you're feeling better, Omega," La Virgen says. "We were so worried."

The lampshade tilts. "I was sick of watching you puke."

Clau looks out the window. I know she's thinking about Romeo and Julieta again. "It's going to feel so lonely here tomorrow while you're at school."

"You'll have Abuela and Abuelo and Mami...."

"Your abuelo's always napping and your mom will be busy getting ready for the party. And all your abuela does is talk about when she was a girl and try to get me to do chores. You know, making a bed takes a lot of energy for a ghost."

"I'm sorry, Clau. Maybe you shouldn't have—"

"No…" She shakes her head. "I told you. They were making you worse."

"I know," I say, "but I still don't understand why."

"I used to be allergic to cats," Selena says. "That's why I was always more of a dog person."

"Maybe that's what it was," Clau says. "You were allergic to them or something."

"They were dead." The lampshade tosses its tassels. "Dead cats don't have fur, therefore you can't be allergic to them."

I take a second to check in with my brain, with my body. I search for an emotion I can name, something left behind from the past few days. Not only are the nausea and the fever gone, so is the fear. I hadn't realized before how heavy it had been, so tight around my chest and lungs that I was barely breathing.

I turn to Clau. "What if it wasn't the fact that they were dead that was making me sick? What if it has *how* they died in the first place?"

"What do you mean?" Clau asks.

"If the cats were"—I lower my voice—"*murdered*, that means their souls didn't pass peacefully. Like it stained them somehow and they carried that energy over with them."

Clau hugs her knees, thinking. "Like it was stuck to them like glue and then that glue got stuck to you too."

I nod. "That's how hauntings always happen. People come

in contact with a disgruntled ghost and the next thing they know there's an evil spirit following them home."

"So there *is* a cat killer on the loose." Clau scrunches her brow. "Our only lead was La Lechuza, but your mom *and* Soona said she isn't real."

I remember Soona's hand on my shoulder, how she'd jerked away. "She said La Lechuza wasn't real, but that doesn't mean it's true."

La Virgen gasps. "You think she was lying?"

"Of course she was lying." The lamp sways. "Who's going to admit to a child that the world is full of monsters?"

"Maybe she's protecting me from something."

"Or maybe La Lechuza scares her too," Clau says.

My insides go cold. What kind of monster could scare Soona? She's the most powerful person I know.

"Whether she's trying to protect me or she's...afraid of something, she's not going to tell me the truth. Which means..." I look from the hall to my bedroom window, the very one I was almost lured out through a few nights before.

"Which means what?" Clau asks.

"We're going to have to find out another way."

CHAPTER 8

"I THINK I SHOULD GO BACK AND CHANGE again." I stop in the middle of the school parking lot. "This shirt feels too—"

"You changed clothes six times," Clau reminds me.

Abuela's starting to loosen the reins with Clau and actually let her walk to school with me today. Well, I walked. She floated.

"What if he forgets?" I rub my sweaty palms on my jeans. "What if it's a prank?"

"If it's a prank, I'll haunt his bathroom mirror for a month." She nudges me forward. "But it's *not* a prank." She wriggles her eyebrows. "It's a *date*."

I swat at her, my hand hitting air as she goes fuzzy. "It's *not* a date."

"Oh, yeah? Then why is he wearing his dad's cologne?"

I freeze. "Clau. You did not."

She looks away with a shrug.

"You *spied* on him? When you were *supposed* to be grounded?"

Instead of answering me she blows me a dramatic kiss and then disappears.

I wish my nerves had evaporated with her, but there's still a swarm of bees in my stomach by the time I find Aiden in the corner of the library sandwiched between the comic books and copies of Shakespeare.

"Hi." He stands.

"Hi."

"Do you want to … ?"

I nod, sitting next to him. That's when I notice his text-book is already open, a Rebanadita resting in the spine.

He picks it up, twirls it between his fingers. "You like these, right?"

I take it from him. "Yeah. How'd you know?"

"You and Abby used to …"

I smile, remembering. And then I stop, thinking about how many other sentences could start with *me and Abby used to.*

"I'm sorry if I freaked you out yesterday by coming to your house."

"No, it's …" The bees in my stomach turn to tiny fire-works. "Thanks for checking on me."

He taps the eraser end of his pencil. "When you and Abby stopped talking, I didn't know it was going to feel like I'd lost a friend too. I know we didn't really call each other that. Friends, I mean. But..." He meets my eyes. "I'd like to be."

My heart squeezes. "Yeah." I smile and try not to blush. "I'd like that too."

"Cool." He flips to the next page in his textbook. "Hey, do you remember when me, you, and Abby were walking home from school and had to outrun that giant dust storm?"

"Oh my gosh! The haboob!"

His eyes widen. "The haboob!"

"I almost choked to death on dirt because I couldn't stop laughing at you screaming, 'The haboob is coming! The haboob is coming!'"

"It's officially my favorite word now."

I hear a loud *shush* from the other side of the stacks. Soona.

Aiden grows quiet, the smile falling from his face. "Sometimes...I wish I could bring her back." He looks up at me. "The Abby that used to laugh until she cried. That used to be happy."

I lean closer like I did with Clau. Letting him know I'm here.

"Yeah," I say. "I miss that Abby too."

We'd hidden behind one of the silos as the dust storm blew through, Abby using her jacket to shield us both.

"Close your eyes," she'd said so I wouldn't get dust in them.

Then we held on to each other as the wind rocked us.

Afterward, we ran through the sprinklers in her front yard, trying to wash off the dirt. Until it turned to mud and we were covered in that too. Then Abby's mom chased us around with the water hose until we were finally clean.

As the sun started to set, Mrs. Montgomery sat between us on the porch steps, wrapping an arm around us both.

"You girls be good to each other." She squeezed us tighter. "Be there for each other. You understand?"

"Pinkie swear." Abby reached out her hand.

I reached back. "Pinkie swear."

Mrs. Montgomery sighed, hugging us close, and I felt the warmest peace wash over her. But beneath that was something tender. Like a bruise. Except more painful than that.

The next day she told Abby and her brothers that she was sick and I realized why she'd told us to take care of each other. Because she wasn't going to be able to take care of Abby for much longer.

Except I couldn't do it. When she needed me most. When she asked me to bring her mother back. I broke my promise. I broke us.

Now Abby feels so far away. A part of the past. Our friendship more like a story instead of something that actually happened.

A part of the past.

The past…

My heart races. *That's it.* I've been so busy worrying about La Lechuza in the present. But what if that's not where the answers are?

What if they're in the past?

What if I could talk to someone who was there too?

I failed Ms. Schulz's pop quiz that she had me make up during lunch. Carlitos offered to give me the answers, but I didn't want that bad luck hanging around. When you put bad out into the world, it always comes back, even if that "bad" is just cheating on a math quiz. Besides, I need all the good energy I can get for the séance tonight.

Well, the séance we'll be having once I actually know how to have a séance. Which is why Carlitos is walking into the library approximately forty-five seconds before me so he can distract Soona while I search section O for any and all materials on summoning the dead.

Talking to ghosts who have actually crossed over is much more complicated than communicating with someone like Clau, who refuses to follow the rules. A séance does have very specific protocol that usually takes years of training to master, but I only have a couple of hours, so fingers crossed that I don't blow anything up or leave someone permanently possessed.

That's the other thing about communicating with ghosts that used to be animals. You have to give them a human voice.

"Did you tell him yet?" Clau asks.

"If I told Carlitos we were going to have to use his body as the vessel for communication, he would not be helping us distract Soona right now."

Up ahead Carlitos greets Soona, saying something that makes her laugh and I roll my eyes. Then he knocks over a pencil holder on her desk, careful to make sure it falls on her side.

That's our signal.

As she bends down to pick them up, Clau and I tiptoe across the library before disappearing into the stacks. My heart pounds as we inch toward section O. When I hear Soona laugh again, I know we're in the clear, the two of us slipping behind the beads without a sound.

The second I see the rows and rows of books stretching into infinity, my heartbeat ticks up and I wonder if sneaking into a mystical library that is practically a maze, and has the power to trap you with your own curiosity, was actually a great idea or a very, very bad one.

"What are those?" Clau points to the alebrijes still turning in slow circles above our heads.

"Those are alebrijes. They're sort of like spirit guides.

Supposedly they're around to protect you from danger, but other times they can be kind of mischievous."

"Which type are these?" Clau asks.

"I don't know. I think they belong to the books."

"You mean they're protecting them." Clau's head sways, still watching them. "But from who?"

There it is. The first itch this mystical library is tempting us to scratch. Suddenly, I feel like I'm hooked to the end of a fishing line, something tugging me deeper into the stacks.

But we're not here to learn about *these* giant birdlike creatures. We're here to learn about a giant birdlike creature that might possibly be eating the cats in our neighborhood and also how to contact those cats from beyond the grave.

"What kind of library is this?" Clau grazes the spine of one of the books. A tongue slithers out from between the pages and licks her. "¡Uy! What the heck was that thing?"

"Just a book." I try not to let myself get distracted by her questions or mine as I search the endcaps for the letter *S*.

Clau accidentally brushes against one of the shelves, the book stacked on top instantly growing thorns. "These aren't like any of the books I've ever seen. Not even the creepy ones in your attic." She looks closer at one of the titles. "*Basic Bone Baking for Witchlings: Volume One.*"

"We're still in the *B*s?" I quicken my pace, scanning from left to right.

"So are you and Carlitos witchlings? What's a witchling? Can I become a witchling? How many of them exactly are there in this little town?" Clau's questions come at lightning speed.

Before I can warn her about the effects of the library, about the fact that all those questions running through her mind are a trap, Clau's gone.

I spin in a circle, but of course Clau leaves silent footsteps. Instead, I listen for recently awoken books. Hissing. Snapping teeth. Leaves rustling.

Somewhere in the distance, I hear a strange sound. A soft

tapping. Like water dripping onto a hard surface. I follow it, swatting away all the questions that are chasing me like gnats. About the sound. About Clau. About the cats and La Lechuza and witchlings and Carlitos's stupid jokes and why exactly Soona would lie to me.

"Clau! Where are you?"

I try to focus on just that one thing—finding Clau. *Where are you? Where are you? Where are you?*

"Clau! Answer me!"

I keep chanting the question. I keep picturing her face. Then I round the corner, turning down a row of books that are covered by low-hanging storm clouds, rain pooling on the shelves, in the creases between books.

Clau is holding one of them, the pages translucent. That's when I realize that it's glass, the book made of broken shards, her fingers trembling around them. The rain pitter-patters against the pages, both the book and Clau drenched.

I move to her side. "Clau?"

She doesn't answer, the rain slipping silently down her cheeks.

I lean in to take a closer look at the words, but there are none. Behind the glass is a shadow, swirling like the clouds above our heads.

"Clau, we need to get out of the rain." She blinks. "Clau, can you hear me?"

She finally looks up, and her expression is just like it was yesterday morning when she told me she made Romeo and Julieta cross over. And I wonder what questions dragged her to this spot, what answers she did or didn't find.

She closes the book and puts it back on the shelf. "Clau, are you okay?"

She nods once.

"I think I saw the *S*s." I take her by the hand. "This way."

We get farther and farther from the storm clouds, but Clau is still quiet.

"The library's enchanted," I say. "It wants you to ask hard questions, the kind of questions that could have you searching the shelves for hours. But it isn't real, Clau." I stop in front of her, meeting her eyes. "Whatever you're feeling, whatever you're wondering about right now, it isn't real, okay?"

"It's like a spell?" Her voice is small.

"It's just a spell," I say. "A very powerful spell."

She exhales, relieved.

The two of us wind down the row marked *S*. It curves like the letter, the second bend bringing us right to the books on séances. There's *Snappy Séances for the Witch in a Pinch* and *Seasoned Séances for the Serious Summoner*.

"What about this one?" Clau points to a book titled *Séances for Beginners: The Quick-Start Guide for Communing with the Dead*.

"Perfect." I pull it off the shelf, waiting for the binding to grow vines or the pages to snap at my hand like teeth. But the book doesn't stir. More questions appear, coming like a flood. I quickly stuff the book in my bag, ignoring them. "Okay, let's get out of here."

Clau and I exit section *S*, but we're so deep in the stacks now that I don't really know where *here* is.

"Do you remember where the entrance is?"

Clau shrugs. "I think I got a little turned around."

We both move in slow circles, waiting for the path to open up, for a sign that we aren't lost. Even though, according to Soona, this far in the stacks, we're supposed to be.

Which way? Which way? Which way?

The question strikes like a giant bell, reverberating until it's drowned out all my other thoughts. But it's another trap, the sound inside my head almost hypnotic.

Instead of letting it drag me even farther into the library, I try to imagine the beaded entryway, Carlitos and Soona on the other side.

But there's something else needling its way into my mind. Crisp but faint. And then it sharpens, wedging itself between my thoughts.

A whistle.

La Lechuza.

The millions of questions I have about her hook themselves

around my arms and legs, and I start walking, knowing we're not nearing the exit. Not caring either way.

"Omega, are you sure this is the—?"

"This is the way."

We reach the row of birds' nests, books nestled under twigs and down. They coo, and Clau reaches out to pet one. It jostles, waking.

"They're so cute," Clau whispers.

And that's how I know they're not what I'm looking for. I spot the book Soona showed me about the history of owls, gently pushing it to the side before scanning the shelves beneath and behind. I feel a tug, another hint from the library itself. *Dig deeper.*

"What exactly are you looking for?" Clau creeps up behind me.

I shush her, trying to think. To listen.

Where are you?

That's when the shelf begins to groan, something splitting the wood. Wild roots slither out, thick and covered in thorns. There's something bound in them, the vines wrapped so tightly all I can see are its eyes. Two bulbous moons shining as bright as a flashlight. It blinks, watching me too.

The vines loosen, sliding forth an old book that looks like a pile of leaves, except for the eyes protruding from the front cover. I grip the binding, pulling it closer.

Clau reads the black letters stitched sharply with something like thread, or maybe hair, across the cover. "*The Legend of La Lechuza.*" She takes a step back. "Wait, but..."

"I knew it," I breathe.

"Do you really think you should open that?" Clau asks. "Maybe Soona had a good reason to lie. Maybe she'll explain it all to you if you just ask."

"I already asked. She made her choice." I graze the letters with my finger. "This is mine."

The eyes close, slowly, an invitation.

Clau shivers. I hold my breath. And then I turn to the first page.

I remember how Soona had summoned the history of owls and I let that breath go, blowing the words on the page into being. This time it isn't another owl. It's a shadow, slowly stretching into long limbs. A woman, her dress old and covered in lace.

For a long time the stranger just looks at me and I wonder if she can even see us or if she's trapped somewhere between this world and the one within those fragile pages. She seems fragile too, like something wounded waiting to be hurt again.

"You're safe," I promise.

Her fear dwindles.

"We just want to know who you are. What happened to you..."

"A child has never opened this book. Has never demanded to know what's inside." The woman's head makes tiny jerks to the left and right.

I stand perfectly still. "Are you going to hurt us?"

She frowns. "That's what they told you, what you thought you'd find in these pages." She can barely meet my eyes. "A monster. But what they didn't tell you is that I was a child once."

"You were human?"

She softens, remembering. "I was a little girl who loved trees. Who loved singing. Who loved the moon." Her face falls.

"What happened to that little girl?" I ask.

"They took her." Her gaze wanders off like she's still looking for that little girl. "They stuffed her into dresses and made her stop climbing trees. They told her the moon was evil and she believed them."

She's talking about a different time, her memories of being stuffed into dresses sounding just like the stories my abuela's always telling Clau and me about when she was a girl.

It makes me think about all the things I get to do that Abuela couldn't. She married Abuelo when she was only fifteen, and even though she loved him, she also wanted to be so much more than just his wife. She always tells me, "Mira, Mega, you make your own way, you make your own rules. Don't let anyone stifle the power inside you, ¿entiendes?"

132

It wasn't until she left my bisabuelos that she understood her own power, which is why I always think it's funny when she tries to convince Carlitos not to leave our small town. That's not exactly letting him make his own rules. But I guess that's how it goes when you become an adult. You finally get to tell yourself what to do, which makes you feel like you can tell other people what to do too.

I sense the woman slipping away, being dragged down by something dark.

"But you grew up," I say, trying to drag her back. "Didn't you learn that they were wrong?"

"I grew up and I met a man who told me I could be anything I wanted, if first I became his wife. So I did. We were married and I loved him." Her voice quakes. "But he lied." Her hands form tight fists, her body shaking.

"Oh, she's not playing." Clau shudders behind me. "Omega, let's go!"

"I left him, in search of the moon. It found me first."

"What do you mean *it?*"

"Two bright eyes, dancing among the treetops. Watching over me as I ran." Roots take hold at the woman's feet, a strange forest rising up around us. Suddenly, she's in a nightgown, running barefoot among the trunks of the trees, something swooping down over her head. "The owl waited, luring me in with a song, with a promise much stronger than the one that man had given me." The shape of an owl looms over her, giant wings spread wide like the sails of a ghostly ship. "It said:

> *Be my skin*
> *avenge his sin*
> *let your life begin."*

Behind me, Clau gulps. "You killed him?"

The forest disappears, night fog swirling around La Lechuza. She smiles, her teeth razor-sharp points. Her mouth stretches into a beak, her eyes swollen with moonlight.

"I had to. To complete the transformation." She takes a step toward us and in her eyes I see her husband's face, contorted in fear, mouth open wide. She blinks and his body is lifeless.

"Transformation?" I croak.

"I wasn't the first the moon turned." Her grin is wicked. "And I won't be the last."

La Lechuza jerks, like something's struck her from the inside. "No no no no…" Her head hangs, fists still clenched. Fighting something. "I won't. I won't."

"Won't what?"

Her fists stretch into talons, then back to fingers. The woman and the witch fighting for every inch of skin.

"Let them go!" Her beak recedes, lips spread in a scream. "Let me go!" And then she is made of sharp points again, beak and claws all arrowed in on me and Clau.

She cackles, meeting my eyes. Swimming in them is something human, the woman trapped and staring back at me. Her features get fuzzy, everything growing black.

"Omega?"

I blink; Clau is fuzzy too. "Omega, wake up!"

"Enough!" Another voice. Powerful. Familiar.

The darkness loosens its grip on me. I blink and see Soona standing between me and La Lechuza. She snaps a finger and the blank pages of the book begin to shred, fluttering into the sky like locusts. They swarm the monster, beating it down with their wings. It shrinks, screaming, until the swarm collapses with a gasp.

Everything is quiet. The wind is gone.

Soona snaps her fingers again. "Broom."

A broom and dustpan appear, moving on their own to sweep up the mess. The dustpan empties over the book's binding, the pages reforming before the cover slams shut.

Soona snaps one more time, sending the book back to its spot on the shelf, where it's swallowed by the same vines that were safeguarding it earlier. Now I know why it wasn't so easy to find.

She reaches out a hand, pulling me to my feet.

I'm still staring at the place where La Lechuza just stood. "She had a broken heart."

"There's nothing more dangerous," Soona says.

"It's still no reason to give up your soul," Clau adds, even more pale than usual.

Soona stares at the same spot. "You'd be surprised what you'd be willing to give up for love."

"But she didn't want to do it," I say. "She was trapped in there. I could see it." I shudder. "I could *feel* it. Whatever the monster was making her do, it wasn't her choice." I kneel, brushing the ground where she'd stood, her pain still radiating from the spot. "It seemed like she didn't have a lot of choices in her life." I look up at Soona. "You knew she was here all along, didn't you?"

"Omega…"

I examine her more closely. "Why did you lie to me?"

She crosses her arms. "I don't think someone who sneaks into an enchanted library without permission should be pointing any fingers." She pushes me toward the exit.

"How did you find us, anyway?" Clau asks.

"Carlitos told me the same joke twice in a row. Also, he was sweating like a pig."

I roll my eyes. "I knew he'd screw it up somehow."

"Well, that screwup may have saved your life."

"But it was just a book. That wasn't the real La Lechuza, was it?"

"How many times do I have to tell you that stories are truth?"

We pass through the beaded archway, time racing down my spine like a cold piece of ice.

Carlitos stands at Soona's desk, cheeks reddening the second he sees us.

He mouths the word, *Sorry*.

I scowl, cracking my knuckles.

Once she has all three of us together, Soona raises an eyebrow. "Now, I hope your little adventure has taught you a valuable lesson."

I grin. "To always trust my instincts?"

Her scowl is even fiercer than mine. "That some things are better left unfound."

"But if we didn't even know she was out there, how would we be able to stop her?"

"*We* are not going to do anything." She spins Carlitos and me toward the exit, Clau sandwiched between us. "You're going to let the adults handle this. Do you understand me?"

I stare down at my feet.

"Omega…"

I exhale. "I understand."

"Good." She waves us off. "Now get home before I tell your mother where you've been."

When we're outside the school, I punch Carlitos in the arm. "All you had to do was distract her for five minutes."

"Ow! I tried, okay? But she's, like, a genius. She probably knew we were up to something before we even got there."

I smile, unzipping my backpack. "If she's all-knowing, then how did I leave the library with this?"

He squints. "*Séances for Beginners: The Quick-Start Guide for Communing with the Dead.* Really, Omega? I thought we told Soona we'd learned our lesson."

"So I lied."

"Well, I didn't. We shouldn't be messing around with this kind of stuff. It's dangerous."

"Oh, don't be such a loser," Clau teases.

"Yeah," I say, "since when are you afraid of ghosts?"

Clau creeps up behind him, trailing a cold finger down his back again.

He jumps. "It's not just ghosts we have to worry about. Once you open that door, anything can come through it. And you're not a powerful enough witch to be able to stop it. You're barely a witch at all."

My cheeks burn and I grit my teeth, trying to hide the sting of his words. The same sting I feel around every birthday, every holiday, and every family get-together. All because I can't make the kind of magic you can see; because I can barely control the invisible empathic abilities I *do* have. And all because Papi's not a brujo. Because Mami dared to fall in love with someone "ordinary," not just making my magic weaker but making it defective.

"Look, I didn't mean…" Carlitos sighs. "It's just, I'm scared, okay?"

"It's okay to be scared," I admit because I'm scared too. Because I know that my humanness means every spell I ever try to cast will be tricky, that it might go wrong.

But that doesn't stop me from being drawn to it. Maybe that's because a small piece of it *does* belong to me. But if I'm too scared to even try, how can I ever claim it?

Besides, I don't need to be powerful enough to open the door between this world and the next. All I need is to make a crack wide enough for a couple of dead cats to step through. But most importantly, if I don't open this door, I'll never learn how to close the other one. How to send La Lechuza back to where she came from.

"What do you even need to talk to the cats for, anyway?" Carlitos asks. "Didn't you just get the answer you were looking for—that La Lechuza is real?"

"Which only leads to more questions," Clau says. "Like where is she hiding?"

"So ask the trees if they've seen her again. We'll go back

to Señora Avila's so you can talk to the bird fountains in her yard."

I shake my head. "That won't work."

Carlitos clenches his fists, his fear slowly turning to anger. "Why not?"

"Because they can't move," I say. "And we're not looking for La Lechuza. We're looking for her nest."

CHAPTER 9

The Allsup's stands like a mirage at the edge of the road, a tumbleweed blowing in one direction while a semitruck idles in the other. It's blocking the only pump at the gas station, three trucks behind it in line, all honking their horns. The parking lot's full too. Kids bounce out with fried burritos and sundae crunch bars, chimichangas and helados.

"You're drooling," Clau whispers unnecessarily.

Carlitos wipes his mouth. "I'm starving."

"It's four o'clock in the afternoon," I say. "Besides, we're not here to eat."

Carlitos rolls his eyes. "Yeah, yeah, pull out your list of contraband so we can get this over with already."

Séances for Beginners: The Quick-Start Guide for Communing with the Dead conveniently listed ingredients for a basic séance in the index of the book, which I then copied onto Mami's normal shopping list. Well, it's not exactly *normal*.

Normal would be things you could walk in and buy at the grocery store without having to learn a secret knock. For all other necessities—heart of toad, rat tails, cow eyeballs, human bones, et cetera—there's Allsup's. Well, the secret potions shop beneath the Allsup's.

On our way in, Belén Ochoa gives us a wave from behind the register. She's worked here forever, mostly because her post behind the counter is the perfect spot for people watching, which means she never runs low on gossip.

She leans over the counter to the viejita in line, whispering a little too loudly about one of the teachers at our school who showed up on Monday with purple hair.

"I heard it was a nervous breakdown. There were ambulances. Straitjackets. Todo el asunto."

The viejita in front of her gasps. "And they're letting her be around the children?"

I roll my eyes, whispering to Carlitos from behind the Cheetos display. "I heard Mrs. Smith just went to a cosplay convention and couldn't get the purple dye out of her hair."

Carlitos rips open a bag of hot limón Cheetos. "Belén doesn't care about the truth. She cares about making herself seem like some all-seeing profeta, even though she's really just one of those wacko conspiracy theorists that posts pictures of burnt toast online that she swears looks like the Virgin Mary."

The viejita wags a finger. "You think she's one of those... what do you call them? Punk rockers?"

Belén narrows her eyes. "I think her true identity is much more sinister than that."

"Ay Dios." The viejita shakes her head before taking her Fabuloso and walking away.

"See?" I groan. "This is why everyone in town hates each other. Because people like Belén are constantly making up rumors."

We don't stick around to hear what other lies Belén's come up with and instead head for the narrow hallway in the back. It's full of truckers and a family of four, all waiting for the single working bathroom. The other one is marked OUT OF ORDER, which is code for *Keep Out Unless You're Here for Magic Stuff*.

Clau disappears, gliding straight through the freezers to the back of the store to await our signal.

"Hey, Omega."

I turn and see Aiden. He's holding a blue Powerade, some beef jerky, some peanut M&M's, a bag of gummy worms, and a fried burrito.

"You going on some sort of quest?" Carlitos asks.

Aiden looks down at his bounty and blushes. "Uh, just making sure I don't need to go home before it gets dark."

"So where do you go?" Carlitos asks.

"Carlitos." I flash him a look that says, *Mind your own business.*

"What?" He looks Aiden up and down. "With all those cats going missing, everyone should be a suspect, right? Not *just* us."

"Fair," Aiden says and I can sense his guilt all over again. "There's just this spot I like to go to sometimes. It's got the best view of the woods east of town. Seriously, you can see everything from up there." He clears his throat. "Maybe if you're not busy…we could…"

"Actually, we're very busy," Carlitos interrupts.

I pinch his hip the way Abuela does and he yelps.

"It sounds cool."

"So cool," Carlitos deadpans. "But we're sort of on a time crunch." Carlitos pushes me toward the bathrooms. "We really got to go."

"Okay, see ya."

I smile over my shoulder, not wanting to break eye

contact just yet. But then Aiden sets his stuff on the counter and Belén starts talking his ear off.

"You can stop shoving me now."

"I wasn't shoving you," Carlitos says, "I was saving you. That family is trouble, Omega. I know you like Aiden but—"

"What?" I practically yell so loud that everyone in line waiting for the bathroom turns around to look at us. When they turn back around, I whisper, "I *do not* like Aiden."

Carlitos rolls his eyes. "It's coming off you stronger than the smell of hot garbage."

"What is?"

"Love."

"Psst!" Clau appears at the end of the hallway and I realize she's been waiting all this time for my signal.

I give her a small nod and then she uses all her energy to knock over a display of toilet paper, causing a distraction that allows me and Carlitos to slip inside.

The door slams closed behind us, making Carlitos jump. I'm knocked back by something else—the sour smell of formaldehyde wafting from the dimly lit space down below.

Last year in science class we dissected rats, and now whenever I see Señora Delarosa or enter her potions lair, I think of cutting open their bulbous bellies. Then fainting, not because I had a weak stomach myself, but because Joon Lee passed out at the first sight of a spleen, bumping into me on his way down. His horror and nausea were like quicksand, making me look like a total lightweight.

But Señora Delarosa isn't just pickling rats down here. As we descend the concrete steps, we see all sorts of critters floating in jars lining the back wall: lizards, tarantulas, baby birds. Some are just the parts: chicken feet, pig ears, cow tongue. The harsh desert around our little town means she has access to an endless supply.

Beneath the jars of dead animals are pots of fauna. Flowers, cactus paddles, cactus needles, aloe vera juice, wild mushrooms, and seeds in every color of the rainbow. There are other ingredients tucked away on the shelves or spilling into one another on her various work spaces.

Kuku, Señora Delarosa's alebrije, comes bounding up the steps, tail wagging as he slobbers all over Carlitos. His front half looks like a hairless dog while his hind is shaped like a fox. He's got giant bunny ears between two bull horns, and his tongue is as long as a lizard's.

"Kuku." Señora Delarosa whistles and he retreats, turning in circles before rolling up in a ball at her feet.

She sits at a table in the center of the room, stitching what looks like human hair onto a beige doll.

"Who's that supposed to be?" Carlitos plops down in the chair in front of her.

She pauses her stitching, eyeing him over the rims of her glasses. "You," she says dryly.

"Or is it that teacher Belén was talking about upstairs?" I rest my elbows on the table, leaning in closer to examine the doll's crooked eyes and railroad-track mouth. The energy pouring from it tastes bitter on my tongue. Like vengeance.

Señora Delarosa sighs. "Belén thinks she knows what evil looks like. But if she did, she'd notice it in herself and stop gossiping all the time."

Carlitos and I laugh.

Señora Delarosa lifts a finger.

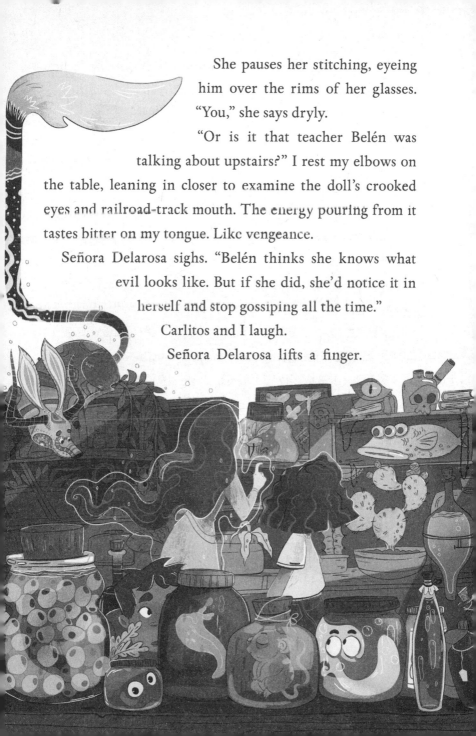

"Tell your friend not to touch." She's pointing at Clau who's examining some bright yellow berries up close. "She'll suck the energy right out of them."

Señora Delarosa can't see Clau, but she can sense when the energy in a place has shifted and also where or who that energy is coming from.

When it comes to the dead, there's definitely a very specific energetic signal they give off. When my bisabuela died last year, I remember approaching her body in the casket and feeling this cold, heavy dread. Like her body had become a black hole, sucking up all the life and light around it. I've been to other funerals and those bodies exuded the same thing.

But Clau's different and I wonder sometimes if she knows it. That she doesn't exude death, even though she is…dead. But that she gives off something else. An emotion I can't even name. An emotion so pure it probably doesn't have one. Because it's probably not supposed to exist. Like Clau.

She frowns, backing away from Señora Delarosa's overstuffed shelves. That's when I notice a glass bottle full of something red and sticky. There's a tag around the corked end—*Para Avila*.

"Are you here to gawk or to buy something?" Señora Delarosa finally says, huffing a strand of black hair out of her face.

"Yes, sorry." I hand over the list. "We came to pick up a few things. Just the usual. For Mami. Business has really been booming and we keep getting orders nonstop. Especially this week. She's got so many new orders to fill, not to mention all of the things she's making for Marisol's quince tomorrow...."

Carlitos nudges me and I realize I'm rambling. And sweating.

Señora Delarosa narrows her eyes at me before taking the shopping list. I tuck my hair behind my ear, trying to look relaxed.

She looks from the list to me, then back to the list. "Ah-huh, I see...." She lifts an eyebrow. "For the quince..."

"Yes." I swallow, afraid she can see straight through me, that she can sense the energy shifting again, making room for my lie.

She exhales. "Let me see what I can find."

Carlitos and I exhale too, grinning at each other as she begins to pull things from the shelves.

On a shelf on the other side of the room, I notice a pot almost bubbling over, the fuchsia liquid inside as bright as bubble gum. Next to it is a vial with Mrs. Villarreal's name on it.

"Do you think that's supposed to help her find Oscar?" Carlitos whispers.

"Or to help her forget him," I whisper back.

"It's for her bunions," Señora Delarosa interrupts, still perusing the shelves. "Not that it's any of your business."

"Bunions from all those miles she's walked searching for Oscar," Clau says. She passes through some of the bubbles floating up from the potion. "Maybe we should tell her the truth."

"Maybe," I agree, suddenly feeling guilty, "but not until we have proof. Otherwise, she'll just think we're a bunch of weirdos like everyone else does."

"Unless we're killed in the process of getting that proof," Carlitos hisses.

"All right." Señora Delarosa makes her way back to her worktable. "Let me wrap these things up."

In a few minutes everything is neatly bagged and tied with string.

Señora Delarosa punches out numbers on an old calculator. "Okay, so that'll be thirty-four dollars and eighty-nine cents." She blinks. "Now will that be cash or charge?"

My heart jumps into my throat. All I have is ten dollars in cash and a couple of quarters I found in the school snack machine.

The door at the top of the stairs creeps open. Belén waves down at us and even from here she smells like fried dough.

Carlitos starts drooling again.

"Señora Avila is here to see you," Belén says with a raised eyebrow, code for something that makes Señora Delarosa shake her head.

Belén looks back over her shoulder through the crack in the door. "She says it's *urgent*."

"Tell her we're almost done here."

Belén nods before heading back to the cash register.

"Now." Señora Delarosa turns her attention back to us. "I said, will that be cash or charge?"

"Oh, um…" I'm sweating again.

She narrows her eyes, looking between me and Carlitos. And I know for certain this time that she's caught on. That she knows exactly what we're up to. That she's going to tell Mami and I'm going to be grounded for, like, ever.

Suddenly, the door's thrown open again and Señora Avila comes bounding down the steps.

She looks rattled.

"You said it would work! That if I—"

Kuku jumps in front of Señora Delarosa, his teeth bared and snarling. His tail stiffens, hackles up like he's ready to attack.

"Kuku!" Señora Delarosa claps her hands, but he doesn't move.

"Here, Kuku." Clau whistles and his ears perk up.

But his eyes are still tracking Señora Avila's movements.

"Kuku, do you want a treat?" Carlitos tosses a hot Cheeto and Kuku chases it underneath Señora Delarosa's worktable.

Señora Delarosa grabs Señora Avila by the shoulders. "You need to calm down."

"It's taking too long," Señora Avila says behind gritted teeth. "I paid for your services."

"And I warned you the cost might be more than you can bear." Señora Delarosa glances at us like she's suddenly remembering we're still there. "That's enough of this." Then she lowers her voice. "Not in front of the children." She turns to me and Carlitos. "Tell your mother I'll just use the card she has on file."

We take the bags. "Gracias, señora. I'll let her know."

Señora Avila is still on the verge of tears, and as we head for the stairs, she sways, knocking into me, and everything she's feeling hits me at once. Like an electric shock.

She doesn't even look up, her eyes down as she mutters to herself. I try to pull myself up the stairs before the *feeling* pulls me to the ground. Something loud and wild and angry.

Slowly, the sensation grows arms and legs, wrapping itself tightly around me. Like being hugged by a storm cloud, flashes of heat and cold crushing me until I can barely keep my eyes open.

I feel the bag of ingredients slipping from my grasp as I wobble on weak legs.

"Omega, what's wrong?" Carlitos takes my arm, trying to help me up.

But I can't move forward. The only direction I can move is down. Down. Down.

"It's the second time this week." Mami whispers from the hallway.

Abuela sighs. "Maybe it wasn't the flu after all."

Then another gruff voice. "All I know is she's been sweating like a pig."

I look down, and Abuela's worry doll, which four-year-old me nicknamed Mr. Patches, is tucked under my arm. Abuela made him out of a pair of her father's jeans, which means that instead of cuddling with a sweet stuffed doll meant to take away my worries every night, I am forced to endure the insults of an eighty-year-old man.

Nowadays she only brings him out when she really needs some divine intervention, whispering prayers into his ear that she hopes he'll speak over me as I sleep.

He hacks up something awful. "Yick! I'm soaked."

"Where's your compassion?" Selena tsks.

"You're not the one who's been nearly smothered to death for the last few hours," he growls.

"What kind of guardian angel are you?" La Virgen puts her hands on her hips. "You have a *sacred* duty."

"Sacred?" He scoffs. "I'm not touching this kid's dreams with a ten-foot pole." Then he turns to me. "You've got some serious problems, niña."

Selena tries to comfort me. "He doesn't know what he's talking about."

Unless he does, I think. *Unless he's right.*

I scour my memory for La Lechuza, but I don't remember anything after the fall. It doesn't matter. I'm still scared anyway.

I groan, so sick of feeling afraid, and then I toss Mr. Patches onto the floor where he lands face-first.

He grumbles words I'm not allowed to say into the carpet.

"Omega, are you awake?"

Mami and Abuela both rush in from the hallway, Mami kneeling to press a hand to my forehead.

"I'm fine," I say, trying to sit up. My bones still ache and I try to hide my grimace.

"Ay, how did you end up on the floor?" Abuela scoops up Mr. Patches, placing him back on the bed.

He glares at me. "You toss me around again and I'll—"

This time I press him into the mattress, smothering him for real.

I can tell by the looks on Mami's and Abuela's faces that they have moved way past concerned and straight to angry, which is Mexican for terrified. I also know that if I don't pretend to be all right, they'll never let me out of their sight, which means we won't be able to do the séance tonight. And we have to do the séance tonight because there's not another full moon for four weeks.

So I sit up straight, smile, and say, "So, what's for dinner?"

Mami quirks her head. Abuela's eyes widen.

"Dinner?" Mami repeats. "You passed out in Allsup's and have been asleep for almost four hours. Before we get to dinner, why don't you tell us what happened?"

I feel my temperature rising, but this time it's not a fever. It's the fact that Mami is dangerously close to discovering why Carlitos, Clau, and I were at Allsup's in the first place.

"Carlitos was hungry," I avert my eyes, "and then I bumped into Señora Avila. Her energy overwhelmed me, that's all."

"That's all?" Abuela puts her hands on her hips. "That woman has the personality of a wet mop. What do you mean her energy overwhelmed you?"

Mami rolls her eyes. "You're just saying that because she used to have a thing for Papá."

"A thing which he did *not* reciprocate. *Because* she has the personality of a wet mop."

"Ah-huh," Mami says. "Is that why she was your best friend until you were in ninth grade?"

"You two were friends?" I ask. "I didn't think Señora Avila had any friends."

"You're right," Abuela snaps. "She doesn't. Because she has the personality of—"

"Ya, we get it, Mamá." Mami turns to me. "Go on, Omega."

I knot the sheets in my fists, trying to think of what to say next.

"She was in a hurry." Clau appears, minus her usual theatrics. "She seemed upset about something, right, Omega?"

I nod fast. "Yeah...it was weird. She...she was weird."

Abuela raises an eyebrow. "Upset, you say..."

I swallow. "Yeah, and there was a glass bottle of this red sticky stuff with her name on it."

"And she was angry with Señora Delarosa," Clau goes on. "She said, 'It's taking too long.'"

"'It'?" Mami repeats.

This time Clau and I both nod.

"The veladora she ordered. I wonder if..." Mami purses her lips, shaking her head.

Abuela nods this time, looking at Mami. "I was wondering the same thing."

"I'll call Belén," Mami says, drifting toward the door.

Abuela beats her to it. "After I call Dolores."

Once they're gone, I immediately rip off the blankets, searching for my shoes and then the bag of supplies.

"What are you doing?" Clau hisses.

I stuff the supplies in my backpack before tossing it over

my shoulder. "It never takes Mami and Abuela more than three phone calls to get the chisme. That's ten minutes tops."

"But ten minutes before what? Where are you going?"

I face the window. The one I was almost lured out through the other night. I can already see the moon shining bright above the trees, beckoning me closer. I press a hand to the glass, silently pushing it back. The breeze tangles in my hair, reaching for me too.

"Can you pop over to Carlitos's and tell him to meet me at the spot?"

She taps her chin. "Should I tell him why?"

Down the hallway, I hear Abuela cackling on the phone with Dolores.

"Tell him whatever you have to." I slip out into the darkness. "Then meet me there in ten minutes."

CHAPTER 10

SOMETHING RUSTLES IN THE GRASS JUST BEYOND the tree line. I freeze, listening for footsteps.

Instead, I hear panting, Carlitos and Clau appearing through the darkness.

"I thought you were a pack of coyotes," I say.

"Why'd you have to go so far?" He drops his backpack next to mine. "The moon's not actually any closer all the way out here."

But he's wrong. The moon *is* brighter out here, the glow it casts making the salt ring I poured look like snow.

"Stop being such a baby and get inside." I push Carlitos over the threshold.

"You sure you know what you're doing?" He shivers, even

though the humidity out here has my hair sticking to the back of my neck.

I gesture around the makeshift force field. "I followed the directions exactly." Then I hand him one of Mami's veladoras. "All I need you to do is hold this."

He raises it, watching the flame dance. "What's it for?"

Clau snickers as Carlitos cuts his eyes between us.

"You two are up to something." He sniffs. "I can smell it."

"It's just a light for the ghosts to see by," I say.

"Yeah," Clau adds, "some of them are a little nearsighted."

This time I roll my eyes.

"Okay, now I need you to hold very still."

Clau swirls around Carlitos, making sure he doesn't move an inch.

"Okay," he snaps, annoyed, "got it."

I check the salt to make sure there are no breaks in the circle. Then I light a few more candles around the perimeter, the moon's magic driving the flames higher. They're so bright the night around us looks pitch black, and I almost get lost in it, waiting for something to crawl out of the darkness.

Instead, it's a feeling that creeps toward us. Like a guitar string that's been pulled too tight. Like the dull thud of bone on bone. I can tell something is happening. I'm just not sure if it's *me* making it happen.

Until a breeze brushes my cheek, an invisible hand lifting my chin.

Now, it whispers.

The insects grow silent and the fluttering leaves stand still. As if nature itself is waiting. I take a few deep breaths, the sweat on the back of my neck suddenly going cold.

I sense the door between this world and the next, that strange, taut feeling turning into a sound. A steady drumbeat, low and long and ancient.

I trace the words on the page as I speak them aloud:

> *Dust and bone*
> *Upon thy throne*
> *Let light and breath*
> *Guide you home.*
> *Borrow this voice*
> *This body too—*

"Whoa, whoa, whoa!" Carlitos drops the candle in the dirt. "What do you think you're doing?"

"Seriously?" I hang my head back. "Now I have to start over!"

"Start over?" He stomps over to me. "You are *not* starting over. Are you serious? You were about to let a ghost possess you."

Clau and I exchange a look.

Carlitos's eyes widen. "No." He waves his hands. "No. No. No! Absolutely not!" He grips his head in his hands, searching the dark for any signs of the supernatural. "Oh my God." He clutches his chest, breathing heavily. "What did you do to me?"

"I didn't even complete the spell. You're *fine*."

"Fine? You almost turned me into a human puppet!"

"Yeah, but for a very good reason," Clau says.

She's right. We were so close to finding out where La Lechuza's been hiding. Literally, one sentence away.

I scan the page again.

"Oh no you don't." Carlitos jumps out of the force field.

I press a finger to the final line.

"Omega..."

"Hush," Clau shushes him.

I clear my throat and then I read. "*Fill it up like an empty room.*"

The candles blow out with a gasp, the three of us letting out one too.

Carlitos shudders beside me. "What's—?"

"Shh." I swat at him, trying to listen for a voice. I close my eyes, feeling for a shift in energy.

Just the hint of something magical. Proof that it worked. *Please. Please.*

But there's nothing. Just silence.

"Is that it?" Carlitos asks.

I stare into the night, still waiting for something to step through it.

When nothing does, a lump swells in my throat. "I guess you were right." I drop the book in the dirt. "I guess…I'm not a real witch after all."

"Maybe there was something wrong with the spell," Clau says. "Like a typo or something."

"Yeah, maybe…" I say, even though I know the truth. The reason why people's energy has been overwhelming me more than usual. The reason why the spell didn't work.

It's because I'm not strong enough.

I'm not strong.

"Omega." Carlitos is frozen, finger pointing toward the tree line.

"What is it?"

"Do you hear that?" he whispers.

We both hold our breath, listening for the dead.

Twigs snap. I blink and there are lights flickering between the trunks of the trees.

"What is that?" Clau asks.

I hear laughing, footsteps breaking into a run.

Before I can knock over the candles and scatter the salt, Abby's leading a group of our classmates straight for us. Each of them is wearing a shirt with pictures of the missing cats printed on them, some holding cans of catnip while others hold belled collars. Her Friday night search party, which we were very publicly not invited to.

They shine their flashlights over our faces and then on the strange objects at our feet.

Abby aims her flashlight on the spell book in Carlitos's arms. Her eyes widen. But instead of calling us evil like she usually does, she stays tight-lipped, just staring. Taking it all in.

Betrayal. She burns with it.

"Abby was right?" Naomi faces the other kids. "Omega is behind all of this?"

I step to her. "I'm not the one stealing people's cats! How many times do I have to tell you—?"

"Then what is all this?" Joon waves his hands around. "Sure looks like some satanic stuff to me."

"You lied...." Abby's voice is so small I almost don't recognize it. But then she meets my eyes. "You *lied* to me."

Before I can respond, she steps to me and I stumble back. Then her eyes well up and I know that her thinking I'm a freak is only the half of it. Because the spell book and the candles prove something else—that I could have helped her connect with her mom. That I could have used magic to do it.

"You've *always* been a liar." She grits her teeth. "Always!" Then she shoves me and I almost land on one of the candles, still warm.

Before I can react, Clau is gnashing her teeth, gathering as much energy as she can before charging straight at Abby and knocking her to the ground. Abby lands in the center of the circle, scanning the dark for what just hurled itself at her. Her eyes finally land on me, but the moment she tries to speak, no sound comes out.

She mouths something, still silent. The other kids back up, afraid.

Naomi stutters, "Wh-what did you do to her?"

I don't know what to say, just as speechless. I turn to Clau, eyes pleading.

She throws up her hands. "That was not me. You know I can only control things that are battery-powered!"

Carlitos and I exchange a look. Suddenly, there's a twinkle in his eye.

"What's wrong, Abby? Afraid to finally tell everyone the truth?"

"The truth about what?" Joon asks, impatient.

"That rounding up strays is all part of her dad's plan to clean up Noche Buena. So what if a few pets got caught by mistake? This little search party was just meant to throw everyone off the scent so he can win reelection."

I gulp, impressed by the lie and even more impressed that they actually seem to be buying it.

Joon stands, slack-jawed. "Abby, is this true?"

But she doesn't answer. *She can't.*

"Say something!" Naomi demands.

Abby clutches her throat, face turning red with rage. She still can't speak.

Naomi narrows her eyes at her. "I can't believe you tricked us."

Joon huffs. "And all for some stupid reelection campaign?" He looks her up and down. "Tell your dad he just lost my parents' votes."

"Let's go." Naomi leads the other kids back through the trees. "Looks like we've got a bunch of missing flyers to tear down."

We wait until they're out of earshot and then Carlitos and I start panicking again.

"What the heck did you do to her?" Carlitos hisses.

"Me?" I turn to Clau. "You! You're the one who pushed her inside the force field."

"Because she pushed you first!" Clau huffs. "But I didn't steal her voice. I'm not Ursula from *The Little Mermaid.*"

"It was the witch."

We all freeze at the sound of the voice. But it isn't Abby's. The three of us turn, slowly.

Abby's sitting up, a wicked grin on her face.

"Holy smokes!" Carlitos shudders. "Is she possessed?"

"Not bad for your first try," the voice says.

I feel a rush of heat. The spell really did work. I made it work. And I don't know if I'm relieved or terrified.

Suddenly Abby's grin evaporates, her eyes locked on Clau. "Oh no, not her again."

Clau frowns. "Romeo?"

Abby's voice changes to something softer. "Be nice. She's dead."

Clau stutters. "Ju-Julieta? Wait…" She turns to me. "You summoned them both?"

"You…" Romeo growls. "You tried to make us your prisoners."

"Why do you have to be so cold?" Julieta says.

"I don't know. Maybe it has something to do with being murdered."

"Murdered?" I take a step forward as Carlitos and Clau take a step back. *Finally. The answers we've been looking for.* "Who was it?" I swallow. "*Who* killed you?"

"It was dark." Abby hangs her head as Romeo speaks through her. "The smell was so strong I thought it was a dream. But then I saw it, moonlight glinting off the aluminum can, top popped open as the salty scent traveled on the breeze. I followed it, but before I could mash my face into that oily lump of tuna, I was snatched up by the neck." Abby grits her teeth. "I thrashed and hissed, but I couldn't wriggle free. We approached a house, and in the sheen of the windows, I watched her transform, her body gnarled like the branches of a tree. Her beak...so wide I could hear the screams of the ones she'd devoured before."

"No...no..." Abby shakes her head, Julieta in distress.

"It's okay," Clau says. "We just want to make sure it doesn't happen again."

"You think you can stop her?" Romeo again, mocking us.

"Was it La Lechuza?" Carlitos asks.

Julieta wails like her name alone is a weapon.

"That's what humans call her," Romeo says.

"And what do you call her?" I ask.

"Animals know a thing like that cannot be named."

Shadows spread over Abby's face. I look up and the moon is gone, hidden behind something low and moving fast. There's the flap of wings. And then the quiet is pierced, the sound as sharp as a knife.

The whistle lassos me until I'm so tangled up it feels like I'm in shackles. Like I can't move...like I *won't* unless *she* wants me to.

Omega...

The sound takes shape, until it's suddenly...a song.

This way, Omega. Come to me.

My heart begins to sing the same song and I know that I am being summoned. For the first time in my entire life I feel something transforming inside me. I feel moonspun and mighty. I feel like magic.

"Omega? Omega!"

These voices are different, hammering away at whatever trance I'm in. "Omega!"

The shackles around me loosen and I whip around, spotting Mami and Abuela running toward us. But they're not alone. Soona and Luisa are with them, holding hands, chanting something that makes Abby twitch and wail. Their chanting grows louder as they approach, but I can't concentrate on what they're saying. All I can concentrate on is how furious Abuela looks. She swishes her skirt, huffing and puffing like she wants to throw one of her chanclas at us.

Mami's angry too, but there's something else in her eyes. Relief. That's when I realize how scared they must have been when they noticed I was gone.

"I'm sorry," I say, but the sound is swallowed up.

Wings beating, wind rushing past. It sounds like a giant storm. Mami and Abuela stumble back, looking up at the sky.

Soona and Luisa are steadfast, making their way toward the circle, toward Abby. She's scared too, her head back, hissing. I can't tell if it's Romeo or Julieta who's gotten ahold of her, or both, the spitting loud and feral. Soona and Luisa kneel in front of her, still chanting, and then Soona pulls a small vial from her bag.

The liquid inside is bright red. Just like the one I saw in Señora Delarosa's potions shop with *Para Avila* written on the side.

Abby twists, trying to pull away.

Luisa holds Abby's head back. Soona forces her mouth open, pouring the liquid inside, and then Abby is paralyzed.

After a moment, she gags, clutching her throat and gasping for air. Beneath the wheezing it sounds like her voice again.

When she glares at me and says, "What did you *do* to me?" I know she's back to normal.

Before she can claw my eyes out, Soona and Luisa drag Abby away, leading us all back through the trees.

Mami snatches me by the shirt. "Don't say a word."

Abuela snatches Carlitos by the ear. "And don't you squirm."

Then they drag us under the cover of the trees, Soona and Luisa chanting again as wings beat overhead.

"Una es la Santa Casa de Jerusalén donde Jesucristo crucificado vive y reina por siempre jamás. Amén."

It's Las Doce Verdades del Mundo—The Twelve Truths of the World—a prayer I've heard Abuela say when she felt that evil was close.

"Las dos, son las Tablas de Moisés donde dejó grabada su Divina Ley."

I join them, mouthing the words under my breath as we race toward home. "Las Tres Divinas Personas de la Santísima Trinidad, Padre, Hijo y Espíritu Santo."

The sky above me boils, the being screeching against the sound of our voices. I try to look up, but we're practically running and I don't want to trip.

But now I know for certain that the darkness chasing us isn't a storm or a shadow. Just like it wasn't on the ride home from the doctor's office when the rain beat down on the windows and the car swerved. It was never just a dream. The monster above our heads was *never* just a nightmare.

CHAPTER 11

THE ADULTS SEND ME, ABBY, CARLITOS, AND Clau inside
with the threat that if we sneak out again, it's pelas for us
all, and with the correa, not the chancleta. I haven't gotten a
spanking since I was seven and I certainly don't plan to start
now. Not to mention, almost getting eaten by La Lechuza
tonight has definitely forced me to learn my lesson about
sneaking out.

Inside, Abuelo is standing in the middle of the living
room, a maze of cups and bowls and buckets around him.
They're spread out across the floor, some sitting on shelves,
the windowsill, and the radiator.

We sidestep glassware as he places another bowl on top of
his old record player.

"What are these for?" Carlitos asks.

"Storm's coming," Abuelo says.

"Don't open the doors or windows, ¿entiendes?" Papi kisses me on the forehead. "We'll be right back."

Abby stomps her foot, almost knocking over one of the cups. "I want to go home!"

"And get eaten by a giant bird witch?" Carlitos motions toward the door. "Be my guest."

"What are you talking about?" Abby wraps her arms around herself, shaking.

"Do you want me to push her outside?" Clau circles Abby, wrapping her in an icy chill. "We could use her as bait."

"We're not using her as bait," I shoot back. "We're going to stay inside like we were told."

"Bait?" Abby takes a step back, knocking into one of the metal buckets. "Who are you talking to? What are you trying to do to me?" She's hysterical now, scanning the windows and doors, shrinking back, though I can tell she wants to make a run for it.

She takes a step, but Carlitos blocks her path. She tries to head for the back door, but Clau pushes a chair in the way. The sight of it moving on its own stuns her, her chest heaving like she's having trouble breathing.

"Abby..." I take a careful step in her direction. "Just stay calm, okay?"

She shakes her head. "I don't trust you."

"Well, you're going to have to. If you go outside, you might get hurt. That thing that was following us, it's dangerous."

As soon as the word slips from my lips, it feels wrong somehow. Because beneath the fear I felt when La Lechuza's voice was inside my head, there was also familiarity—a strange longing deep in my gut.

"And what about in here?" Abby says. "You had me possessed and now you're talking about using me as some kind of bait." She pinches her eyes shut, still trying to process. "And that's not even the worst of it...." Her lip quivers and she's quiet for a long time before she says, "You know, I used to wish that we were sisters." She looks away. "I used to think maybe we were supposed to be. Like it was just an accident where we ended up. I wanted it so much I told you everything— about my mom being sick and my dad disappearing and how scared I was all the time. Because you were my best friend." She sniffs. "You were *supposed* to be my friend."

"I *was* your friend, Abby."

"No." She shakes her head. "Friends help each other. Friends tell each other the truth." Tears rush down her cheeks. "You knew how much I missed her."

I remember all those mornings before school, the two of us sitting in the courtyard, me holding Abby's hand while she cried. I remember all the cat videos I sent her to try to cheer her up. The dances to her favorite songs we spent hours making up on the weekends so she wouldn't have to think about it.

I tried to help her. I would have done anything.

Except for the one thing that would have actually worked.

Maybe she's right. Maybe I am a terrible friend.

"You knew how much it would mean to me to be able to see her again. To talk to her just one more time." Abby shakes. "And you said you couldn't do it."

"It was the truth. Back then I didn't know how. I'm still not sure I understand how it all works. But if I could go back—"

"I don't believe you." She huffs. "My dad was right about you and your family always making everything worse."

"Abby, I'm—"

"Omega, don't bother." Carlitos's chest heaves, turning his back to her. "She's not worth it."

She turns away from us too, her reflection in the window still wiping away tears.

Outside, I hear the sound of tires on gravel as Tía Tita and Tío Juan pull up in their truck.

Chale comes crashing through the front door, flying one of his superheroes around while he spits out sound effects.

Tía Tita gives Carlitos a look through the window and mouths the words, *Watch him*.

The adults huddle in the yard, speaking in whispers.

Then they fan out, traveling in pairs until they've disappeared again into the trees surrounding the property.

Then we're alone, the lights eerily bright in the kitchen, the sound of the television humming low behind us.

"Do you think that was really her?" Carlitos whispers, his arms covered in goose bumps.

"What else…?" I swallow. "*Who* else could it be?"

"Maybe something else came through the door to the other side," Clau says. "Like a demon or something."

Carlitos and I both shoot Clau a look.

"Yeah," Carlitos says, "because a demon would totally be better than a flying owl witch."

A flying owl witch that seems to be following me, I want to add, but I'm too scared to actually say it out loud.

This way, Omega. Come to me.

Her voice was so clear, like she was whispering the words right into my ear.

I don't understand what she wants from me. And why *me?*

Clau shrugs. "Well, if it is a demon or something else that followed Romeo and Julieta through the portal, at least that means the spell worked and you were wrong about not being a real witch, Omega. In fact, it probably means you're a super powerful witch because you were able to summon a demon."

"Can we stop talking about demons?" I snap.

Chale crashes his superhero into Carlitos's leg. "Demon! Demon!"

"I'm not a demon," Carlitos swats him away. "At least one of us isn't scared."

"Demon!"

"No, Chale, ¡no malas palabras!"

Chale's eyes widen, his mouth forming a little O shape. A few seconds later and he's pouncing on the couch, superhero still held high.

"Why did you tell him demon is a bad word?" Clau asks.

"I tell him lots of things are bad words just so he'll be quiet. So far he thinks he'll get in trouble if he says, 'ice cream,' 'PlayStation,' 'bubble gum,' and 'Santa Claus.'"

I narrow my eyes at him. "You're a terrible big brother, you know that, right?"

"Hey." He shrugs. "Whatever works."

With the volume turned down on Chale, my ears tune to the sound of the wind outside. It's still howling, tree branches slapping one another and sounding like static. Like this entire night is operating on the wrong frequency. And yet, I can't help but want to take a closer look, to see if she's really out there, staring back.

But the thought of seeing those eyes, of them peering into my soul, of them possibly snatching that soul out of my body, keeps me frozen still.

Chale jumps down from the couch, the only one brave enough to get near the glass. He stares into the darkness, standing on his tiptoes.

Then he points and says, "Demon."

My heart stops. Carlitos freezes. Abby gasps. And I know I *have* to look.

"Chale, get back here!" Carlitos pats his knees like he's calling a puppy.

I move first.

Clau floats to my side. "Omega, what are you doing?"

"I need to know what's out there."

I reach the window, leaning in close. I can barely make out the chicken coop out back. My eyes adjust and I can see the breaks between the trees. I look up and the sky is perfectly clear, stars twinkling like diamonds.

I blink and the stars disappear. The moon splits in two. Honey pots. So sweet I want to reach out and touch them. And then I hear it, a low piercing whistle; the moons growing bigger and brighter until…

The front door crashes open.

We all scream, my body jumping back from the window.

"Sorry, kids." Papi waves us away from the glass.

"Did you find her?" Carlitos asks.

"Coast is clear." He smiles. "The women have it all under control."

"But I…" The words are caught in my throat and all I can do is point. "You saw it." I turn to Clau. "Didn't you?"

Her eyes soften like they did the night the lightning struck and La Lechuza appeared in the flash. I was the only one who'd seen her.

Then she admits, "I was too afraid to look."

I yank on Papi's arm. "She's still out there. I saw her."

He places a hand on my head, sighs. "We'll take another look, sound good?"

He calls out to Tío Juan on the porch, telling him to start the truck so they can do another pass of the property.

"We'll be right back," Papi says. "In the meantime, why don't you all watch some TV, eat a late-night snack?" He winks. "I won't tell Mami."

"Uh, we've got a problem." Tío Juan pops up behind the screen door.

"What's wrong?" Papi steps right through Clau.

"Do you have any jumper cables? Truck battery's dead."

"I'll grab my tools."

Chale launches himself from the couch onto Carlitos's shoulders. "Demon!"

"What did I tell you?" Carlitos rips Chale off like a Band-Aid. "Tío Tomás says to go watch TV."

"I don't think that's going to be possible." Clau hovers her hand over the remote. Nothing happens.

"Wasn't it just on?" I hold down the power button. Still nothing.

"Ugh." Clau rolls to the other side of the couch. "Now what are we going to do?"

The lights flicker and then they go out.

Abby freezes, looks up. "What's happening?"

Carlitos looks from me to Clau. Then he says, "Run!"

The four of us bolt for my room, Chale chasing after us, his face scrunched like he wants to cry.

Clau whacks Carlitos. "You're scaring him."

"Ouch! Come here, Chale. It's okay. We're just playing hide-and-seek."

"Hide-and-seek?" Chale rubs his eyes.

Something cracks overhead. We all look straight up, following the sound. The crunch of giant feet taking one step and then another as dust trickles down from the ceiling. Jagged lines snake across the plaster as the weight above us shifts.

The roof groans, something scraping across the metal shingles. Wings beat and I hear something giant descend, landing like thunder on the hard earth.

Clau floats to the window, the only one of us daring to peek out. "She's…she's…"

"Spit it out!" Carlitos crawls over next.

And then I can't help myself. I make my way to the glass and then I see her, wings like two giant wall clouds. And then I see her eyes—see where they're trained on my shadow behind the glass.

Abby shimmies across the carpet to see. "What *is* that thing?"

"She's not a *thing*," I shoot back, still staring, still too afraid to even blink.

"She's talking to Soona," Clau whispers.

My hand grazes the glass and I push it open, the breeze carrying in the sound of her voice.

It's ragged and rough. "I've been patient."

"Is that what you call stalking a poor child? You've made her feel like prey. I can see it in your eyes, Luna. You're not waiting. You're *hunting*." Soona steps to her. "Maybe it's been so long, that's all you know how to do."

"Time has changed you too." La Lechuza cranes her neck. "So that all you can do is see the ugliness in things."

"Am I wrong?" Soona says. "About you…about what you've become. Tell me I'm wrong, Luna."

"She doesn't have much time."

"She's not like you," Mami cuts in. "She will *never* be like you."

La Lechuza looks down, shame hanging from her neck like deadweight. "The transformation has already begun. Soon the moon will get what it wants. It always does."

"Not this time." Abuela glares at her. "So take your hunger and go. Leave this place!"

The women all join hands, their voices calling out the Twelve Truths of the World again, even more forceful this time.

La Lechuza winces against the sound. Then she bares her teeth, her body tensing like there isn't blood flowing through her veins but fire. It burns behind her eyes and she lets out a beastly scream. The flap of her wings is like thunder, then the night grows even darker.

All I can see are the women's silhouettes, their heads hanging back, looking up as La Lechuza heaves herself into the sky.

The window still open, I smell the storm first. Then rain begins to beat down on the roof. A moment later, I hear the pitter-patter as it strikes the bottom of bowls and buckets and glass cups.

When we make our way back to the living room, Abuelo and Papi are swapping out full glasses for empty ones.

A few minutes later, Tío Juan's truck starts, no tools needed. The TV clicks back on, the lights in the house flickering to life.

It doesn't take long for Carlitos to start hurling questions at everyone, but the adults ignore them all. Soon, Tía Tita ushers him and Chale out the door. Then Soona places a hand on Abby's shoulder, erasing this entire night from her memory before taking her home.

In the quiet, I wait while Abuelo starts a pot of coffee and Mami and Abuela bless the exterior of the house. I wait while Papi finishes washing the dishes from the dinner I didn't eat. I wait as he kisses me good night before going to bed himself.

I wait and wait for the courage to ask my own questions. For the chance to say I'm sorry. Mami waits too. Until I've stewed long enough in my own fear and shame and regret.

When she and Abuela finally come into my room, I'm still not ready, their words swirling around me like a tornado.

"Since when did you become such a malcriada?"

"And let's not forget about the money you spent at—"

"Did you think Señora Delarosa wouldn't call me to—"

"We leave you alone for one second and—"

"You spent all day in bed and then you think it's a good idea to go—"

"Do you know how scared—?"

I hang my head, trying to hide the tears. "I know. I'm sorry."

Mami kneels, grabs my chin. "No, you don't know."

"¡Estás terca!" Abuela stamps her foot. "¡Estás una mocosa!"

"Mamá…" Mami's voice is cool, the anger loosening its grip on her. She turns to Abuela. "Let me talk to her. Alone."

Abuela shakes her head, still angry. She blinks back tears the same way I am.

After she closes the bedroom door, I finally meet Mami's eyes. "I'm sorry," I croak and I mean it. I mean it *so much*.

She sighs and sits beside me on the bed.

"It's just that I had questions and everyone was lying to me and…I needed to know.…" I hiccup, but she doesn't interrupt, letting me explain, letting me get it all out. "I needed to know if she was real and if…if…" Mami puts an arm around me. "I needed to know if she was the reason I keep getting sick. If I should be afraid. If I'm getting worse."

I sob into her shirt, everything slowly coming into focus. Why I can't let this go. It's not because I'm curious. It's because I'm afraid. Because when I dream about La

Lechuza, there is something familiar, some invisible connection between us growing stronger.

"You're right," Mami finally says. "We did lie to you, and for that I'm sorry."

I wipe the tears from my cheeks. "Y-you are?"

She nods, brushing my hair back. "We thought it would be easier, but we were wrong. And I'm sorry. I'm sorry that you've been so scared and worried and that the lie only made it worse."

"It's okay," I say because it's a strange thing when your parents apologize to you. "So…" I tread carefully. "What's the truth?"

She exhales, thinking, and then, "The truth is, La Lechuza is real."

Yeah, got that, I want to say, but I'm on thin ice as it is so I don't. "But why did you lie about her?" I ask.

Mami sighs again, meeting my eyes. "If you could pretend like Abby never existed, would you?"

I think about La Lechuza's human form, the woman in the library who fought so hard to keep from becoming a monster. I try to think about her life before the man. Before the moon. When she was just a girl with a family and friends and a whole life before it was stolen from her.

"La Lechuza was your friend?" I say.

Mami stares out the window like she's waiting for her to appear behind the glass. Then she says, "No, she was family."

CHAPTER 12

Sage is burning. I hear Abuela shuffling around in her slippers, cleansing the house. But sage isn't the only thing I smell. I follow the scent of panqueques on the griddle. Papi's cooking breakfast.

"Buenos días, mija. ¿Tienes hambre?"

"I'm starving." I yawn, stretching my arms. "Where's the syrup?"

"On the table." Mami comes around the corner dressed in her Blanca's Blooms shirt, her long hair pulled back into a ponytail. "But don't mess up any of these decorations. Tía Tita and Tío Juan are on their way over with Carlitos. After the two of you eat, you're helping me load up the car."

With all the commotion last night I'd forgotten that Marisol's quinceañera is today. She invited the entire school and I know everyone's going to be there. In a town so small that we don't even have our own grocery store, birthdays are a key means of socialization. Too bad I don't exactly like socializing.

Plus, the more people in a place, the more energy there is, and the more energy, the more likely that I catch something that doesn't belong to me. Now that my empathic abilities seem to be going haywire, it's back to navigating public spaces the way I used to, which means standing alone in a dark corner all night. *Unless…*

"You know, Mami, I was thinking that maybe I shouldn't go with you tonight. I broke the rules by sneaking out and I'm feeling very guilty about that. You should probably ground me to teach me a lesson."

Mami smiles. "You know, Omega, guilt can sometimes be a good thing." She looks over at Papi; the two of them both have the same strange look on their faces. "I'm glad you regret what you did and that you're never going to do it again. And on second thought, I think grounding you is probably a good idea."

"Just to make sure the lesson really sinks in." I take another big bite of my panqueques, relieved that I'm not going to have to bump into Abby again. Soona may have wiped her memory of last night, but that doesn't mean Abby's forgotten how much she hated me before.

"I agree." Mami pours me some more freshly squeezed orange juice. "We want this to be a valuable lesson learned. One you never forget. Which is why you will definitely be coming with me to the quinceañera tonight. I can't think of a better punishment, can you?"

I choke on my orange juice.

"You and Carlitos can help me set the tables and clean up afterward."

"Mami, please, I don't want to see Abby. I don't want to be surrounded by all those people. What if I get overwhelmed again?"

Mami comes to sit down next to me. "One: This is a small town and you'll have to see Abby eventually. Two: You can't let the fear of being overwhelmed stop you from living your life. If magic isn't working, then we have to figure out another way to help you get better and that might mean exposing you to what's triggering, helping you build up your stamina. And three: I know you don't always feel like a normal kid. Let's both take a night off from the supernatural and just try to have fun."

A night off from the supernatural. *Tell that to La Lechuza*, I think. Because either she's got a grudge against our family that would put Abuela's cold shoulder to shame or she's trying to tell us something. Or more specifically, *me*.

She doesn't have much time.

The words echo inside me and I reach for my moonstone again, trying to comfort myself: *You don't even know who she is. La Lechuza could have been talking about anybody. Besides, what would she want with a witch who can't even cast a possession spell without completely screwing it up?*

"Do you think you can try?" Mami asks.

There's no point in arguing with her so I just nod.

Luckily, I don't have to sit in the awkward silence my punishment has left behind because Carlitos and Chale are already bounding up the porch steps. Chale pretends to be a rocket ship crash-landing himself into Papi's legs.

Papi laughs, hoisting him up before tossing him in the air.

"Well, *he* doesn't seem traumatized," I say.

"My mom told him it was all a bad dream. Then she let him stay up late watching *Mao Mao* until he forgot all about it."

I shake my head in disbelief. "To be young again..."

"I know," Carlitos says. "Last night scarred me for life."

"Uh-uh." Mami pushes a plate of pancakes in front of Carlitos before forcing a fork into his hand. "We've agreed to take a day off from the supernatural. Now eat, stop talking about La Lechuza, and let the adults handle it like you should have done from the beginning."

Carlitos raises an eyebrow. "Are these pancakes full of magic meant to dull our curiosity about La Lechuza?"

Mami grins. "That's none of your business." She squirts a giant dollop of syrup on top of Carlitos's pancakes. "Now eat up."

Suddenly, Clau turns up her nose, hands on her hips as she makes a grand entrance into the kitchen. She fluffs her hair. "How do I look?"

Carlitos raises an eyebrow at me, confused. She's wearing the same thing she always wears.

The clothes she died in.

"It's for the party tonight," Clau says.

Just go with it, I mouth.

She does a twirl, looking at Carlitos over her shoulder.

"Oh, yeah, you look great," he finally says.

She grins before snapping a finger and igniting the old stereo under the TV. It's playing "Golpe y Estribillo" by an old band from Venezuela as she shimmies across the room. "I've been practicing for the dance contest tonight. No way those kids at your school are better than me."

No, they're just more alive than you, which means you'll automatically be disqualified.

"I heard Marisol's parents hired Medicina to play at the party." Carlitos squeezes more syrup on his pancakes, while Clau continues twirling in circles across the room.

I roll my eyes. "That's ridiculous. If they had that kind of money, why would they live in Noche Buena?"

Abuela comes around the corner with her sage. "You two are lucky you live in a small town. You're much safer here than in the city. People are murdered there every single day."

Carlitos and I exchange a look. Abuela always uses the safety argument to try to convince us to stay in Noche Buena and live with her forever. But after last night, I'm not so sure if she's right.

"I bet they have less supernatural beings," Carlitos murmurs. "Those kinds of things don't usually hang around big cities."

"Because there's plenty of evil there already," Abuela corrects him. "So much sin everywhere you look."

"There's sin *everywhere*." Mami tosses two Blanca's Blooms shirts to me and Carlitos. "Speaking of which, I don't want to see any inappropriate dancing from either of you tonight." She smiles and we both bust out laughing.

Mami knows we don't dance. We people watch, gorging on food while we make fun of all the kids who make our lives miserable. Of course, Clau dances (sometimes inappropriately), but no one can see her so it doesn't count. Although, she'll have to keep it PG tonight in front of Mami unless she wants to risk being grounded again.

"And more importantly," Mami goes on, "if Abby's there, I don't want any fighting."

"If she keeps her mouth shut, everything will be just fine," Carlitos huffs. "She's the one who always starts something."

Mami puts her hands on her hips. "I don't care if she says something to you. You should be the bigger person and walk away."

"But being the bigger person is exhausting," I groan.

"Which is exactly why not everyone can do it." Mami rummages through some boxes before snapping a finger in our direction. "After you two finish eating, I need you to go up to the attic and grab another box of vases."

"On it." I chug the rest of my orange juice before following Clau as she floats up the stairs to the attic.

The last time I was up here was when I brought back that old children's book that played that creepy song about La Lechuza. Back when we still thought a story was all she was.

As I come upon the book where I'd tossed it before racing back down the stairs, the hairs on my arms stand on end, goose bumps trailing all the way down my spine. Like the black-and-white drawing is somehow a piece of her. Like looking into those bulbous cartoon eyes means that she's somehow looking back.

"Who else votes that we should burn that thing?" Carlitos nudges it with the toe of his shoe.

I hear a cough and dust puffs up from the speaker on the front cover of the book. A child's voice dribbles out, raspy like they're choking on sand. "Excuse me, but how would you like it if someone burned you?"

Carlitos kneels. "I should have known this dang thing would be enchanted with some annoying person's energy."

The speakers cough up more dust. "You kiss your mother with that mouth?"

I flip open the cover and read the inscription. "To Gume Mendoza, age seven."

"This book was Tío Gume's? The Tío Gume who dresses up every year as Pancho Claus and the Easter Bunny so all of the cousins can get a photo without having to pay for one at the mall?" Carlitos laughs. "Okay, now I'm definitely not scared of this thing."

"Really?" Clau swirls around him. "Because you were crying like a baby last night."

"I wasn't crying."

"Fine, you were wailing."

"I wasn't wailing."

"You were screaming."

"I *wasn't* screaming!"

"Enough!" I shove the book back into the box where we found it, but then my hand grazes the leather-bound binder underneath and I see that it's embossed with the year 1975. Then I remember what Mami said about La Lechuza being family. If that's true, then she'll have ended up where all of our long-lost relatives have—in one of our old family photo albums.

I scan the other dust-covered boxes stacked around the attic, kneeling to swipe at the dirt and search for more dates.

"What are you looking for?" Carlitos asks.

"Do you see any boxes from when Mami and Tía were our age?"

He crouches, searching the boxes on the other side of the room. "Do you really think stuff that old will still be intact?"

I glare at him. "They're not a hundred. And old photos last forever."

"Let me take a look." Clau gets fuzzy and then she swan-dives into one of the boxes.

I hear pages rustling before she pops back out, appearing for half a second before slipping into the next box.

A few minutes later and she springs from one of the boxes like a jack-in-the-box. "Bingo."

Carlitos and I rush over, folding back the flaps. There are stacks of old photo albums, pictures stuck behind plastic pages. I grab the one on top, opening it against my knees. "Look, there's Abuelo and Tío Gume."

Tío Gume has his hands raised like he's telling one of his never-ending stories. Abuelo's gripping his shoulders, smiling, like he can't believe what he's hearing.

And then the images begin to shift and it's like watching an old black-and-white movie. Carlitos touches the corner of the photo and with both of our empathic abilities focused in on their faces, Abuelo and Tío Gume suddenly begin to talk.

"It was as big as a whale, chavo!"

Abuelo laughs. "Let me guess. Then it swallowed you whole?"

Tío Gume slices his hands through the air like he's running. "I was too fast. Like lightning."

Abuelo pats him on the belly. "I think you mean thunder."

They both hang their heads back, laughing.

We pass photographs of Mami blowing out birthday candles and of Tía on a swing set, pausing to watch their faces light up, to hear their voices when they were still just girls.

There's one of Abuela in the garden and Abuelo in his workshop. I can hear the flowers rustling in the wind and the clank of a hammer on the head of a nail. Their faces smoother, brighter.

Sometimes being an empath really bites. Especially since pain and suffering are such a big part of being human. Sometimes it seems like that's all there is. But other times I get a glimpse of something truly magical and I realize that being an empath can actually be pretty cool.

Because when I look at these old photos, I don't just see familiar faces. I'm not just guessing what they were thinking or feeling. *I'm* feeling it too. I'm watching them *being alive.* And it feels like hugging the sun.

We turn to the next page, a small polaroid stuck in the center.

As soon as I hear the cackle, I know it belongs to Soona. She's sandwiched between a few faces I don't recognize, a thick corsage pinned to her party dress. The group around her looks dressed up too.

Carlitos points. "Is that Abuela?"

Her voice ignites next. "Does Noel know you stole that dress out of my closet, Paulina?" She's talking to a young Señora Avila.

Señora Avila swishes her skirt. "Maybe it looks better on me."

"And maybe you need to get your eyes checked." Abuela gives a twirl, batting her lashes in Señora Avila's direction.

Tucked behind Abuela, his face half hidden behind another girl's over-hair-sprayed do, is Abuelo, a flower pinned to his lapel.

"And what am I?" He moves forward to take Abuela's hand and gently dips her like they're already dancing. "Chopped liver?"

She slaps his lapel. "Oh, Roberto."

"They were going to some kind of dance or something," I say.

"Date night," Clau says.

"There..." Carlitos's finger trembles. "Does she look familiar to you?"

The face is slightly blurred, in motion, the woman turning to laugh. But even out of focus, the eyes give her away.

And then the figure comes to life, joining the party. "La Lechuza."

I can't help it. My finger grazes the photo, her face. Her head tilts as she smiles, but there's a shyness to it. Like she's uncomfortable among the crowd. Like the camera's too close. She blushes before smoothing her dress and then she looks right into the lens. Right into my eyes.

I gasp, shuffling back. Then I turn to Carlitos. "Last night..."

"What is it, Omega?"

"Last night Mami came to my room. She told me something about La Lechuza."

"What?" Carlitos huffs. "Like finally admitting she's real. It's a little late for that, I think."

"No. She said...she *said*...La Lechuza is...our *family*."

"What!" Carlitos's voice bounces off the walls.

I swat at him. "Would you be quiet?"

He barely lowers his voice. "She's our...? We're related to...?"

"Oh no, I think he's hyperventilating," Clau says, blowing ice-cold air on him until his eyelashes are covered in crystals.

He scrubs at his face. "I'm not hyperventilating!"

"Then you're in shock."

"I'm not in shock!"

"Then you're having a panic attack."

"No!"

"A heart attack."

"Clau, stop it!" I wave my arms, trying to separate them. "No one is hyperventilating. It's just…a lot to process, that's all."

"I guess if La Lechuza is *somehow*…our *family*…" Carlitos grimaces. "That must mean they know how to deal with her, right? Like when Tío Gume comes to visit. He's always telling stories way too loud and overstaying his welcome and everyone knows the only way to get him to leave is to literally pack his bags for him and stick a fifty-dollar bill in his pocket."

"You think La Lechuza is like Tío Gume…."

"You know what I mean," he says. "Like maybe there's a trick with getting her to leave. Maybe they figured it out last night and that's why it's safe enough for all of us to go to the quinceañera."

"Abuela and Mami do go at it a lot. Maybe family's good at that. Making up and moving on."

"Are there any other pictures of her?" Clau asks, suddenly moving closer.

I turn the page and there's a close-up of the women in the group, skirts swooshing around their ankles, dark lips spread into wide smiles.

I know Clau can't see them the way we can, alive in two-dimension. Laughing and swaying.

But as she stares at the image, something flashes across her face. Abrupt. Confused.

"What is it?" I ask.

Clau's mouth quavers. She points.

But all I see is the woman La Lechuza was. *Luna.* Young and beautiful, but desperately trying to hide. She squeezes into frame beside Abuela. Abuela whispers something in her ear that makes her laugh. Señora Avila takes her hand, trying to pull her forward. To coax her out of her shyness. Nothing menacing about her.

Until she finds my eyes again in the camera. Until she stares at me like she knows I'm watching. Like she wants me to be.

My heartbeat ticks up.

If Clau's heart was still beating, hers probably would too.

"What's wrong, Clau?" Carlitos asks.

And then in a voice so small it doesn't even sound like hers, Clau says, "She looks...*familiar*."

"Duh," Carlitos says. "She tried to eat us last night."

"No. Not...the owl." Clau touches the bent corner of the photograph. "Her face." She pinches her eyes shut. "Maybe I'm wrong."

"Wrong about what, Clau?"

"I don't know." She exhales, waves a hand. "Just forget it."

The attic door creaks open and we all jump, knocking into the vases we were supposed to be carrying downstairs.

It's Abuelo, one hand stretched out as a vase tumbles to the floor. He catches it just before it shatters. Then he uses the hem of his shirt to shine the glass.

He winks at us. "Not every stranger is a monster." He hands me the vase. "And not every monster is a stranger. Remember that, mija."

CHAPTER 13

WE GET TO THE VENUE BEFORE ANYONE else. The "ball-room" is actually just an old barn that someone covered in twinkling Christmas lights. It smells like dirt and cafeteria food. There's a box fan in each corner, the air on full blast, but it's still too warm for dancing. That won't stop anyone, though. If they paid the DJ for four hours, then they're going to dance every minute of those four hours.

I nudge Carlitos before pointing to where the DJ is setting up his equipment. "I told you Medicina wasn't going to be here."

"I guess it was just a rumor."

"It's always just a rumor."

"Start unboxing everything on that long table," Mami says as she and Papi pass by, carrying in the giant flower archway.

Carlitos sneaks a bite of something from the refreshments

table while their backs are to us. "Do you…them…we're…jer?"

"What?"

Carlitos swallows, wipes the powdered sugar from his lips. "I said, do you really believe them that we're not in danger?"

I watch Mami and Papi from across the room. Now they're busy arranging some bright birds-of-paradise on the cake. Mami's always stressed the day of a big party, but today she seems even more on edge. Papi too. He notices us looking and I quickly get back to unboxing.

"They wouldn't have dragged us here if it was dangerous."

"Unless they're lying again." Carlitos raises an eyebrow.

Clau raises one too. "Maybe they're lying to *themselves.*"

"Well"—I turn my back so Mami can't read my lips from across the room—"there's one thing that never does."

Carlitos follows my eyes to the candy bowl at the end of the table. "Reese's test?"

I nod. "Reese's test."

Carlitos swipes one of the Reese's Peanut Butter Cups and gently tears the package open. It flutters to the ground as we both stare at the perfectly round hunk of chocolate. Then he begins to peel back the brown wrapper.

"You're shaking."

Carlitos tries to hold his hands steady.

"And sweating," Clau remarks.

He glares at us.

I clench my fists, suddenly realizing that I'm shaking too. I still don't know which version of La Lechuza is the real one. The monster that  chased us through the trees or the young woman going out dancing. *Luna.* There was something beautiful about her. An innocence that makes me feel silly for ever being afraid.

But every time her eyes caught mine, even though we were years and dimensions apart, there was still a tiny piece of me that shuddered. And it's that part, the part of me that feels *too much*, that needs to know what's true. Whether she is evil...or good. Ugly...or beautiful.

Or...if some monsters...some *people* exist in between. That the *gray* is where we all belong because the gray is where life happens.

"Easy..." I glance over my shoulder to make sure Mami and Papi still aren't looking. "Careful..."

Carlitos's nostrils flare. "I got it!"

The wrapper peels free and this time the chocolate left behind looks like the wax seal on one of those old-timey letters. Something sent from the past.

We all stare at the strange shape and suddenly La Lechuza

stares back, pointed teeth wedged into a sharp smile. Like she's *happy* to see us.

Carlitos yells, hurling the entire peanut butter cup across the room.

"Be quiet! Mami's looking over here!"

She has her hands on her hips, eyes narrowed in warning. *No funny business.*

"It was a spider," Carlitos calls. "Just a spider."

"Don't worry," Clau says, "I'll distract her."

While I fan Carlitos's face, Clau makes her way to the center of the dance floor. She raises her arms in the air and then with one shake of her hips, the DJ's speakers blare "El Baile del Gorila" at full blast. The DJ rushes over to his equipment, trying to turn down the volume while Clau spins from one end of the dance floor to the other.

The DJ finds the volume button and shuts the music off right when Clau tips herself back like some chambelán has just dipped her. He walks away from the equipment, messing with some extension cords against the wall.

Clau spins and the music blares again. The DJ falls backward on his hands, blinking wildly like he knows the music is possessed. This time Carlitos and I can't hide our laughter. We clutch our stomachs, almost knocking over the flower corsages we're supposed to be setting out for the escorts.

This time Mami knows exactly what's going on. She

glares at us from across the room, but instead of marching over and yelling at us, she smiles, she and Papi laughing too.

Maybe she's not worried after all. Maybe we shouldn't be either.

I use a napkin to wipe up the smeared chocolate, La Lechuza's face now a glob in my hand. I close my fist, open it, and the glob changes shape again. It looks like something from an inkblot test. I squeeze the napkin again and this time it looks like Winnie the Pooh.

The energy changes too, and suddenly, the sensation feels like tiny threads tied to the tips of my fingers. I wriggle them and I feel the threads twist up my arm, stretch across my chest, and tug right at my heart.

Mami always says that in order to make someone *feel* something, you have to make yourself feel it first, which is why age and experience are an empath's secret weapons. The more memories you have, the more emotions you can tap into.

But it also means that I can't make someone feel something I haven't, even if that feeling lies somewhere deep in their own heart. Those memories are off-limits, the human mind much more sacred than the random objects we can read by touch. Some empaths train for a lifetime and still can't access a person's past.

So if I want to learn to control my abilities, I've got to work with what I've got.

I concentrate, trying to draw out the negative energy and replace it with something good.

But that's not specific enough. I try to focus on a *feeling*.

Tenderness.

Wonder.

I let the feeling fill me up and then I push it out, the energy vibrating along those invisible threads until I feel everything around me shift.

"Omega, we need your help over here," Mami calls from across the room.

I take one last look at the chocolate mess before crumpling the napkin in my fist again and tossing it in the trash.

I don't know if the feelings will stick, if the janitor who takes out the bins at the end of the night will absorb any of what I've tried to leave behind. But there's no harm in trying, right?

Maybe Clau was right when she said I just needed a little practice. Carlitos might not have to devote as much time to honing his abilities. But maybe I'm different. And maybe that's okay.

Soon people start entering the ballroom and someone dims the lights, the vela centerpieces Mami created to make the night even more special sparkling like stars. The DJ has lost his battle with Clau, the music on and ushering people onto the dance floor until she's hidden behind their jostling bodies.

Slowly, the barn begins filling up with people, kids rushing to the dessert table early while their parents try to drag them toward the buffet line. It's packed too, people carrying away plates of cabrito and rice and beans.

Once the barn is completely full (and people's bellies are full too), the DJ gets on the mic, holding it away from himself like he's still scared his equipment might bite him. "Damas y caballeros…" When nothing grows fangs, he begins introducing the damas y chambelanes, Marisol Montoya led out by a procession of girls in purple dresses and boys in suits and shiny shoes.

There are fifteen couples, one for each of Marisol's birthdays, and they're made up of Marisol's sisters and cousins and closest friends.

I try to imagine what my court will look like. My cousins, Tío Gume's kids, will probably drive in from out of town. But there's only three of them, and Papi's family mistakes our magic for strangeness so they don't come around a lot. Abby is definitely out of the question and so are all the people she's convinced we're evil. And my best friend is a ghost no one else can see.

So I don't have to imagine what my court will be like. Because there won't be one.

I try not to focus on the pang in my chest as I watch them perform a choreographed waltz, the music fading out as the boys dip the girls. I think it's over until the music scratches, switching to a fast-paced cumbia.

Suddenly, my gaze is pulled toward the entrance as Abby and her brothers barrel in like a pack of wolves. They even howl like them too, whooping when they see the table of food.

Except for Aiden.

"You're drooling."

"What?" I snap my attention back to Carlitos.

He rolls his eyes. "They're the enemy, Omega."

"Aiden's not like them. He's nice."

Until he knows my secret, I think. Then maybe he won't be so nice. It makes me wonder if our study session was a mistake. What if I get close to him the same way I got close to Abby and he ends up rejecting me too?

"Oh no, she's spotted us." Carlitos tries to duck behind the refreshments table. "Omega, get down here."

But it's too late.

"Nice outfit." Abby looks me up and down. "I'll take some punch."

I clench my fists behind the table, wishing I could give her a different kind of punch. Instead, I pour her a glass and shove it into her hand. A little spills on her dress. The same dress she wears to every party and it reminds me of all the reasons Abby is so spiteful. Because she's jealous. Because she has insecurities too.

She looks down at the drop of red, then back to me. "You're going to regret that."

I could apologize, but I don't, and her anger strikes me as she saunters off.

"Tell me that wasn't an accident and you'll be my new hero," Carlitos says.

I slump down onto the floor next to him. "I wish."

"Well, your clumsiness just might get you killed." He peers over the table. "She's got her gang assembled. I guess Naomi and the others forgave her for playing that prank on them." Carlitos takes another peek. "Oh, crap, they're looking over here." He ducks again.

"We can't hide down here all night."

"Says who?"

"Omega?"

I shoot up, dusting off my jeans.

It's Aiden and I'm suddenly aware of the stains on my shirt, of where it hugs me too tight, of where sweat is beginning to form on my upper lip. I try to smile and it comes out crooked.

I quickly motion to the table, trying to act normal. "Can I...Would you...What do you want?"

He raises the plate of food he's already holding. "Uh, I just wanted to say the room looks really good. You and your mom did the decorations, right?"

"Oh, uh...yeah...we...uh..."

Carlitos nudges me in the knee. "Just say thank you."

"Thank you!" I say a little too loudly.

"The music's good too." Aiden bobs his head. "I just don't know how to dance like that."

We watch the partygoers march in a circle, some adding in fancy footwork like crisscrossing their feet or walking backward and turning in circles. But most are just stomping to the beat.

"Cumbia is like the easiest dance ever." I finally remember to breathe, but it sounds like a snort. I pretend to cough.

"If you say so…" He laughs. "Maybe you can teach me?"

I blink, not sure if I heard him right. *Aiden wants to dance? With me?*

His face reddens. "Unless it's not your thing. I'd probably just mess—"

"No." I stop short, still trying to figure out how to respond. "I mean yes!"

Aiden furrows his brow, confused.

"I mean, yes, I can teach you. I want to teach you. We can…" Then I feel a rush of heat as I notice Mami watching me from across the room, *watching* me talk to Aiden. If she knows I have a crush on a boy, I'll never hear the end of it. I'll die of embarrassment.

"We can…?" He shrugs.

I exhale. "Later." Then I jerk my head in the direction

of Mami. "Maybe once all the food's gone. I'm sort of… grounded right now."

"Oh…"

"It's a long story. But now she's watching me like a hawk."

"I get it." He gives me a small wave. "Maybe later, then."

And as he walks away I can't help it. My knees wobble as I take in the feelings he leaves behind—curiosity, anxiety, joy.

None of what I expected, what I feared.

I'm relieved, letting his emotions linger, swirling at the base of my stomach until he's far enough away that my body latches on to something else.

It's faint at first, hidden beneath the loud music and all those dancing bodies. People hugging and eating and laughing. I take a deep breath and try to concentrate, reaching for the feelings closest to me, letting them slowly rise to the surface. I spot two girls glaring at a couple on the dance floor and taste the bitter chalkiness of their jealousy. I clutch my moonstone in my pocket, shaking it off.

Just breathe, Omega. Like with the chocolate. Concentrate.

The bad taste dissolves as I focus on an old woman dancing from her chair. She's clapping and laughing and exuding a kind of wild joy that feels like sunflowers and tastes like root beer floats. I smell the bright yellow petals and feel the fizzing of the bubbles on the tip of my tongue.

None of it overwhelming me. None of it knocking me off my feet. I grin. *Maybe I'm not so hopeless after all.*

I release the feeling like a helium balloon, imagining it traveling over the crowd, and filling them with joy too.

Then one by one, I home in on Clau's smugness at being the best dancer here, Mami's relief that everything's gone off without a hitch, and then to Marisol's annoyance at having to dance with every man and boy at the party.

They've started the dollar dance, the line wrapping around the room. Basically, it's when the male partygoers pay money and in exchange they get to dance with the birthday girl. It's old-fashioned and I can tell she's hating every second of it. Until Michael Evans takes her by the waist. Then the feeling radiating from her is a sticky sweet glee.

I look down at Carlitos, who's still hiding on the floor. "Why don't you go get in line?"

He laughs. "Yeah right. How big of a loser do you think I am?"

His words form a knot in my stomach. I watch him, the way he crosses his arms, shrugging off the sight of the people dancing. But I can't quite put my finger on what he's feeling.

There's an incessant tapping like annoyance, but beneath that there's something softer. Embarrassment maybe? I reach for him, resting a hand on his shoulder and it's like I'm sinking to the bottom of the ocean. And I can finally name it. The feeling that has him hiding.

Loneliness.

Carlitos has always acted like he's too cool for everyone, but I know deep down he's just worried people will make fun of him. Or worse, that Marisol will reject him in front of everyone. No matter how hard Carlitos tries to pretend that he doesn't care what people think, the truth is he cares too much. So do I.

I slide to the floor next to him. "I feel it too, you know."

He doesn't look at me. "I don't want to tell Abuela that I agree with my dad about leaving. But the truth is, I can't wait. Maybe then I'll finally be able to make friends without them being brainwashed by some small-town gossip."

"Is that why you hate Abby so much?"

"Don't you?" He picks at the edge of the tablecloth. "I know it's not right. Abuela doesn't even like when we say the word. But it's how I feel."

"You're allowed to be angry," I tell him. "I'm angry too." It burns at the back of my throat—twelve years' worth of tears over not being included in stupid things like trick-or-treating or book clubs or sleepovers or school dances. Twelve years' worth of tears over feeling like a misfit and a mistake.

And I don't even want to be included anymore. I just want it to stop hurting every time I'm not. I just want it to *stop* hurting.

"I'm way past angry," Carlitos admits. "I'm...I'm *sad.*"

He closes his eyes and as I lean against him; our loneliness swells like a storm cloud over our heads. I feel the cold pitter-patter of the rain, but I don't know how to stop it.

As the night goes on, all the emotions around us start to jumble, pinging from one thing to the next until I can't find my focus. I can't sift them out one at a time. All I can do is breathe.

Breathe, Omega.

"Are you all right?" Carlitos asks.

"I'm just getting a little overheated." I pull myself to my feet. "I'll be right back."

I head for the bathroom, but it's just as crowded, girls reapplying makeup to their sweaty faces. As soon as I walk in, I'm pouring sweat too.

"Did you see what she was wearing?"

"I can't believe she was dancing with him."

"Who does she think she is?"

Jealousy is a barbed wire around my insides, pulling tighter. I reach for the sink, gripping the sides to hold myself up. The girls give me a look, but they don't say a word. Then they file out, their anger turning to a rancid stench I can practically taste.

I turn on the faucet and the water is lukewarm. I wait for it to cool down, but it doesn't. I splash some on my face, not worrying about my makeup running since I never wear any.

I take a few more deep breaths, rubbing the moonstone between my fingers and waiting for this molten lava to let go of me. But it just keeps sloshing back and forth until I'm dizzy again.

"Oh, it's you." Abby's voice. "I should have known you'd be hanging out in here."

There's laughter, but the sound is fragmented. Then it disappears altogether and all I can feel is Abby's disgust.

"I'm not…" I try to say, *I'm not feeling well.* I try to say *something*, but I can't.

I slump down to the floor, even though it's filthy. My head spins, black dots filling my vision. I try to blink them away, but they're pulling me under. Down. Down. Until all I see is black.

"Omega! Omega, wake up!"

I'm sticky and wet, my hair pressed to my face.

Carlitos touches my cheek, then my forehead. "Omega, stay with me."

I groan, my stomach rolling.

"Omega, I'm here. It's okay."

"What happened?"

Carlitos's face hardens. "You fainted again. And…"

"And what?"

He helps me to my feet before bringing me to the mirror. "Oh my God."

My face is covered in permanent marker. Someone's drawn on a thick unibrow, devil horns, and a beard and mustache. Underneath I'm as red as a beet, the lava sloshing around in my stomach about to erupt.

"Abby…" I growl.

I try to charge for the door, but I'm still too weak. Before I can reach it, someone throws it open.

Mami rushes over. "Who—" But then she stops. She knows who did it.

Then she's the one charging into the ballroom. She crosses the dance floor, searching for Abby's dad. But he's not here. He never shows up to the parties on our side of town—just drops his kids off and then picks them up at the end of the night.

As I peer out, I don't see Abby either. She must have run off to avoid my wrath. But the more time that passes, the less angry I feel and the more...the more...*devastated*. I feel sad. I feel lonely. All of those emotions Carlitos and I were just wallowing in. But more than that, I feel like I want to crawl inside a hole and never come out.

I throw myself into a bathroom stall instead, slamming the door closed behind me.

"Omega, you know she's a miserable jerk." Carlitos presses a hand to the door. "She picks on you because she's jealous."

I'm crying so hard I can't answer.

Carlitos sighs, leans against the stall. "I'm not leaving, Omega."

I hear the bathroom door thrown open again. Mami comes inside.

I finally force out, "Why can't she just leave me alone?"

"Because she's broken and now she has to break everything around her to make herself feel better," Mami says.

"And you said we should forgive her." I can practically hear Carlitos shaking his head.

Mami swats him. "Don't talk to me like that."

"Ow."

I can't help but laugh. I ease the door open a little.

Mami grabs me by the chin. "Your face covered in permanent marker is prettier than her insides will ever be." She presses a hand to my chest. "And in here, you're beautiful. Because you will forgive her. That's how you show your strength."

"But she's awful. She's a...she's a—"

"Uh-uh." Mami gives me a look. "She's a little girl, Omega. Just a girl." She leads me out of the stall. "And so are you. But someday you'll be a grown woman and you'll look back on all of this and realize that Abby bullying you was such a gift. Because it made you strong. Because it made it possible for you to overcome so many other things. Abby may never be happy. But you will, Omega. You will live the life you've always wanted and you'll know you did it because of this. Because Abby made you ready for the ugliness of the world."

I fall into her, crying into her Blanca's Blooms shirt.

"I love you, mija."

"I love you too."

I don't know if what Mami says is true. If I'll be grateful that Abby bullied me, if it'll make me strong. Right now all I feel is weak and scared and angry. But Mami's heart beats with knowing. Like she's sure. So I trust her, letting that feeling sink into my skin, up through my veins, until my own heart beats with it too.

CHAPTER 14

"OMEGA?" CLAU WRAPS HER ARMS AROUND ME, her face scrunched in concern. "What happened?"

I look up, letting her see.

She gasps.

"I think I've got some rubbing alcohol in the car." Mami scrubs at the lines on my face. "I'll send your papi to go out and get it. Carlitos, you come with me before someone catches you hanging out in the girls' bathroom. Clau, you'll stay with…"

But Clau's gone, the feeling she leaves behind hot on the tip of my tongue. *Revenge.*

I lock eyes with Mami. "She's going after Abby."

Before we even reach the door, the lights go out. The music cuts off. I imagine Clau, hovering over the crowd, absorbing their energy. At home, it's more like charging a battery. With this many people, it'll be like igniting a rocket.

Mami leads us out of the bathroom, people murmuring as they make their way off the dance floor. I'm relieved there's nothing but candlelight, the shadows hiding the marks on my face. It's barely enough to see by, but I don't need to see.

All I need is to follow the feeling that's driving Clau.

When people in Abuela's telenovelas talk about the "thirst" for revenge, I never really understood what they meant. But the feeling Clau leaves behind *is* thirst. Something wild that needs to be quenched.

"Any sign of her?" Carlitos whispers.

We sidestep people who are huddled together, still eating and drinking, waiting for the power to come back on. The barn is old and this isn't the first time the generators haven't been able to keep up. It's probably better this way, everyone thinking this is normal, no one freaking out. But the darkness is just the beginning, hiding whatever Clau has up her sleeve next.

"There's Abby." Carlitos points.

She's standing with Naomi and Aiden.

I stumble to a stop. "I can't go over there. Not looking like this."

"Do you see Clau?" Mami asks.

I scan the darkened dance floor and search every corner, but she isn't there. I shake my head.

Mami sighs, pressing a finger to her temple. "This is why I told your abuela to stop treating her like another grandchild. This is exactly why she doesn't belong in this world anymore. Because she's more powerful than any person in it."

I swallow, my throat throbbing at the thought of Clau crossing over. But beneath that is an even deeper pain at the thought of Clau actually hurting someone. Even if it is Abby. So I know I have no choice. If Clau's going to go after Abby, she's going to have to go through me first.

I push my way through the crowd until I finally reach Abby. She looks at me, stunned, terrified that I've come to finish what she started.

Aiden stares at me, just as wide-eyed. "What happened?" He squints in the dark. "Omega, are you all right? Who did that to you?"

Naomi snickers and Aiden looks between her and Abby. He knows they're responsible.

He shakes his head. "Abby, what is wrong with you? I told you to stop this! Omega hasn't done anything to you but try to be your friend. You *used* to be her friend, remember? Or did you forget?" His lip quavers. "Did you forget like you're forgetting Mom…like you're forgetting who she raised you to be?"

But Abby's barely listening. She's waiting. For me to yell or push her the way she pushed me, for me to make her feel as small as I do right now.

But instead of attacking her, I reach out my hand. "We have to get you out of here."

"What are you talking about?" she says, taking a step back.

"Abby, please. Just trust me."

She hesitates, still waiting for me to strike.

"Omega…?" Carlitos has finally made it through the crowd, Mami right behind him. They're both looking up.

"No." Mami clutches her chest. "Clau, no!"

Clau hovers above us and so does Marisol's three-tier birthday cake. It glides over our heads, pausing right over Abby.

Next to me, Mami's slack-jawed.

No, Clau, no...

Abby finally looks up, and at the same time we all yell "Clau!" the cake falls, landing with a splat. It hangs off Abby like moss, the buttercream stuck in her hair and her mouth. She scrapes it from her eyes and then she screams, unleashing a wail that has everyone holding their ears.

The music blasts again, the lights flickering like we're in one of those haunted houses on Halloween. That's when people realize that it wasn't just the shoddy generators that cut the power.

And that's when they start running.

But Clau's not finished yet. In the brief flashes of light, I can see her eyes still narrowed, still thirsty for something. The moment I realize what it is, what she's been longing for all this time, I know it's not just Abby that Clau's angry with, it's the living. Every single one of us who isn't invisible.

Her thirst is actually longing. The *longing* to be seen.

"Clau!" I try calling her name again, but she doesn't hear me.

As people run, she turns her attention on them, ripping the tablecloths from under plates of food, tossing chairs as people head for the exits.

Mami grabs me with one hand and Carlitos with the other. We spot Papi near the doors, holding them open for people as they rush past. Mami pulls us in the same direction.

"But Clau…," I say.

Behind us, Aiden takes Abby by the arm, leading her out too. We get all tangled up on our way out the door, but when we finally make it outside, the parking lot is in just as much chaos.

The street glistens like after a storm, but the air isn't just ripe with the smell of rain. I smell oil, a line of it spilling from an overturned truck still smoking on the side of the road. Out of the dust, something moves in the glow of the taillight. Red bleeding across sharp edges, layers and layers of glistening black.

The crowd shifts back, women whispering prayers, men cursing, some holding their breath.

Mrs. Villarreal clutches her rosary. Señor Rivas clutches his pocketknife. Everyone terrified, except…

I take a careful step, leaning to see where Señora Avila stands, unshaken. *Smiling.*

It's a small, almost invisible thing. But I can *feel* the reason why. As she watches La Lechuza, all the people cowering in fear, she…she likes it.

I remember running into her in Señora Delarosa's potions shop, the vial of red liquid with her name on it. She was frantic that day. *Impatient.* And when I bumped into her, something wild exploded inside me, knocking me to the floor. Kuku had sensed it too, his teeth bared like she was something dangerous.

Señora Avila's grin widens, the moonlight catching a flash of teeth. Sharp and pointed.

Like the woman in the library who was fighting so hard to stay human.

I wasn't the first she turned. And I won't be the last.

She was trying to warn us that there were others.

Suddenly, the crowd shifts back again as La Lechuza's wings stretch, feathers fanned like knives. Then she turns her head, slow, smooth, like it's not even attached to the rest of her body. She scans the crowd, searching. *Searching. Searching.*

When her eyes lock on mine, the air is snatched from my lungs. I wait for her to attack, for her beak to spread into that jagged, wicked grin. But she doesn't come for me.

She doesn't come.

Instead, she beats her wings back and forth, fanning the crowd as if we're flames.

She leaps into the sky, her body swallowing the moon, and then those flames erupt, people shouting, running, throwing rocks and trash and anything else they can at her.

Because they think this mess is hers. The overturned truck, the driver bleeding as a group of partygoers carry him out of the busted window. The chaos inside the barn, the inanimate objects brought to life by something supernatural. Something *sinister.*

My mind races back to Clau spinning out of control. I

expect her to have vanished or to still be inside wreaking havoc. But when I turn to head back inside the building, she's floating behind a crying Marisol, staring through her, through us all, to the spot where La Lechuza just stood. But not just the spot. She's staring at the debris. The twisted metal. The broken glass.

I remember the shards of it she'd found in the library. The way she'd gazed into her own reflection, waiting for answers to questions I'd had no idea were tormenting her.

It's the feeling coming off her now—*torment*.

I look closer and there are tears.

She shakes and I can't help but rush to her side. "Clau? Clau, what's wrong?"

Clau just points.

"Clau...what is it?"

"She was there."

I inch closer, trying to read the memory behind her eyes. "Who? When?"

She squeezes her eyes shut, hiding what's there. "La Lechuza," she finally says. "She was there when they... when *we*...died."

CHAPTER 15

CHURCH IS ALMOST AS PACKED AS MARISOL'S party last night. That's usually how it works after una pachanga, everyone waking up early the next day to repent for their sins. This time it's mostly the threat of demonic forces that has them squeezed ten to a row and leaning against the church walls because there's nowhere else to sit. Some people even look like they're wearing the same clothes. Guess I'm not the only one who barely slept.

Luckily, I don't have to worry about running into Abby here. She goes to the Pentecostal church on the other side of town where they speak in tongues, don't play music, and only take the sacrament a few times a year like on Easter and Christmas. Carlitos and I go to the Catholic church where the service is in Spanish, the music is depressing, and we take the sacrament every single Sunday.

My stomach knots with memories of the night before. Collapsing on the dirty bathroom floor. Abby's grubby hands drawing in permanent marker all over my face. Clau's revenge-fueled (and then jealousy-fueled) freak-out. The car accident. The debris.

La Lechuza.

Her eyes found mine the same way they had in every daydream, in every nightmare, in every old photograph. She found me in the crowd, and as I struggled to make sense of that invisible connection flowing between us, Clau was realizing something too. About her family. About herself.

Last night was the first time I ever heard her admit that she's dead. I don't know what exactly Clau remembered, or how much, but the sorrow of those memories followed her all the way home. Then she disappeared, drawn to the attic again. A little later, I heard Abuela's footsteps up the stairs. I fell asleep before I heard her come back down.

Unlike the silence I woke up to this morning—no nine AM dance party with Clau—the energy here is buzzing, people's hands wet with too much holy water as old women march in wearing black veils like someone died.

As far as I know, Mr. Iglesias, the man in the truck, is going to be fine. No broken bones. Just a bump on the head from where he struck the steering wheel because he drives an old Chevy with no airbags.

But, of course, Mr. Iglesias's lack of serious injuries is not as interesting as the theories about his connection to La Lechuza. So far, I've overheard that Mr. Iglesias is a Satan-worshipper, a "miscreant" being punished for his sins, a reckless drunk driver, and a zombie.

"I heard that when he woke up, he was speaking in Latin," Mrs. Villarreal says.

"I heard that bump on the head of his was actually horns," Doña Maria adds.

At first I think all the gossip has drowned out the sound of Belén's obnoxious organ playing as people find their seats. But she's not even on stage. Instead, she's busy comforting Marisol Montoya's mother, who is still wailing over the party being ruined.

"El Diablo always goes after the holiest among us," Belén says, patting her on the back. "You're raising a little angel."

Carlitos makes a gagging sound. "Do you think we should tell her that her little angel is complaining to anyone who will listen about her birthday presents being destroyed and asking for new ones?"

While Mrs. Montoya is in tears, Mr. Montoya is as red as a tomato. He shakes his fist, riling up Señor Rivas and Mr. Huerta, who are both nodding their heads.

"Tonight. We're going to find that monster and send her back to el infierno where she belongs!"

Even quiet Señor Jimenez is listening intently.

But as the conversations about La Lechuza rise to a steady rumble, Father Torres takes to his pulpit. "Gente, por favor."

No one's listening, Belén still comforting Mrs. Montoya, Mr. Montoya still yelling and waving his fists in the air, Las Chismosas still talking a mile a minute.

Then Father Torres lifts his giant leather-bound Bible and slams it against his pulpit with a bang. Everyone turns to look as he adjusts his robes before forcing a smile.

"Please..." He motions for everyone to sit.

Belén slides onto her organ bench and lays into the keys, igniting one long drone. "Basta, Belén." He waves his hand like he's shooing a fly.

Her hands fall off the keys.

He continues in Spanish. "Needless to say, after the events of last night, you all have come to the right place. I hope now, more than ever, you understand the importance of fortifying one's soul, devoting your life to Jesus Christ, who died on the cross of Calvary so that you may be saved, so that no evil may stand against you, so that Satan may not lay claim to what has already been purchased with the blood of the only son of our Heavenly Father..."

"Do you think Father Torres will break his record today?" Carlitos asks.

Father Torres is notorious for his two-hour sermons that sometimes stretch into three, depending on how much the Holy Spirit needs to say that day. I swear, they make me feel like Moses wandering in the desert.

"It's the second Sunday in a row."

"Yo sé. I heard no one's seen him in days."

Abuela flashes Mrs. Villarreal and Doña Maria a dirty look for talking during Father Torres's sermon.

"My husband said he was missing work. Then one day he just stopped showing up altogether."

"Do you think he walked out on her?"

"After thirty years? ¡Qué lastima!"

Carlitos nudges me before looking in the direction of Señora Avila, the target of their gossip. I hadn't noticed her walk in or the fact that she's dressed in all black, a thick lace veil covering her face.

Her face.

I remember the way it looked last night. Almost gleeful. Definitely not scared. And then she smiled, moonlight revealing a flash of teeth.

Sharp. Pointed. Teeth.

I stare, waiting for the veil to shift so I can get a better look. Proof that what I saw last night wasn't another fever dream or my fears getting the best of me again.

Come on ... show your face.

Suddenly, she turns—slowly, slowly—until she's looking right at me.

My heart lurches into my throat and I quickly stare at the hymn book in my lap. I still feel her eyes and my pulse pounds. I hold the hymn book up in front of my face, but instead of turning around, she quietly gets up from her pew and walks to the back of the sanctuary before disappearing through the double doors.

I'm not the only one who notices. Mrs. Villarreal and Doña Maria both watch her leave, their mouths slightly open.

"Do you think it was another woman?"

Doña Maria crosses herself. "Ay Dios."

"Maybe we should check on her later."

"Yeah, to get some more dirt," Carlitos says under his breath.

I snort, covering my mouth.

Abuela flashes us another look, this one sharp as a knife.

"She shouldn't be home alone," Mrs. Villarreal says. "Especially after that wicked thing showed up last night."

They bristle with fear. But even after all of Father Torres's references to the "winged demon" that appeared last night, even as the people around her shuddered and clutched their children tightly, Señora Avila did not flinch. She did not feel afraid.

And for some reason, that fact, plus the fact of her missing husband, has me itching with questions. Like why Señora Avila doesn't seem to be worried about her husband's disappearance and what that has to do with the fact that she doesn't seem to be worried about La Lechuza either. Maybe because she knows where her husband is. And maybe... she knows where La Lechuza is too.

Carlitos and I take quiet steps up the stairs, as if it's possible to sneak up on a ghost.

"She still hasn't talked to you?" he whispers.

"She hasn't talked to anyone but Abuela."

"Maybe because she overheard your mom talking about making her cross over."

I shush him, hoping Clau didn't hear.

I know why Mami said it—she was scared of what Clau might do—but I wish she hadn't. Because knowing how Mami really feels, knowing the truth about Clau, is just going to make it harder to pretend like she belongs here. Because she doesn't. And yet, the thought of Clau disappearing forever doesn't feel right either.

When the attic door creaks open and there's no sign of Clau, I think maybe we've spooked her, but then Carlitos points to the window. Clau is even more translucent than she normally is, her body blending in with the dusty window and the smudged sky on the other side.

"Clau?"

She doesn't turn at the sound of my voice, just keeps staring into the glass, as if even the piece in front of her is a clue to what happened to her family, to what happened to her.

"Clau, we don't want you to leave." Carlitos steps forward. "You know that, right?"

Clau finally turns around, both of us startled by Carlitos's honesty. He and Clau are always picking on each other, her jokes always rubbing him the wrong way. But suddenly I sense his annoyance change and I know that all the things I thought bugged him about her are actually the things he would miss the most.

"Yeah, Clau," I say. "No matter what you do, we'll always forgive you."

"And what if I can't forgive myself?"

I've never seen Clau so serious, so sad. So I have to ask, "Do you mean about the party... or something else?"

Clau goes pale like she's covered in frost. "The accident..." She pinches her eyes shut.

"That wasn't your fault," Carlitos says. "It was La Lechuza. If she was there..."

"She was." Clau swallows tears. "But that was after...when the car was already in pieces. When they were already..."

I reach for her and it's like clutching ice. "Do you remember *everything?*"

I don't ask because I want to drag her back there but because I'm hoping there's something she's missing, some piece of the puzzle that doesn't put all the blame on her. Because the guilt she's carrying is strong and made of lead. As I hold her hand, it presses on my lungs until I'm chained down by it too.

Clau nods. "...Everything." She looks down. "We were driving. It was late and we were on our way home from a weekend at the beach. It was my twelfth birthday and Papi said we could go anywhere I wanted." She shakes her head, trying to get the words out. "It was time to leave, but I kept begging him for five more minutes. For another hour. We ended up driving home in the dark, Noche Buena just a town we were passing through. Then it started raining, a terrible storm that tossed mud against the windshield." She closes her eyes for a long time. "My little sister was asleep in her car seat. I was falling asleep too and then..." Tears stain her cheeks, her eyes still closed. "And then the car swerved, spinning fast. Mami screamed." Her voice shakes. "Papi looked back at me. He was scared too."

Carlitos reaches for Clau, both of us holding on to her before she slips away, trapped in the memory.

"The car turned over and over, everything breaking. I hit

my head and when I woke up, everything was upside down. My face was wet and I blinked, looking for Mami and Papi. For Candela. But I was tangled in the seat belt, everything fuzzy. And then I saw her, crouched over the car, her wings opened so wide I couldn't even see the sky."

"I don't understand," I say. "If La Lechuza didn't cause the accident, why was she there?"

"She was there"—Clau finally opens her eyes—"for Candela."

"Your sister?" Carlitos says.

"She was out of the car, La Lechuza's wings shielding her from the rain."

"Wait." I can barely breathe. "But that would mean..."

Clau nods. "She survived." Then she starts sobbing again. "All this time...I never knew. She's been out there all this time."

Suddenly, Clau's gripped by a feeling I can't even name. Something between regret and longing, mixed with dread, and the tiniest shard of hope. I find it like a needle in a haystack, and even though I don't know if it'll work, if my empathic abilities are actually getting stronger, I take that bit of hope and plant it like a seed in my own heart.

Then I close my eyes and imagine it sprouting leaves, turning green, growing up and up and up. I let hope swell inside me until my heart is a forest, and then I squeeze Clau tight and lead her into the trees.

She exhales and I pray that she can feel it.

But as I hold on to her, that hope doesn't just sink in. It begins to rise, carrying with it Clau's memories from before. When she was still alive. When her family was still intact.

I can see it all.

They're at the beach, Candela on their father's shoulders as Clau and her father jump over wave after wave. They make it to the first sandbar and wave back at her mother on the beach. She's wearing a big floppy hat, a big smile on her face as she snaps photos of the three of them.

Candela squeals as their father dips her toes in the warm

water. Clau hugs his leg, bracing against the waves, laughing when one knocks them onto their backs. The sun shines bright on their faces, so warm that I can feel it on my own skin.

But I'm not supposed to be able to see her memories. Abuela says they're off-limits. And yet, here they are playing behind my eyes like a home video. That's exactly how it feels. Like I've rummaged through the attic of Clau's mind, pulling out something old and lost. Something *powerful.*

"Omega, look…" Carlitos stands back, staring at the air around us.

It's golden, like I've taken the sun from Clau's perfect beach day and placed it over our heads. When she opens her eyes again, they're suddenly dry, and I know she feels me tuning her from the inside, like she's not just a person but an instrument.

She smiles and I smile back.

Because it's working. Because some part of Clau is healing. Because I'm not as broken as I thought I was.

"Thank you," she says.

"Always." I pull her into a hug, filling her with my gratitude next. Because she believed in me. She *always* believed in me.

I want her to know that I believe in her dreams too.

"We'll help you find her, Clau." I squeeze her tighter. "I promise."

She buries her face in my neck and I fight hard to keep her from sinking into those dark feelings again. "I've been trying to think...but...last night. I keep replaying it in my head. I keep thinking that Candela shouldn't know that person."

"You were upset...."

She sniffs into my shoulder. "At first I was just angry with Abby. But then, when everyone stopped to look, it felt like they were looking at me. *Finally.* Like I was real."

"You *are* real," I say.

She shakes her head, unsure. "I wanted them to see me. I wanted them to remember."

"Well, mission accomplished." Carlitos smirks. "The kids at school are going to be telling that story to their grandchildren."

I punch him in the arm. "Not helping."

"Ouch! It's not like it matters. People think it was all La Lechuza's fault."

"But...was it?"

I can't help but remember the way everyone looked at her, attacked her with trash and harsh words. My stomach twists, not at her ugliness but theirs.

"You mean for the car accident?" Carlitos asks. "My

mom said it wasn't the first time Mr. Iglesias has crashed his truck."

"So she could have turned up after." I look to Clau. "And you said she wasn't what caused your family's accident?"

"It's not what I remember," Clau says. "It was just a flash, but I remember that I wasn't afraid of her. Neither was Candela."

"There's one other person who wasn't afraid of her last night," I say.

Carlitos's forehead wrinkles. "Señora Avila."

"Which could mean that she knows there's not actually anything to be afraid of..."

"Or," Clau says, "she just *thinks* there's not actually anything to be afraid of. I don't remember being afraid of La Lechuza, but when I told your abuela that I saw her with Candela, she didn't look relieved. She looked worried. So I asked her if La Lechuza saved Candela or if she...took her."

"What did she say?" I ask.

"She said she didn't know."

Carlitos is frozen. "So maybe she's not at all like Tío Gume."

"Obviously not." I shake my head. "But if La Lechuza's own family isn't sure if she's evil or not, how could Señora Avila be?"

"I guess it depends on the answer to Clau's question. Was Señor Avila saved or was he taken?"

"And if he was *taken* and if that was what Señora Avila wanted, there'd be no reason for her to fear."

Just like the familiarity I've been feeling between La Lechuza and I...Señora Avila seemed to feel it too. A strange knowing. But what does she know that Mami and Abuela and Soona don't? And more importantly, *how* does she know it?

CHAPTER 16

"I want you there and back in ten minutes. ¿Entienden?" Abuela hands me a five-dollar bill.

Carlitos snatches it from me. "And after we get the masa are you expecting change back or...?"

She grabs him by the chin. "You think you're off the hook? Ask me again if I want my change back and you'll both be grounded until the end of the year."

He shudders. "Okay, 'buela, got it."

"¡Rápido!"

We jog down the porch steps, Abuela watching us until Tía Tita calls her back into the kitchen. They're making sopes for lunch, but we ran out of masa, which means Carlitos and I get to experience exactly ten minutes of freedom while we pick up a new bag at Allsup's.

"Do you think she's getting crankier in her old age?" Carlitos asks.

"No." Clau laughs. "I think you two keep breaking the rules y ella tiene harta."

"Us two? I think you mean *us three*. I'm not the one who dropped an entire cake on someone's head last night."

"No, but you did run screaming like a little baby."

He whips his head around to face her. "Because you completely lost it! And I wasn't screaming!"

"Fine. You were shrieking."

"I wasn't shrieking."

"So you were squealing...."

"I wasn't squeal—!"

"Quiet!" I yell. "We're in public."

The bell rings as we enter the store, the three of us ambushed by the smell of fried dough and cleaning supplies.

Belén is behind the counter, talking on her cell phone. "Ay. ¡Ya pues! Don't believe me. But I'm telling you...uh, hold on," she says after I drop a bag of masa on the counter. Then to us, "This plus the usual?"

We nod, mouths already watering.

She drops two fried burritos into paper sleeves and slides them into a bag before dumping in a fistful of hot sauce packets.

Carlitos snatches the bag, breathing in the smell.

"Anyway, if you're inter-
ested, Germán should have
Señor Avila's truck fixed up
by the end of the week. The
old woman gave it to us for
practically nothing—said
she just wanted it gone—so we can give you guys a good deal.
All right, let me know."

As soon as she hangs up, I ask, "Were you just talking
about Señor Avila's truck?"

Belén leans against the counter, fanning herself with a
Spanish tabloid. "Yeah, why? You about to get your license
or something?"

"No. I was just wondering…when did Señora Avila sell
it to you?"

"A couple of days ago."

"You said she just wanted it gone? Why? Was she upset?"

Belén narrows her eyes, examining us. "You heard those
viejas at church gossiping about the Avilas, didn't you?
Those old ladies just can't keep their mouths shut."

Neither can you, I want to say. But I don't. "Do you know
anything about why he left?"

"Or how?" Carlitos adds.

She waves a hand. "I shouldn't be talking to you about
this. It's gossip. Pero…" She leans toward us. "I heard he'd

been all around town without his wedding ring. Talking about running away to the city."

"So maybe he just ran away," Carlitos says.

Belén raises an eyebrow. "Without his beloved Rosita? No. He loved that thing more than anyone."

"Rosita?"

"His truck."

She goes back to fanning herself. "Anyway, like I said, I shouldn't be talking to you about this. Now go on home before that wicked thing snatches you both and eats you for dinner."

I grab the bag of masa. "Thanks, Belén."

Outside, Carlitos tears into his burrito. He scarfs it down in four bites before eyeing mine too. "You gonna eat that?"

"Of course I'm going to eat it. I'm just thinking."

"About what?"

"About Señor Avila's truck and how weird it is that Señora Avila got rid of it in such a hurry."

"Do you think she got rid of the body just as fast?" Clau says. "Or do you think La Lechuza swallowed him whole?"

I sigh, annoyed. "She didn't *eat* him."

Carlitos shakes his head. "Are you sure?"

I'm not and it's an even worse feeling than knowing the truth one way or the other. At least if I was certain, I might be able to actually *do* something about it. But instead, I feel like I'm in this limbo just helplessly waiting for more bad things to happen.

We finally near home, reaching the end of the block. When Carlitos slams into me, I realize that I've come to a complete stop. Right in front of Señora Avila's house.

It looks even worse than it did last time—the windows smudged black with something thick like tar while a foul green gas pours from the seam beneath the front door.

Carlitos holds his nose. "It's like it's rotted."

"I know I can't see what y'all can, but there's definitely something creepy about this place," Clau adds.

I feel a soft nudge, forcing me to take one step toward the house and then another.

"Omega, what are you doing?" Carlitos hisses.

I nod to the carport. "She's not here."

"And?"

I shush Carlitos, wondering for a second why he doesn't feel it too.

"Psst!"

I whip around. "What was that?"

"Down here."

Nailed to the trunk of the giant oak tree on the side of Señora Avila's house is a brown plastic squirrel, some of the paint chipping off. I kneel, examining it more closely.

"Yeah, I'm talking to you," it chirps.

Carlitos kneels next to me.

Then the plastic squirrel says, "She's been feeding that thing, you know?"

"What?" Carlitos stumbles back.

"She's been feeding it at night."

Carlitos's eyes widen. "Is that what happened to Señor Avila?"

"I don't know. Sometimes they'd leave the lights on late at night while they yelled at each other."

"Do you remember when the yelling stopped?" I ask.

The squirrel is silent and for a moment I question whether it had actually spoken at all. But then it says, "The screaming stopped...the night the whistling started."

My stomach drops.

"Whistling?" Carlitos says.

"La Lechuza..."

"It's how she lures her victims," the squirrel says.

And I know it's true not because Abuela told me but because I can feel in my bones that I've been hunted. That it's the source of our strange connection. *She's been calling to me.* Except...I don't feel like prey. Not anymore. Not after seeing all those people attack her as she flew away last night at Marisol's quince. Not after her showing up in Clau's memories from the night she died.

"You know how to get rid of her, don't you?" the squirrel says.

Carlitos narrows his eyes. "*You* know how to get rid of her?"

"Sure." It chirps. "You need a piece of rope." Carlitos and I both lean in closer, listening. "You tie it into seven knots. Then, while one of you is tying the knots, the other one is shouting curses at her. Nastiest, most terrible words you can think of."

"What?" Carlitos snorts. "That's ridiculous! You're full of it...."

"Mmm...," the squirrel muses, "I think you meant to say, I'm full of—"

"Whoa, whoa! Enough!" I turn my back on the squirrel. "No one is going to curse her out." I cross my arms. "We're already grounded as it is."

"Then what are we going to do?" Clau asks.

The nudge returns, only this time it's more of a sound. I follow the knocking up the back porch to the rickety screen door. The wind is tossing it against the frame. *Knock. Knock. Knock.*

I reach for it. "It's unlocked."

"Probably by accident," Carlitos hisses. "It's not an invitation, Omega."

But he's wrong. Something *is* luring me inside, the nudge growing stronger as I step one foot over the threshold and then the other.

"Omega, no..."

I step inside the house, Carlitos watching me through the mesh screen.

The rot we sensed from the outside covers the walls, something damp like mold sprouting in the corners near the ceiling, goo dripping down like giant scratch marks. It smells like roadkill in here and I hold my nose, trying to focus enough to search for clues.

My arm brushes a teakettle on the stove and the kitchen changes color, the black and gray turned to sepia as I watch the Avilas arguing at the kitchen table, Señor Avila getting to his feet before kicking the chair under the table and storming out the screen door.

"Why do old ladies love covering their furniture in plastic?" Clau floats over to the couch, her voice breaking the vision, and I follow.

I rest a hand on the arm and there they are again, Señora Avila standing in front of the television with her hands on her hips while Señor Avila sits on the couch, elbows on his knees, head hanging.

"Oh my God!" Carlitos chokes as he finally steps inside. "She's been *living* here?"

I let go of the couch and motion to the mold. "And she's not the only one." Then I motion to everything else. "Touch anything in this place and you'll get a front row seat to two people who really did not like each other."

Carlitos reaches for one of the dead house plants to give it a shot. A few seconds later he jumps back. "¡Uy!" His eyes widen. "Yeah, she *definitely* killed him."

"Yeah, well a feeling's not enough," I say. "We need evidence."

"Okay, what are we looking for?" Clau asks. "An evil diary where she makes all of her villainous plans? A giant leash that she uses to take La Lechuza on midnight walks? I mean, *flights*."

"That's actually a good idea," I say, making my way across the living room. "The squirrel said she's been feeding it. What if she treats La Lechuza like some sort of pet?"

Carlitos gulps. "Pet? As in, maybe it sleeps here? As in, maybe that's why the back door was open?"

We all freeze. But as I search the stillness, I don't *feel* her.

"Clau, check the other rooms."

"You got it." She gives me a salute before sliding behind each closed door. "All clear," she calls. "Except...y'all might want to see this."

We follow Clau into Señora Avila's bedroom. I know it's her bedroom because it's even filthier than the rest of the house and because the veil she wore to church today is on one of the nightstands.

"What is it?" Carlitos asks.

Clau points to the open jewelry box on the dresser. Gold winks from the tangled mess. Bells.

"Are those what I think they are?" Carlitos shudders.

"Cat collars." I flip over one of the tags, confirming what we already know. "KitKat." I flip another and the same feeling floods me as when we first found their ghosts.

There are at least a dozen others, each one belonging to someone's missing pet.

"What a sicko," Carlitos says.

"Speaking of sick..." I press a hand to my forehead, already clammy.

"Yeah..." Carlitos takes a step back. "Touching this stuff is definitely going to give us ojo."

"Look."
Clau points. "I guess he really did take it off."

"What?"

I spot something at the bottom of the pile. Round and gold and gleaming.

"Señor Avila's wedding ring," Carlitos breathes.

I set down the bag of masa before reaching for it. The second I touch the cold metal the air around me shifts. I see Señor Avila standing right where we are, buttoning his work shirt as he stares at himself in the mirror. His face droops like he barely slept.

Behind him there's yelling. Señora Avila is tossing clothes around and waving her hands. But her voice is a warble like Señor Avila is listening to her underwater.

The scene disintegrates, replaced by a fog, wisps of smoke trailing behind Señor Avila as he breaks into a run. I hear the pounding of his feet on the dirt. I *feel* the pounding of his heart in his chest.

He's being chased.

Overhead, wings beat like they did the night La Lechuza chased us after the séance. She's gaining on him.

He glances back, almost stumbling. But then he gets to his feet again, pumping his arms even harder.

He stops, searching the darkness, and I can barely make out what he sees. It looks like a farm...like one of the silos near the train tracks.

Where are you?

I hear La Lechuza let out a shriek and then there's a splash, Señor Avila disappearing into something black and wet. He holds his breath, fighting to stay beneath the surface. My own throat tightens too, lungs squeezing.

I drop the ring on the floor, gasping for air.

"Omega, what happened?" Clau swirls around me, concerned.

Carlitos slaps my back like he thinks I'm choking.

"I'm fine," I croak. "I'm okay." I straighten, taking giant gulps of air.

"What did you see?" Carlitos asks.

"I saw..." I inhale. "I saw Señor Avila." I look from Carlitos to Clau. "And I think I know where he went."

When we step outside, the wind has changed, knocking the screen door like an angry visitor trying to get inside. I swipe my windblown curls out of my face as I come around the side of the house. The oak tree's branches thrash wildly, sending something fluttering down over our heads.

The feather falls, dipping from side to side before landing at my feet. My body moves to reach for it before I can stop myself. But suddenly, it's swept up again, twisting and turning on the breeze. Floating in the same direction as the desert. As the vision I had of Señor Avila running for his life.

I nod to Carlitos and Clau. "It's this way."

I let the feather guide me across the road before cutting through the open field ahead.

"Whoa, whoa." Carlitos tries to cut me off. "Where do you think you're going?"

I don't answer. I just keep walking. Following the feather as it dances ahead of me.

"What if it's a trap, Omega? What if La Lechuza is trying to lure you to her nest so she can eat you?"

I stomp through sand, dodging rocks and cacti. "It's taking us to Señor Avila."

"How do you know that?" He yanks my arm. "Do you hear yourself right now? You sound delusional!"

I shrug him off of me. "Something's happening. My powers, they're...they're actually *working*."

"You don't know that either."

His words hit me in my gut, stopping me for the first time. The sky overhead feels endless, stretching bright blue in every direction. The sun beats down. Heat steams up from the sand.

But I know what I saw. I know it.

I see the silos up ahead, and then the giant cattle trough starts to peek up over the horizon.

The feather hangs in the air and it feels like another invitation. Like it finally wants me to reach out and touch it. I hold out my hands, and the feather lands perfectly within my open palms.

I twist and turn the feather in the light, igniting flashes of purple, then green, then blue.

And it doesn't feel like last time. Like an omen. Something wicked. It feels like holding the stars.

Like I'm waking up from a dream.

A dream where I was afraid and helpless and hopelessly ordinary. I hold the feather and I feel its power because somewhere, deep down inside me, I have power too.

I hold tight to the feather as we approach the silos, and the closer we get, the more I expect to see Señor Avila still hiding inside that cattle trough. But suddenly there's more than one voice riding on the wind and it sounds like yelling.

"I said give it to me!"

All three of us stop, searching for the sound.

"Crap!" Carlitos glares at what looks like a mirage in the distance. "I think we wandered too far into Montgomery territory."

I spot the water tower to our left. Carlitos is right. We're almost to the trailer park where Abby lives.

"Let's see if they can swim."

Carlitos hangs back. "Let's go before they see us."

Instead, I move closer, my insides latched on to a new feeling. Disgust. *Terror.*

I squint. "What are they doing over there?"

"I don't know and I don't want to know."

I start walking, knowing that Abby's brothers are up to no good.

As we approach, I see Abby's older brother Brian shove

Aiden. They're right next to the cattle trough. I hear the splash of water as Abby's middle brother, Caleb, drops something to the bottom. Aiden lunges for it, about to throw himself into the dirty water.

"Why do you have to be such a buzzkill all the time, Aiden?"

My footsteps crunch on the hard ground.

Caleb whips his head around to look at me. "Speaking of buzzkills." He's clutching a horny toad.

"What are you doing?" I snap.

He holds up the horny toad and locks eyes with it. "Teaching these things how to swim. Wanna see?"

"Don't do it, Caleb." Aiden glares at him, his eyes glistening.

Caleb looks from his brother to me. Then he smiles and tosses it into the cattle trough.

"It'll drown!" Carlitos clenches his fists, angry.

Brian narrows his eyes. "And what are you gonna do about it?"

Caleb laughs. "Yeah, what are you gonna do? Sit on us with your fat butt?"

Carlitos's face burns red. Then he runs straight for Caleb, tackling him to the ground. Brian rushes over, trying to yank Carlitos off his brother. Until Clau rushes him too, throwing him on his back.

While Aiden just stands back and watches.

"Help me!" Caleb groans.

But Aiden ignores him, jumping into the cattle trough and scooping out the horny toads.

While Caleb and Brian are both tangled with Carlitos and an invisible Clau, I run over and place a hand on them both. I don't know if it'll work again like it did with Clau, but if I could just reach them a little, if I could just make them feel an ounce of what I am, maybe I can get them to stop.

But as soon as I touch them, the past plays before my eyes the same way it did with Clau. Only this time, the memory I find isn't a perfect day at the beach.

They're at the hospital, Brian and Caleb arguing about something. Brian puts Caleb in a headlock, nurses turning toward the commotion. Their mother is a few feet away, tubes hanging out of her shirt as she tries to tighten the blanket around her.

"Boys," she pleads. But she's tired, barely able to keep her eyes open.

The blanket falls to the ground and Brian moves to pick it up. He lays it across her lap and then he spots her purse.

He looks to Caleb. Caleb gives him a nod. Then Brian reaches inside and pulls out her wallet. I let the regret fill me like melting wax, but instead of slow and warm, the feelings rush in, fast and on fire. So much more powerful than before. Wilder too.

That's when I notice the feather, still gripped in one of my hands, the changing colors trapped in its sheen more like flames. Everything is amplified and I'm afraid I just might burst.

Then I turn back to Brian and Caleb and force the feelings inside them, dragging the memory to the surface until they're rolling onto their hands and knees.

I stare at my hands, shaking, but Aiden doesn't notice. He's too busy desperately trying to bring the horny toads back to life. As Brian and Caleb watch, the regret they're feeling suddenly turns to fear. Their eyes fill with tears.

"Y'all are sick," Carlitos spits.

"I'm sorry," Brian blubbers. "I'm sorry, Aiden."

The horny toads move slowly at first, coughing up water. The first one takes off and then the others follow, skittering across the sand.

Aiden hangs his head, relieved. Then he looks back at them, disgusted. "What would Mom think?"

Suddenly, they're sobbing, as if for the first time, they're considering the fact that she might be watching.

Judging them too.

"I'm sorry, Aiden. Please..."

Aiden walks right past them, kneeling next to me. "Are you okay?"

That's when I realize that I'm on the ground and that every cell in my body is buzzing. But the fire doesn't burn. It feels safe. It feels *good*.

"They're scum," Carlitos says.

"You got that right." Clau shakes her fist at them.

"I'm so sorry, Omega." Aiden tries to help me up. "Did they hurt you?"

"No." I get to my feet. "I'm okay."

The four of us stare after Brian and Caleb as they run all the way home, and I think about what Mami said about how not all monsters are supernatural. Some monsters are human. And I can't help but wonder if that's what Brian and Caleb are.

But there's another question making my heart race. I stare at the feather until the sun and the clouds and the bright blue sky disappear. Until all I can see is black. Then I beg the darkness to tell me: If Brian and Caleb are monsters, then *what* exactly am I?

CHAPTER 17

"¡OYE!" WE ALL TURN AT THE SOUND of Abuela's voice. "We've been looking everywhere for you three. What part of grounded do you not understand?"

"Sorry, Abuela, we were just—"

She waves a hand, not wanting to hear excuses. "¡Basta ya! Now get inside and get cleaned up." On the way she swats at each of us with her chancla. But before we can make it to the front door, she wrenches Carlitos by the arm. "What's that in your pocket?"

"Wha—?"

She snatches the Allsup's wrapper from his jeans. "What is this? Where's my change?"

He shrugs. "A pre-lunch snack?"

"We got a little hungry, that's all." My whining only makes her turn on me.

"And why is that?" She taps her foot. "Hmm? What exactly were you doing that caused you to be so hungry that not only did you miss lunch, but now it's practically dinnertime and your entire family could have starved and you two wouldn't even care?" Abuela waves a hand. "And where's the masa I sent you to get?"

My heart stops. *Oh no.* I left it in Señora Avila's bedroom.

Someone calls, "We'll see you tonight, Tomás," and when the front door opens, I realize the house is full of people.

There's Mr. and Mrs. Gallegos, Mr. and Mrs. Nguyen, and Mr. and Mrs. Dubois. All getting up from the kitchen table to shake our parents' hands.

"What's going on in there?" I ask.

But no one answers me.

Carlitos and I get caught up in the goodbyes as everyone begins to leave.

"It's nice to see you," Mrs. Gallegos says.

"Nice to see you too," I say, unable to hide my confusion.

"Listen to your parents." Someone pats me on the head. "Be careful out there, now."

I smile and nod before finally being able to wedge myself inside the house. "What's going on?" I say again.

Papi sighs. "Some people in town are forming a search party."

"What kind of search party?" Carlitos asks.

"For La Lechuza," I answer, remembering how angry Mr. Montoya was this morning at church.

"It's not their place," Mami cuts in. "Us magic folk just want to make sure no one gets hurt, that's all. Luckily, Father Torres has helped us convince the church community to hold off for tonight; that it's safer if everyone just stays inside. But if there's another sighting and people decide to go after her on their own, that's when things could get dangerous."

"Do you think someone might?" Carlitos asks. "Get hurt, I mean."

I know when he says *someone* he means someone *human*. But I can't help but think of La Lechuza and how if there's even the slightest possibility that she might not be responsible for any of the terrible things that have happened in Noche Buena, we can't just let them go after her.

"What if they're wrong about her?" I say, turning to Mami and then Abuela. "What if *everyone* is wrong about her?"

Mami sighs. "Omega…"

"She's our family, isn't she? Aren't we supposed to try to help her? To warn her?"

"We have," Abuela says. "She knows what can happen

when she stays in a place too long. Why do you think she's avoided Noche Buena for the past *forty* years?"

"Wait," I say. "So this has happened before? *Why?*" I demand. "How?"

"Why? Because humans are driven by fear. They'd fight their own shadow if they could. But trust me, Omega. She can take care of herself. She's been doing it a long time."

I wasn't the first she turned. And I won't be the last.

She doesn't have much time.

The transformation has already begun. Soon the moon will get what it wants. It always does.

I remember La Lechuza's warnings and I can't help but wonder if the strange things that are happening to me—being able to read memories, the feather making my powers stronger somehow—aren't just a coincidence. If they're happening now for a reason. If La Lechuza *knows* that reason. If she knows me. Maybe better than my own family does...

"Is that what you would do to me?" The words come out before I can stop them. My face gets hot.

"What are you talking about?"

"If I was like her..." I finally meet Abuela's eyes. "Would you leave me all alone? Would you make me take care of myself too?"

Mami grabs my shoulders, gripping me hard. "You are *not*

like her. Do you understand me?" She shakes me. "Omega, do you understand me?"

All I can do is nod.

She quickly lets go, smoothing out her dress.

But I still can't speak. Because in her touch were the same secrets I sensed when Soona looked me in my eyes and said La Lechuza was *just* a story. The same *knowing*. The same *regret*.

The same lies.

She's *lying* to me. Again.

Only this time, it's not about La Lechuza existing in only fairy tales. It's about La Lechuza *existing*…in me.

That night when we take hands for the prayer circle before dinner, I'm immediately struck by Mami's anger and Abuela's worry.

"…and may you steer us away from bad decisions, from our cruel curiosities that will only get us grounded." Abuela peeks an eye open at me. "Amen."

"Amen."

Mami's made pozole tonight. I squeeze out a lime over my bowl before pressing the rind to my teeth.

"Uh, knock, knock…"

We all turn toward the front door. It's still open, Mr. Montgomery on the other side of the screen.

The lime falls out of my mouth.

"Sorry to bother you," he says.

Papi gets up first, giving Mr. Montgomery the same hundred-watt smile he gives everyone.

Even though he doesn't deserve it.

Papi reaches out a hand to shake. Mr. Montgomery reaches back, but he doesn't smile.

"What can we do for you, Jack?" Papi asks. "We were just sitting down for dinner. You hungry? We can grab you a bowl."

"No need." He stuffs his hands in the pockets of his work jacket. "I just came to talk to you about something."

Papi steps out onto the porch, letting the screen shut behind him.

"Stop staring," Mami says. "It's rude."

I stop staring, but I don't stop listening. Even when Mami and Tía Tita start talking about the next quinceañera Mami needs to make decorations for, their voices louder than usual as they try to drown out the sound. But I hear Mr. Montgomery's words loud and clear.

"Omega's been giving my kids a hard time. More than a hard time, actually. I'd go so far as to call her a bully and I'm—"

"Wait a minute." Papi switches to the voice he uses at work. To the voice he never uses at home unless I've done something really awful that I need to feel regret for immediately. "My daughter is not a bully."

"Look, Abby's been coming home in tears for weeks. Just this afternoon, your kid ran my sons home in tears too."

Papi crosses his arms. "And what exactly did she do to them?"

"Listen, they came home with bruises."

"Maybe they deserved them," Carlitos shouts from the table. Tía Tita swats at him. "¡Cállate!"

Mr. Montgomery glares at him through the screen door. "What did you just—?"

"Uh-uh." Papi lowers his voice and somehow it makes him seem even bigger. "Your sons' weekend bonfires have ruined my neighbor's property. Their joyrides in your truck have taken out stop signs and almost gotten people killed."

"This isn't about my kids. It's about—"

"That's enough. Your kids have been picking on Omega and Carlitos and every other kid in this town who is smaller or weaker or different. And my wife and I have still fed them. Still given them rides. Still welcomed them into our home when you had to work late and they had nowhere else to go."

"Now you're gonna throw that in my face? Fine…" He pulls out his wallet. "How much do I owe you?"

"I don't want your money, Jack. But you do owe me your respect."

"Respect?" Mr. Montgomery spits. "You want to talk

about respect? This town used to be a place to be proud of. A safe place. Clean. Plenty of jobs. Then you people came in. Didn't stop coming and now..."

Papi straightens and Mr. Montgomery backs up, almost tripping over the steps.

"It was better before." Mr. Montgomery is as red as a chili pepper.

Mami appears behind Papi. "Before what, Jack? You forget. This family has been in Noche Buena since the beginning. Since before the beginning. Your trailer is parked on land my ancestors used to till with their bare hands."

"And let me guess," Mr. Montgomery says, "that beast that showed up the other night is one of them?" He sneers. "Yeah, I've heard the rumors about you and your *ancestors*. How you all got a little *beast* in you. Is that why you had them call off the search parties tonight?"

Papi stiffens. "You need to *leave*."

Mr. Montgomery points past Mami and Papi. Right at me. "You tell her to leave my kids alone."

"And you do the same," Papi says, no trace of his smile left.

A sharp squealing makes me jolt. Tires skirt across gravel. I finally dare to look, but Mr. Montgomery hasn't even made it to his truck. Someone else is speeding up the driveway, headlights washing over Mami and Papi.

The doors of the truck are thrown open, the engine still

running. Two men in dusty jeans and sweat-stained shirts carry out a limp stranger. He's groaning, covered in blood.

"What happened?" Papi asks, rushing over.

"He was attacked."

"By what?" Mr. Montgomery says, unable to hide his curiosity. He's drawn like a moth to a flame, watching as they carry the man up the steps to the house.

Abuela stands. "Omega, take Carlitos and Chale to your room."

"But—" I want to stay. I need to know what's going on.

"Now," Abuela says.

Carlitos and Chale follow me to my room. I drag my feet, still trying to get a good look.

"I've never seen anything like it. Just swooped down out of nowhere," one of the men says.

"Swooped down?" Mr. Montgomery asks. "Was it a bird?"

"Not just a bird," the man says. "It was an owl."

The sound of engines revving makes the hairs on my arms stand up. I can't stop staring out the window. Even after Papi's taillights disappear up the road. Even after the first stars begin to prick through the cloud cover. Even when Clau and Carlitos try to drag me away.

"She could be out there *right now*," Carlitos says.

He and Chale have made a makeshift fort next to the bed as if a couple layers of blankets will keep them from her claws.

"She *is* out there." I press my hands to the glass. It's cold.

"The mill isn't that far from here," Carlitos whispers. "I recognized the guy's uniform."

I think past the blood and remember the mill company logo on his chest. The same one on the uniform Señor Avila was wearing when I watched him getting ready for work. It's just a couple of miles from here, the silos marking the halfway point. With wings as big as arms, La Lechuza could cover the distance in less than a minute. Maybe she already has.

I take a step back from the window before pulling the curtain closed and squeezing into the fort next to Clau, Carlitos, and Chale.

"Are we playing hide-and-seek again?" Chale asks.

Carlitos nods. "Yeah, and you're winning. Great job."

Chale smiles before turning his attention back to his superhero action figure. Soon, he's dozing off. Carlitos is next, and Clau uses her wintry breath to freeze his drool to his face.

"Do you really think it was La Lechuza who attacked that man at the mill?" Clau asks.

I sigh. "Sometimes I'm certain she's not evil, but then other times...I sense it. Like it's in the air. I just can't tell which direction it's coming from."

"Well, at least no one's turned up dead yet. If Señor Avila was toast, his ghost would have been hanging out around the silos, but there was no sign of him."

"Yeah, that's good news."

I feel a prick, like fingers tracing up my spine. I turn, and in the seam between the curtains, light blooms. I part them with my fingers, slowly, and then I see the light on in Señora Avila's kitchen.

I wonder if she found the bag of masa, if she knows somehow that I'm the one who left it there. As if on cue, she comes to the window, peering out.

I ease back, letting the curtains fall closed, though there's still the smallest sliver, her face cut in half.

I'm hidden. I *know* it. But it's like she still senses me looking. Suddenly, a wild grin slowly spreads across her face and I finally see what I was searching for this morning at church. Proof that she was different. *Wrong.*

But it's not two rows of glinting sharp teeth I find.

It's a dark stain peeking out from her hairline. A red smear under her chin. It's blood.

For a long time, I pretend I'm sleeping. But I'm actually thinking about monsters. About all their different shapes and sizes. Señora Avila and Abby. I think about the bleeding man from the mill and Mrs. Montoya crying in Belén's arms and Mr. Montoya's rage.

I think about Brian and Caleb and those poor horny toads. I think about what Mr. Montgomery said about our town being better *before*, even though for us, there is no *before*.

Abuela says our ancestors used to be nothing but stardust. Over the centuries, bits and pieces fell to earth, lining the landscape like diamonds. We were born from el cielo *and* la tierra and we have lived on this land under these stars for as long as they've been shining.

But Mr. Montgomery doesn't care about the past or even the truth. He probably believes every horrible lie Abby has ever told about me. Maybe she even told him about our magic and about how I wouldn't use it to help Abby talk to her mom again. Maybe he hates me for that too. Or maybe he'd hate me no matter what I did.

In the quiet comes a soft tapping. I go still, trying to sense where it's coming from. But there's no drumbeat in my chest. No fire blazing.

"I think it's coming from the window," Clau whispers.

Behind the curtains, I can see a shape, taller than I am. They tap again and I jump.

"You're not actually going to open it, are you?" Clau hisses.

Earlier, I was so sure the feather was leading me in the

right direction. But what if Carlitos was right about it being a trap? What if La Lechuza was trying to lure me to her?

What if that's her just on the other side of the glass?

I graze the gauzy curtain, then I take a deep breath and throw it back. But on the other side, I don't see La Lechuza. I see Aiden.

He raises a hand, a sad smile on his face.

I push open the glass. "What are you doing here?"

"Don't worry, Omega." Clau's brow furrows. "I'll get rid of him."

I give her a stern look that says, *We do not need a repeat of the other night.*

She turns up her nose. "Fine."

"I'm sorry it's late," he says.

I press a finger to my lips before tiptoeing to close my bedroom door. Through the seam I can see Abuelo still snoring in his recliner and Abuela finishing her cafecito, which signals she's getting ready for bed too.

I tiptoe back to the window and take in Aiden's face, examining every detail to make sure he's not some sort of dream. He smiles, shy, a little goofy, and it's so adorable that I can't help but think that of course it's a dream.

I pinch my arm and it hurts. "Ouch!"

"Are you all right?" Aiden asks.

I blink. "You're real...."

He chuckles and then remembers my instructions to lower his voice. "Yeah, I'm real."

I don't know what to say—I've never found a boy outside my bedroom window before—and I can't help but stare. At his crooked smile, his dimples. There are actually five of them and they look like tiny crescent moons.

"Are you trying to creep him out?" Clau is a cool breeze by my ear. "Say something!"

I cough, clear my throat. "Uh, did...did you need something?"

He looks down, his smile turned tense as he bites his lip. "I wanted to say that I'm sorry." He meets my eyes again. "For Brian and Caleb. And especially Abby." He sighs. "For my dad too. I heard he came over here."

"Yeah..."

"He was out of line." He scratches at the paint chipping from the windowsill. "I think he knows it too."

"But you came alone," I say.

He shrugs. "That's how I do most things these days."

I try to imagine what it would be like if Carlitos and I hated each other's guts, if I didn't have Clau, if my house wasn't bursting at the seams with family. A pit forms in my stomach and all I want is to reach out and hug him, to chase away his loneliness.

He forces a smile again. "It's not so bad. That secret spot I told you about? It helps me clear my head."

"Sounds nice."

Clau nudges me forward and I catch myself on the windowsill.

"Yeah...I'm actually on my way there now." He chews on his lip again. "Would you wanna see it?"

I hear Clau squeal behind me and it makes me blush.

"You don't have to if—"

"Yes." I grin so wide it hurts my cheeks.

"Cool."

"Cool."

He backs up and that's when I realize that I have just agreed to sneak out. Again. I look toward my bedroom door, praying that everyone on the other side is asleep. Praying that breaking the rules this time won't get me grounded... or killed. Hoping that if it does, it'll at least be worth it.

I look past Aiden to Señora Avila's window. The light's still on and I can see her shadow moving behind the curtains. Somehow, I feel safer knowing she's inside, and it makes the trees beyond the property line seem safer too. Even if La Lechuza may be lurking in them...I don't think she's here to hurt me.

Aiden takes my hand, helping me over the windowsill, and then he doesn't let go. Giddiness swells in my chest, but in his touch, I can sense that he feels it too. Along with anticipation and wonder and a million other things swirling like butterflies between us.

"Where are we going?" I ask as we step beneath the canopy of trees lining the edge of the property.

"The perfect place for stargazing. Seriously, you can see for miles."

He leads me over tree roots and across the open field where we held our botched séance, then into another cluster of trees, these taller, with wide trunks I probably can't even wrap my arms around.

Suddenly Aiden stops, letting go of my hand as he leaps for the darkness above our heads.

He pulls down a rope ladder and then holds it steady for me to climb up.

When I reach the platform, my hands brush something soft, an old rug laid across the wooden planks of the tree house. There's a beanbag chair, a small shelf of books, and a case of Coca-Cola.

After Aiden joins me in the tree house, he crawls over to the beanbag, fluffing the stuffing, before gesturing for me to sit.

"It's the best seat in the house."

"The best seat for what?"

"For this." He lies back and points straight up.

There's a break in the trees and beyond them the sky is

glittering. Like it's been covered in powdered sugar. I look closer and not all the stars are burning white. There are shades of blue and purple, colors smeared like someone is painting them right before our eyes.

"That's Jupiter." He points to the brightest star in the sky. "And Venus."

I inhale, pointing too. "And the Big Dipper."

Hovering above us, our fingers tangle, just for a second, before our arms fall at our sides.

"I like to come here to think," he says.

"It's quiet." I sink deeper into the beanbag. "It's so loud at my house. Sometimes it feels like their voices are in my head more than my own."

He laughs. "I know what you mean." Then he frowns. "I thought it would be quieter now. My mom…she was always waking us up with music on Saturday mornings, singing at the top of her lungs while we did chores. When Dad was in a bad mood, she'd put on his favorite song and make him dance. I could never sleep in. I could never *hide*." He exhales. "But now…it's like everything's gotten louder. Brian and Caleb are always fighting. My dad's always yelling. Abby's always slamming doors." He pinches his eyes shut. "Sometimes I think my head is going to explode."

I reach for his hand and I feel the squeeze between my own temples. All the nights with no sleep. All the mornings dragging himself out of bed after he realizes that this day is going to be just like the others. I feel him gritting his teeth, his grief seeping into me like cold molasses.

Slow and heavy with a hint of something sweet.

I remember Clau's hope, just as small, and how I'd plucked it from the mess of all her other emotions, planting it in my own heart like a seed.

I reach for the sweetness, for the bright light buried deep in Aiden's memories. Aiden's mother taking his hands in hers, twirling him across the living room floor, turning the music up so loud that they can feel the vibrations in their whole bodies.

Aiden's eyes are closed as the memory washes over him. He lets out a deep breath, and in the dark I feel him smile. I let go of his hand and his eyes flash open again, wet with tears.

"What did you do?" he says.

I sit up, unsure if he's afraid. If he's...afraid of *me*. "I..."

But then his smile widens as he lets out a breathy laugh. Like his lungs are free. Like his soul is too.

"I knew it," he says.

I hug my knees, still not sure if I just made a huge mistake.

"I always knew you were special."

Then he hugs me, so tight, and while my mind searches him for danger, my heart finds something else. Safety. Comfort.

"It's like what you did to Brian and Caleb, isn't it?"

"I..." I don't know what to say.

"I won't tell anyone," Aiden says. "About what you can do."

My heart squeezes and then the fist around it finally lets go. Like I can finally breathe. Because Aiden isn't afraid. He doesn't hate me.

He *doesn't* hate me.

"Omega, are you okay?" He leans back, looking at my face.

I sniff, not sure how to say it. "I thought if you ever found out…you'd…"

"I'd what?"

"Run away."

He frowns. "My mom always said magic was real. When she died, I couldn't see how that was true. I stopped believing." He smiles. "Until now. Because you reminded me. Because you made me remember her."

"Sometimes it's hard to find those memories. To focus on them and let all the bad stuff fall away. But you can see her whenever you want."

"Thank you," he whispers.

"You're welcome," I whisper back.

I look up to catch another glimpse of the stars, but I face the treetops instead. Toward the long branches stretching into the darkness like beckoning fingers. I stare into the night, into the gray shadow of the fluttering leaves, and I see a knot of darkness. Bald branches tangled and intertwined. Woven together like two open palms.

Like the body of a ship.

Like the folded wings of a bird.

Like a nest.

CHAPTER 18

WHEN I CRAWLED BACK THROUGH MY BEDROOM window and
didn't get busted, I took it as a sign that not only was sneaking
out the right thing to do, but that this close to finding out the
truth about La Lechuza, I had no choice but to do it again.

"Are you sure we're going the right way?" Carlitos huffs
and puffs behind me.

"Yes, I'm *sure*."

"And this time is different because...?"

The leaves above us rustle, Clau swooping down from
the treetops before booping Carlitos on the nose with her
pointer finger. "It's different because she has me."

I crane my neck. "What's it look like from up there?"

"Terrifying." Clau floats down to eye level. "It's just over
that fallen tree stump and to the right."

"And no sign of her yet?" Carlitos shivers.

"Not unless she's camouflaged." Clau's swallowed by some overgrown bushes before popping out a few inches from Carlitos's face. "Boo!"

He jumps. "Stop that!"

"We're going to come face-to-face with her sooner or later," I remind him. "That's kind of the whole point of sneaking out."

"No, that's *your* reason for sneaking out. My reason for sneaking out is so when La Lechuza decides she's hungry, I can run and tell everyone who killed you."

"So you're here to witness my murder."

"Someone's got to do it."

Suddenly, the forest turns a shade darker, the moon smudged clean from the sky. Branches crack and sway, shadows bending up ahead.

We take a right at the fallen tree stump, Carlitos slipping on a loose stone. He grabs my hand, steadying himself, but he doesn't let go. As the shadow swells, stretching wide between the trees, I tighten my grip on him too.

"Is that—?"

"Shh."

Our breathing is too loud and I'm afraid La Lechuza can hear our hearts beating too. Even Clau clings to us, shuddering as we near the clearing.

The nest stretches across four giant oak trees, roots tied in thick braids that wind back and forth above our heads, cracks packed with mud and rocks and twigs. I blink, my eyes adjusting to the darkness, and I notice the nest is surrounded by sharp lines like the bars on a jail cell, the sticks wrapped in thorns.

It doesn't make sense that this is her *home*. The place where she sleeps. Where she dreams. Unless…those dreams are actually nightmares. Unless the thorns aren't meant to keep something in, but to keep something out.

"How are we going to get up there?" Carlitos hisses.

I press a finger to my lips, eyeing the nest. Because the truth is, I have no idea how we're going to get up there.

Up above, I see her giant body shift, dirt falling down over our heads. Carlitos coughs before immediately slapping a hand over his mouth. But it's too late.

I hear La Lechuza heave herself out of the nest and then the ground is quaking beneath us. She lands, wings outstretched, and then she screams. The sound tears at my ears, making my blood run cold. But then I think about the thorns. I think about the partygoers throwing rocks and trash at her. I think about the photos of her and Abuela and Señora Avila all dressed up for a night of dancing.

I stare into her eyes, concentrating on what lies beneath, and then I feel what I knew was there all along. Fear.

She's *afraid. Of us.*

She tries to make herself bigger, to make herself scary. But instead of cowering the way Carlitos is, I straighten. I *keep* staring.

And then I say, "I'm not afraid." I tremble, taking a step toward her. "I'm not afraid of you."

Carlitos wrenches me by the arm. "Omega, what are you doing?"

I move closer, and La Lechuza shifts back. Her giant feet stumble over rocks and twigs as she tries to keep out of reach. Like she thinks I'm going to hurt her.

I reach out a hand. "You're safe." Another step closer. "We just want to talk to you."

"M-maybe she doesn't want to talk, Omega!" Carlitos is still cowering, still begging me to turn back.

"You've been looking for me," I say because I know this connection between us isn't a coincidence. "Now I'm here."

La Lechuza's wings fall at her sides.

I drop my hands too. "Please, we just want to know why you're here."

And why I feel like I know you, I think. *Why it feels like you know me too.*

I feel Carlitos make his way to my side. Clau floats in the corner of my eye too.

"Child, the answer to that is long and hard...."

"We're listening," I offer.

"Does your abuela know you're here? What about Soona?"

"They're afraid," I say. "That's all."

"They should be...." Her face falls, and from this angle, beak and sharp teeth hidden, I can see the woman she was... *before.*

"What happened to you?"

Her head sways as if she's swimming in the memory. "What happens to all empaths who absorb too much hate and not enough love."

"You... you're an empath?"

"L-like us?" Carlitos stammers.

She nods. "Like you. Like your ancestors before you."

"But Abuela's not a monster," Carlitos says.

La Lechuza meets our eyes, her own wet with tears. "Because she has you."

"What does that mean?" I ask.

"It means that your abuela is surrounded by love. It is bursting from her. Every time she sees you, kisses you, holds you, she is renewed."

"What happened to your children?" Clau says in the most gentle voice I've ever heard her use.

"The same thing that happened to my husband. They were killed."

"How?" Carlitos is barely breathing and I know he still thinks she's evil, that she probably killed them herself.

La Lechuza closes her eyes, a torrent of tears filling the deep creases of her face. "The newspapers called it a tragic accident. But Ramon had driven drunk enough times that it was no coincidence. We fought all day, yelling and breaking so many promises. At sunset, he loaded our children into his pickup truck and headed toward the highway. They were found in a ditch, the truck tangled with barbed wire, tires still spitting up mud.

"I was the first one at the hospital. I got there before your abuela could warn me." She chokes. "I held their bodies before I knew how all that grief and death would transform my own."

"It changed you...permanently...."

She nods. "When an empath absorbs that much darkness, the soul retreats and the body takes on a new form. But that alone does not seal the curse. To do that, you must feed on the very thing that transformed you in the first place. You must create it in the world."

She bares her teeth, remembering. "I was so angry. So full of hate. And all I wanted was to seek out more. But even that wasn't enough. I had to plant it in people like seeds. I had to suffocate them with the fear that was suffocating me. That's when I began to hunt."

"I don't think she's talking about just cats," Carlitos whispers.

"Every man who left a late-night bar. Every teenager out for a joyride. Every trucker falling asleep at the wheel. I chased them until their hearts raced, until I could feed from their fear."

Carlitos quakes next to me. "You killed them?"

"Death is a hollow thing and I was so tired of feeling empty. But fear kept me full. Until one day it stopped being enough." This time she looks at Clau, and for the first time I realize that she can see her. "She looked just like my daughter...."

Clau's eyes well up with tears. "What did you do with Candela?"

"I was hunting that night, waiting for someone to drive through my lonely stretch of highway. I heard the crash before I saw it, lightning illuminating the wreckage. The scent of fear led me straight to you. And then I saw her. Those wide, angelic eyes. So much like my daughter Lucia's. My heart stopped for a moment. I thought it was her. I was certain. And what filled me then was a feeling I hadn't felt in such a very long time. *Love.*"

Clau weeps silently against my shoulder.

"It spread through me like wildfire and I felt alive for the first time in years. The woman I used to be, the *mother* I used to be, I remembered her. I *missed* her."

"But then you took her," Clau yells. "You took Candela away from me!"

La Lechuza shakes her head, timid again. "No, I waited with her until I saw the ambulance lights. Until I knew she was safe."

"But why come back now?" Carlitos places himself between La Lechuza and Clau. "Why are you here?"

La Lechuza is quiet for a long time and then she stares into the trees, down the path we walked through the forest, down the path that leads to home. "I discovered something that night. That humans have enough fear without me creating more. I stopped hunting and I started searching. For more children. More victims. A dark highway is already such a dangerous thing. So many accidents. So much death.

"I started waiting with the dying, absorbing their fear so it wouldn't follow them to the other side. But it didn't fill me up like it used to. Even done with love, it still made me feel like a stranger to myself. And the entire time, I couldn't stop thinking about Candela. About the way that memory of my children had awoken something in me. Had helped me remember who I really am.

"I thought…if just the memory of my family could do that, what would happen if we were face-to-face? What would happen if, instead of their hate, I could absorb their forgiveness? That's why I came home. To find forgiveness. To find love."

"Clau and I found a book with your origin story," I say. "The woman who appeared to us...she said she killed her family."

La Lechuza hangs her head. "Altagracia. Your great-great-great-grandmother. She was the first of us empaths to transform into...*this*." Her voice falters. "And I hoped I would be the last."

"What do you mean, you hoped...?"

Rustling in the trees makes all four of us spin. Down the path I see the heads of flashlights, branches bending and making way.

Then above the crunch of twigs I hear Abuela's voice. "Omega Amarissa Ignacia Carlotta Martinez Morales!" And then, "Carlitos Santi Gabino Normando Martinez Vidal!"

"We have to go!" Carlitos tries to pull me into a run.

"Come with us." I reach out a hand again, eyes pleading for La Lechuza to take it.

The footsteps move closer, their shouts just beyond the tree line.

"We can tell them everything. We can help you explain." I reach for her. "We can help you."

"I can't face them again." Her wings spread, slowly, like she's hesitating.

"You won't have to do it alone."

"Omega!" Abuela's voice is full of rage. "Carlitos! Clau!"

He yanks on my arm again. "Omega, come on!"

I lock eyes with La Lechuza, begging her to feel that same thread between us, for her to trust me enough to stay.

She gives me a sad smile and I think she's changed her mind. But then Abuela makes it into the clearing, yelling, her fists raised.

La Lechuza meets my eyes. "I'm sorry." And then she leaps into the sky, the wind cast from her wings wrapping me in the deepest loneliness I have ever felt.

By the time we face Abuela, she's no longer yelling. She's just staring at us, her shoulders heaving as she tries to catch her breath. I wait for her to snatch us by the ears. To call me a malcriada again.

But she doesn't say a word.

Instead, she clenches her jaw as tears fall from her eyes, and then she turns her back on us before heading through the trees toward home.

Mami and Tía Tita aren't quiet. They are loud and angry and their words prick me like tiny needles. Until we reach the house. By then I'm numb, staring straight through them as they tell us over and over again that we should be ashamed.

"That's why she flew away, you know." I didn't mean to open my mouth, but it shocks them into silence. "She flew away because she's ashamed of what she's become and you won't even help her. You won't even try!"

Abuela grabs me by the chin, looking deep into my eyes. "That woman has been doing the devil's work. Is that what's gotten into you too?" She looks to Carlitos. "Both of you?"

"She's changed," I say, tears spilling into my mouth.

"Do you know the things she's done? They're the kinds of things that can't be erased, Omega. Never."

The words punch their way out of me. "But she's our family!"

Abuela grabs me. "*You're* my family." She clenches her jaw. "Do you know what she said to me before she disappeared? That if she ever came back...it would be to take you from me. My children. My grandchildren. Everyone I'd ever loved. So that I could feel what she felt. So that I would become a monster too." Her lip trembles. "From that moment on, she was a stranger to me." Her anger is as thick as mud, but buried under the muck is fear. The same fear Mr. Montgomery felt when he told Papi that we didn't belong.

"She doesn't want to be. She wants to come home. Because she's different. But you won't even let her prove it." I shake my head. "You're just like Belén and Mr. Montgomery and all of the other close-minded people in this town. Afraid of something you don't understand. Even though you could learn to. Even though you could talk to her. You could *listen*. But you don't know how to listen." Then I run to my room before slamming the door behind me.

I don't even make it inside the school before I hear the chatter about La Lechuza, my hand clutching the moonstone in my pocket like it's a life raft as I wind my way through the noise.

"My parents said it's just some weirdo in a feather suit."

"My mom thinks it's a sign of the apocalypse. She prayed over me for an hour last night."

"That's nothing. My abuela made me take a bath in holy water. She even cooked our dinner with it."

Mixed in with the superstitions and spiritual remedies there are kids arguing about what they saw that night at the party, arguing about who was more scared. But once I step inside the building, all I hear is the same mechanical mess on a loop, everyone glued to their cell phone screens. And it's like I'm walking through static, everything too bright and too loud—the moonstone the only thing keeping me afloat.

Breathe, Omega.

One...two...three...

I walk as close to one of the groups as I dare, peering over shoulders as I try to get a good look at whatever they're watching.

It doesn't take much for something to go viral in Noche Buena. If it's even slightly embarrassing, it ends up making the rounds on social media. Like when I puked my guts out in math class. I should have known someone was recording (someone always is). But a few days later everyone was on to the next embarrassing video, this one showing one of the cheerleaders crash-landing after a backflip gone wrong.

I stop trying to see over kids twice my size and find Carlitos at his locker. "What's everyone looking at?"

"You haven't seen it?" Carlitos doesn't have a cell phone so he drags me toward the group of kids huddled together by the library doors.

We lean over their shoulders and watch.

It's a livestream from the Noche Buena Neighborhood Watch Instagram account. I read the time stamp: 11:38 PM. That's around the same time we were at La Lechuza's nest.

At first it's hard to make out Abby's face, but I know it's her since she's usually the one on the other side of the camera when her father goes live to complain about unmowed lawns and the price of gas. But it's so dark I can barely see either of them at first. Until the camera angle shifts and then I see that her face is completely white.

There's a loud bang like something's bouncing off the roof of the truck.

Abby's father grips the steering wheel hard, tree branches beating the windshield as he drives straight through them. The truck jostles, both Abby and her father glancing back every so often like they're being chased.

The truck bucks, sending them both out of their seats.

Abby screams. "It's in the back!"

She turns the camera to face the truck bed and all I see is black. Then steam presses against the window, a thick cloud bleeding in and out. *In and out.*

Then out of the fog come two bright yellow eyes. I stare into them, my entire body going cold. Because these eyes don't belong to Luna.

They belong to the woman who watched me from her kitchen window last night. Whose skin was still smeared with blood.

Señora Avila.

Her bright yellow eyes stare at the camera—at Abby— and then they narrow. The glass shatters and suddenly the screen goes dark.

"I heard a bunch of alien-obsessed losers are coming to try to get pictures." Joon walks by, rolling his eyes.

"Do you think that's what happened to Abby?" Naomi snickers. "Maybe she was abducted." Then they both start cackling.

"People are laughing at this?" My stomach turns.

"I guess there are more monsters in Noche Buena than we thought," Carlitos says.

At the end of the hallway, the crowd has grown. Some of them are imitating Abby's screams. Others are pretending to be the giant bird that snatched her out of the truck. But I can tell by their laughter that they don't think any of it is real.

The "monster" is nothing more than noise in the background. They probably think it's some kind of sound effects Abby and her father have added to the video. Another heavily doctored campaign ad to try to make it seem like there are monsters in Noche Buena that only Jack Montgomery can protect us from.

But it's not fake and Abby's dad can't actually protect anyone.

Which means... "Was Abby really taken?"

"I don't know." Carlitos nudges me. "But you know who will?"

Aiden is behind the crowd, watching them, his face

bright red. I weave through the other students, pushing away phones as people try to shove the video in my face.

"Back off!" I growl.

Aiden rounds the corner, stomping off toward the art building.

"Aiden," I call.

He looks back, slowing when he sees it's me.

"What are you doing here?" Carlitos asks him.

The bell rings, kids scattering like roaches. He doesn't move. He just looks at me and then past me.

"Not here," he says.

We follow him to the courtyard. The teacher on duty has already left and there's no one out here but us. The sun glints off the metal lunch tables.

Aiden shields his eyes. "My dad made me come to school." His cheeks redden again. "CPS has been all over him lately with Brian and Caleb getting in so much trouble. If we were absent, we'd just end up on their radar again."

"I'm sorry."

He exhales. "I guess it's not really important right now, is it?"

"Did they find her?" Carlitos asks.

"No. Dad and some of his buddies spent all night searching. There should be an even bigger group after school."

I see Señora Avila's eyes staring at me from her kitchen

window. I see her eyes on the other side of the glass before it shattered in Abby's video.

"Aiden…I think I know—"

"Please don't tell me you're skipping." Soona appears out of nowhere, arms crossed. "Omega Amarissa Ignacia Carlo—"

"Okay, I know what this looks like…but please…" I hang my head back, exasperated. I'm so sick of being in trouble, but more importantly, I'm so sick of the adults interrupting every time I'm about to make a breakthrough in this mystery.

"Omega…" She raises an eyebrow that says she does not appreciate my tone of voice.

I chew on my lip, thinking. If I lie again, I'll just end up grounded until my eighteenth birthday. But if I tell the truth, maybe Soona will help me. And then maybe we can help Abby.

I take a deep breath, let it out. "Soona, I know where Abby is."

Aiden's eyes widen. "You do?"

Soona looks me up and down. She knows I'm telling the truth. Then she asks, "Where?"

"I'll show you." I take a few steps toward the school entrance, Aiden following.

She blocks our path. "You'll *tell* me."

"I *could* do that." I smile, about to stretch my truth-telling to its final limits. "But after you leave, Carlitos and I will just sneak out to follow you. So probably better if we come along."

"And Abby's my sister," Aiden says. "I'm coming too."

Soona bends over to look me in the eye, an annoyed smile on her face. "Then let's skip the formalities and say that after this little excursion not only will the two of you be grounded until the end of time, but you will also be spending the weekend cleaning out the library. Every shelf. Every nook and cranny. Until you're so bored it feels like time has stood still."

Suddenly, my mouth is the Sahara desert. Because she's not talking about the normal library. She's talking about el Otro Lado where time *literally* does stand still, which means I'm going to be dusting those shelves for an eternity.

CHAPTER 19

THE STORM GREETS US FIRST.

Back at the school there wasn't a cloud in the sky, but in the three miles between there and here, they've tumbled in like miniature mountains, dark and rumbling with thunder.

"It means she's close," I breathe.

"Yes," Soona says, "and also perhaps that she knows we're coming."

But the storm isn't the only one waiting. Abuela and Mami are already on the porch of our house. They knew we were coming too.

As soon as Soona puts the car in park, rain begins to pelt the dirt, sending up dust that makes me sneeze.

Inside, Mami speaks only to Soona. "Señora Avila's house is empty. We searched it top to bottom."

"What?" I step between them. "No. That can't be right."

Mami scowls. "This behavior is becoming a habit."

"But I..." I shake my head, confused. "I wasn't lying, Mami. I promise!"

She exhales before handing Aiden a torn strip of fabric. "Was this Abby's?"

He takes it, running his fingers along the stitching. "Her jacket."

"We found it in the house. But there was no sign of her."

So she *was* there.

"Well, now what?" Carlitos asks. "Where do we go?"

"How many times do I have to tell you there is no *we*." Abuela pushes Carlitos and I each into a chair at the kitchen table, making me feel small.

The adults turn their backs to us again, whispering about where she may have taken Abby.

"Maybe she's not entirely in control of it yet."

"That could be why she ran with the girl. She knows she's vulnerable."

"But where would they go? Her car's still in the garage."

"Wait!" I push out of my chair. "I have an idea."

They only listen to me because I was right about Abby and because I took off toward the tree line before they could stop me.

The sky is so dark it feels like dusk, the canopy above our heads hiding the sharp scribbles of lightning tearing across the sky.

When we reach Aiden's tree house, I almost miss it, the leaves camouflaging the makeshift walls. Aiden jumps up, pulling down the ladder like he did last night.

"Hurry," Mami says, pushing me toward the opening, "before the rain makes it too hard to see."

Aiden climbs up first before reaching out his hand to me. I crawl on my knees, scanning the forest. Leaves shiver from the falling rain, branches bending under the weight. Everything is gray, the rain falling in thick sheets that make it hard to tell if anything's moving, if anything's out there.

"Omega…" Aiden points to the open field behind us.

I squint, trying to see past the rain and fog. There's a prick of light. Then another. And then out of the darkness there are bodies—a line of people stretching from one end of the field to the other. All of them holding torches.

All moving in this direction.

Arrowed in on the darkness beyond the trees. Heading straight for La Lechuza's nest.

"They think she took her." I scramble back down the ladder. "They don't realize there are two of them."

"Who?" Mami reaches for me. "Omega, what are you talking about?"

"The search party. They're on their way right now." Torchlight flashes between the trunks of the trees. "They're going after Luna," I tell her, "and we have to stop them."

When we reach the clearing, the search party has grown.

There's Belén and the Montoyas. Father Torres too, leading the people who, just a few days ago, were sitting in a church pew scared. Plus all the people who go to the Pentecostal church—Mr. Montgomery and his buddies from work. Mrs. Statham and Mr. Fisher.

My stomach tightens. All this time I thought...I *hoped* it would be love that would bring the town together. Instead, it's hate.

"What do you think they're going to do once they find her?" Clau shivers.

"I don't want to think about it," Carlitos says.

Mr. Montgomery weaves through the crowd before getting caught up on something near the front of the line.

Rope. There's at least twenty yards of it, Father Torres tying knots as he mutters a prayer under his breath before passing it to the person next to him, until the rope begins to snake through the entire crowd.

I wave my hands, trying to get everyone's attention. "Please, wait! Stop!"

They ignore me, pushing across the field until they're almost to the tree line, and even from here I can feel how they *burn* with anger, how their hearts are focused on revenge.

"She didn't do it! You're going the wrong way. Please," I plead with them. "Please, just listen to me!"

But they don't listen.

They don't stop.

Until the rain does.

Until something giant swoops down overhead, blocking the storm, before landing with a rumble between us.

La Lechuza looks from me to the angry crowd.

My heart shoots into my throat. "No." I tremble. "They want to hurt you."

"I know. But I won't let you get hurt instead," she says.

Father Torres raises his voice, his prayer more forceful, his tying more frantic. He's on knot number five, almost every person in the crowd gripping some part of the rope, ready to string it around her neck.

La Lechuza flinches, wings flexing. I can see that she's in distress, Father Torres's words striking like fire. He ties another knot and she lets out another cry, lightning striking the earth to match.

"Please." I step in front of her, facing Father Torres. "Please, stop this! You're going to kill her!"

But that's the point. For their rage. For the flames. They didn't come here to listen or even to find Abby. They came here to destroy.

"Father Torres," Abuela cuts in. "We think there's been a mistake. The girl is still out there somewhere. We need to find her!"

Suddenly, I see the rope flung into the air, and Mr. Montoya races to wrap it around La Lechuza's wings. Another piece of rope comes down, this time Mr. Fisher dragging it in the opposite direction until La Lechuza is so twisted up she can't even spread her wings. She can't get away.

And the more she struggles, the louder the crowd becomes. Until their cruelty makes me sick. Until it fills me with rage too. But if I rush the crowd, if I try to tear the rope from their hands and any of that rage rubs off on them, I can't imagine what they might do. *Who* they might become.

But what if I attacked them with something else?

What if the key to stopping them isn't making them hear me but making them *feel* me?

I run straight for Father Torres, grabbing the frayed end of the rope where it coils at his feet. But then I freeze. Because the key to getting other people to feel something is to feel it myself first. Except, I can't. I can't summon joy or

love or any other positive emotion. Not while I watch her scream. While I watch them strangle her.

"It's not out there." Mami stands beside me, taking up part of the rope before pressing it to her chest. "It's in *here.*"

Carlitos appears at my side, followed by Tía Tita and Soona and Abuela. All of us holding onto the rope.

I pinch my eyes shut, concentrating.

"When the Reese's Peanut Butter Cup comes out completely smooth," Carlitos says.

"The first day of spring when my petunias are just starting to bloom," Abuela adds.

I can practically hear Tía Tita's smile. "Christmas morning, Chale yanking me out of bed."

Mami hugs me close. "My family, safe and sitting around the kitchen table."

I let their feelings fill me before making a love list of my own: Papi's goofy laugh and warm tortillas with butter and Aiden's dimples and Mami's pozole and Clau's dance moves and Carlitos's terrible jokes.

The memories lap against my heart, one warm wave after the other until I'm drenched. Then I force that feeling deep into the twisted fibers of the rope, imagining it traveling from one knot, one hand to the next.

But it's not enough to feed someone joy from my own

memories. The real way to make those feelings stick is to feed them joy from their own.

And this is it—the part of me that doesn't fit. The gift that is mine and no one else's.

I blindly feel my way through the crowd one more time. I find Father Torres and in his mind there are so many moments of joy. The baptism he performed last week for Marisol's baby brother, Josef. His mother giving him his first Bible. The first time he saw God.

My thoughts run into Mr. Montgomery next, searching through his memories for something powerful enough to release him from his anger, from his pain.

I see the beginning of everything—the first time he sees Abby's mom working at the post office. Their first date is at the county fair. He wins her a goldfish. She makes him drive her an hour away to set it free in Choke Canyon Lake.

They get married at the courthouse in a dress Abby's mom made herself. They have their first son, and every time Abby's mom has a baby, Mr. Montgomery's heart grows three sizes. But Abby…Abby is his little girl. She makes him soft and patient and kind. She makes him thoughtful and brave and generous. She makes him fall in love with Abby's mom all over again.

I latch on to the memory, dragging it to the forefront of his mind. Until I can sense it slipping over him like a warm blanket.

Then I can't help but open my eyes, the rest of the angry crowd losing steam too, everyone falling quiet. People clutch the rope like it's someone they love, like they know it's feeding some part of their spirit.

There's a low rumble of questions. Then people turn to look at La Lechuza, still trapped, though she's just as quiet.

"Don't let up," Abuela breathes, still clutching the rope. "It's working on her too."

I grip the rope and remember the girl I saw in Mami's old photo albums. Luna. Swishing her skirt. Blushing at the camera.

Do you remember her?

La Lechuza twitches, groaning like there's something awful happening behind her eyes. Like she's fighting herself the same way Altagracia did in the library when I learned her origin story.

But that wasn't the beginning. She had another life before then. She had a family. So did Luna.

I search her memory for them, shoving aside the grief and the pain, until I find a memory as warm and bright as the sun. Luna and her daughters lying under the wide branches of a weeping willow. There's a book on her knees, her daughters resting against her as she reads aloud.

"The girl was tired after all her adventures—and a little hungry too. She followed the path she knew by heart until she finally saw the little house in her memories. Behind the window was her family sitting around a warm fire and she wondered if they would be the same too. She certainly wasn't. She was older and wiser and stronger. But also a little afraid. Until she knocked on the door and they greeted her with the biggest hugs. 'We were waiting for you,' they said. The girl smiled even bigger. 'I'm home,' she thought. 'This will always be my home.'"

She closes the book, pulling her daughters in close.

"I love you, Mami," Lucia says.

"I love you too. So much."

"Read it again, Mami."

Luna laughs, kissing the crowns of their heads. "Okay, otra vez."

I watch her remember every *second*, every *detail*.

Then I see it.

The first flash of her face beneath her ugly mask.

Then a slender hand breaking free from one of her wings.

Her beak retreats. Skin stretches over her feathers. She lets out one last guttural scream and then she collapses on the ground.

I let go of the rope and rush to her side, peeling away her matted hair. Underneath, her face is smooth and round, her lips blue from the rain and cold.

"Luna..." Abuela kneels next to me. She takes her cousin's hand. "Luna, are you all right?"

Luna blinks, examining our faces. "The girl," she breathes. "I know where she's taken her."

I know these woods—the rotten stumps and the old tractor equipment and the rattlesnake holes. But right now it feels like the belly of somewhere I don't belong, the trees whispering warnings for us to turn back.

Luna leads the way and I pump my arms until I'm dripping sweat, no breeze daring to pierce through the trees. I can feel how it stalls, just as afraid as everything else here. We follow the fear as it snakes through the grass before it dead-ends in the darkest spot in the forest.

I tread closer, Mami making sure she and Abuela are always a few steps ahead, Tía Tita and Soona always a few steps behind.

A gust of wind chills me to the bone, making my teeth chatter. Carlitos's knees are quaking too.

Before, when I dreamed of La Lechuza, her whistle was high and sharp. A single pitch. But as the sound suddenly ignites around us, it moves. Bending and twisting into a dreadful melody that makes me feel sick.

I sense her arrival in every cell in my body. Her song straining to get closer, coaxing me forward like a hand. A hand that wants to hold me and strangle me at the same time.

And then the whistle is no longer just a sound. It's light,

a glowing orb in the distance. The light dances and then it splits. Two bright stars. Two wide eyes watching us.

Then I see the bundle hooked in her beak, Abby's blond hair spilling out of the sack. I can't tell if she's breathing or even awake, no sounds escaping except Señora Avila's ragged breathing as she draws nearer.

Her eyes are set deep inside her skull, her face covered in leathered skin, and pinned back by black feathers. She looks older. *Ancient.* The different pieces of her mashed together like some grotesque science project. Like something that's been sleeping at the center of the earth since the time it was made.

I can tell she no longer belongs in this world, and yet beneath those jet-black feathers and that shark-toothed grin, I can *feel* her humanness. Maybe that's the scariest part. Knowing that she used to be human. Knowing that we all have monsters inside us just like Luna did. Just like Señora Avila does.

Monsters that we can either defeat or let devour us. Buried under so much ugliness I wonder if she wishes she'd won. If she regrets becoming something so awful. Or if this is what she wanted all along.

"What I desired..." Her voice slithers out and hooks me. "What was destined for me." She tsks. "You think magic belongs to you, but a curse can be cast by anyone. *On* anyone."

"Why would you curse yourself?" I say.

"What you call a curse, I call creation. Making myself into

whatever I want." Her head jerks. "Sixty years on this earth and most of them have been excruciating. Broken promise after broken promise. Dead dream after dead dream. All these years I've waited for something *more*. A chance to escape.

"When Luna first arrived, I was the only one who was willing to let her in. She told me stories about how grief transformed her. How she'd spent years running, sleeping in a different city every night, hunting and surviving and making her own rules.

"But where she saw a trap...I saw freedom. I *craved* it. But just like he has for forty years, Noel stood in my way." She bristles. "He was *always* standing in my way. So I killed him, bringing myself to the edge of my humanity. Señora Delarosa's potion did the rest."

"That woman!" Abuela shakes her fist. "It's nothing but a costume, Paulina. Can't you see that? Can't you *feel* it? That what you are is temporary? That it's wrong?"

"That's just it, Renata. I *don't* feel and there is nothing in or outside this world that is more liberating than that."

"What about all those cats?" Carlitos demands.

"Something needed to start the transformation. A blood sacrifice, if you will. Soon, I began to prefer the taste." She grins. "But once I kill the child...that's when the process will be complete. My human form laid to rest and all her emotions too. I'll finally be free."

"You're wrong." Luna takes a careful step closer, but it only makes Señora Avila puff up her chest, agitated. "Paulina, please trust me when I tell you that you're *wrong*. This is not freedom. It isn't even living. You kill the child and your soul dies too."

Señora Avila grits her teeth, growling. "They forced this change on you, Luna."

"No, they didn't. I wanted this. It's why I came back."

"You came back because you were scared."

"Scared of what I was becoming. And I won't let you become the same thing."

She reaches for Señora Avila, for her friend, but Señora Avila opens her wings, striking Luna to the ground.

Abuela rushes to Luna's side, just within reach of Señora Avila's beak. She drops the sack, Abby tumbling out and onto the ground. When she groans, I breathe a sigh of relief.

Until Señora Avila lunges for Abuela again. Her beak clamps down on Abuela's chancla as Abuela and Luna scramble away.

Mami and Soona join hands, making a barrier between them, chanting together. "Una es la Santa Casa de Jerusalén donde Jesucristo crucificado vive y reina…"

Señora Avila screams, the sound so piercing that I check my ears for blood. Mami grabs her head too, like the sound is trying to break her open. Abby starts screaming next, holding her ears and rolling on the ground.

Soona throws herself on top of her, trying to quiet the sound with her touch. But Señora Avila is right there, a giant foot on Soona's back, claws digging into her skin.

"Leave them alone!" Clau charges for Señora Avila, her icy exterior burning Señora Avila's cheek.

But Clau's not solid by choice. Now that Señora Avila is supernatural, she can actually touch her. Which means... she can *hurt* her.

Señora Avila beats her wings before pouncing in Clau's direction.

Clau flits between the trees. "Stay away from me, you monster!"

While Señora Avila's distracted, Soona tries to pull Abby away, but their bodies rustling in the grass makes Señora Avila jerk, her head turning at a terrifying angle.

"...Circle." Luna crawls to her feet, mouthing the word to me and Carlitos. "Move in a circle." Then she traces a finger across her throat.

Carlitos and I exchange a look. Then we lock hands.

"Hey, you!" Carlitos chucks a rock at her.

Her head twitches, teeth glinting.

"Over here!" Clau appears, striking her in the wing.

She tracks Clau with her eyes, head making another turn as she lets out a wretched scream.

"You want to eat me?" Carlitos yells.

We take slow steps to the left, careful to stay out of reach.

"Stay away from them!" Abuela chucks her other chancla, hitting Señora Avila right on the beak.

Señora Avila's head spins, someone on every side, egging her on.

"Are you feeling free now?" Luna takes another step to the left.

Abby tries to crawl into the trees.

Señora Avila twitches, panicked. "Give me the girl!"

"Don't let her move," I hiss.

"I know exactly what to do," Clau whispers, and then she pops up behind Señora Avila and lets out a string of curse words so vile my entire body blushes.

I expect Señora Avila to take another swipe at her, but instead she groans, teeth gnashing as she follows Clau with her eyes. Around and around until she begins to gag.

"Hey!" Carlitos waves his arms, getting her to make another achingly tight turn in our direction. "You big dumb chicken!" He takes the squirrel's advice too, even though his insults aren't as impressive as Clau's. "Yeah, I'm talking to you, you rotten ugly witch!"

Señora Avila thrashes, choking herself.

Slowly, we cinch her in, tightening our circle around her. Abuela flashes Carlitos and Clau a look that says, *We'll discuss your punishment later,* but in the meantime we all move as one, calling out to Señora Avila until she's spun herself in circles. Her eyes go wide like they might pop right out of her skull. Mami's almost close enough to finally get a hand on her. Soona is ready with the rope.

I take another step forward, my shoe snapping a branch. Señora Avila turns to look at me and then her neck snaps too, her head rolling right off her body and into the dirt.

"¡Ay Dios!" Abuela clasps a hand over her mouth.

Clau swoops down, examining the head more closely. "Is she...dead?" She nudges it and it rolls toward Carlitos.

"¡Uy!" He jumps out of the way.

"Tying knots isn't the only way to get rid of a Lechuza." Soona kneels, poking at the severed head with her finger. "My abuelito taught me this trick."

"Her predator instincts wouldn't let her look away," Luna says.

Soona nods. "He always said a hungry beast is its own worst enemy. Señora Avila was willing to wring her own neck just to get a piece of one of us."

"She thought she was free...." Luna shakes her head. "But the truth is she would have been slave to those instincts. They would have destroyed her sooner or later."

"But they didn't destroy *you.*" Abuela comes to stand right in front of Luna. She takes her hands. "Forgive me." She pinches her eyes shut. "I should have believed you. I should have been there for you when you asked for help."

Luna squeezes her hands. "After the things I said…unforgivable things said out of anger and jealousy. You were just trying to protect your family." Her eyes glisten with tears. "I would have done the same."

Mami grips Luna's shoulder. "You *are* our family."

"Always," Soona says, wrapping the three of them in an embrace.

They hold each other until their tears have turned to laughter. Until their fear gives way to forgiveness.

"And I'm especially sorry that you had to subject yourself to the likes of Señora Avila," Abuela adds. "That woman has the personality of—"

Clau, Carlitos, and I all exchange a look before saying, "…A wet mop!" And then everyone is laughing.

Well, except Abby.

Instead, Abby breaks through the circle, shoving me and Carlitos aside before she rams a foot into Señora Avila's body. "I told you to keep your grubby hands off of me!" She kicks until feathers start flying. She kicks until she's winded and crying. "Stay away from me!"

"Abby…" I reach for her and she buries her face in my chest, unloading every ounce of terror.

In her memory I see the moment she was taken. How she screamed and cried. How her father sat there, too stunned to fight. Then every painful second after when she thought she was going to die.

But pulsing from an even deeper wound...I find Abby's grief, and for the first time I feel the weight of her loss. I wade through her emptiness until my throat aches with tears. And I finally get it. Why she had to find somewhere to put the pain. Because *this* is agony. What she's been going through all alone...

"I'm sorry." She looks at me, tears in her eyes. "I'm so sorry, Omega."

"I know," I breathe because her regret is just as palpable. "I forgive you."

Then I claw my way out of her pain, dragging her with me. I focus on finding a memory she told me about once as the thing she reaches for every time she can't sleep. Abby and her mother in the kitchen, mixing brownie batter and waffle batter and cupcakes and icing. And every time, her mother scooping up a dollop of something sweet and dotting it on the tip of Abby's nose.

I drag the memory to the surface until we can both taste the sugar on our tongues, and then I tell Abby what I know her mother would. "You're safe now, Abby. *You're safe.*"

EPILOGUE

CARLITOS, CLAU, AIDEN, ABBY, AND I ARE discotheque vampires for Halloween. Abuela made us go outside to cover ourselves in glitter so we wouldn't make a mess, and Chale poked us with a plastic stake until we finally put the finishing touches on our costumes.

Instead of turning us to dust, he led us from one house to the next, jumping to reach each doorknob, jumping even when there wasn't a doorknob, jumping when someone gave him his favorite mazapán candy, jumping when some jerk gave him floss.

We chased him all over town, greeted by Belén the alien, Doña Maria the Queen of Hearts, Señor Rivas as some guy with a bunch of scissors for hands, Soona the Smurf, Mr. Huerta as an astronaut, as well as several others whose costumes are not really worth mentioning, either because they were terrible or because I have no idea who or what they were trying to be.

What is worth mentioning is the way Aiden gives me all of his best chocolate at the end of the night when we're evaluating our haul (and also setting aside the worst of it for next year's trick-or-treaters).

"These are my favorite," he says before handing me his one and only Zero bar.

"Are you sure?" I ask.

He nods. "Yeah, I want you to have it."

I unwrap the chocolate and break it in half. "We'll split it."

He takes his half, holds it out to me. "Cheers."

"Cheers."

"Uh-oh." Clau wriggles her eyebrows at Carlitos. "What do you say? For old times' sake?"

He's holding a Reese's Peanut Butter Cup. "What do you think?" he asks me. "Should we do it?"

"Do what?" Abby asks, her mouth full of Whoppers.

"It's called the Reese's test," I say. "We use it to see if evil is afoot."

"How does it work?" Aiden asks.

Carlitos holds up the Reese's. "We unwrap the peanut butter cup and if it comes out clean, no chocolate stuck to the wrapper, then all is good. But if it doesn't, then there could be something wrong."

"And sometimes that *something* appears in the chocolate itself. Like a bad omen."

"I want to do it," Abby says, grabbing a peanut butter cup.

"Abby." Aiden pushes her back. "Remember what we said about…"

She shakes her head. "Right." Then she hands back the Reese's. "I'm sorry, Carlitos. You go first."

He sucks on his lip, surprised that Abby is actually thinking of others for once. "Uh…" Then he dumps out his jack-o'-lantern. It's full of Reese's. "Why don't we all take a turn?"

Clau swats him. "You were hiding these all for yourself, weren't you?"

"Well, obviously not anymore!"

"Okay, okay…" I slide everyone a piece of candy. "Now, on the count of three. One…" The plastic packages split open. "Two…" Everyone begins to peel back the wrapper. "Three."

There's a crescent-shaped bald spot on the bottom of my peanut butter cup. When I look down at the wrapper I see the sky—a half-moon and three stars. The sight steals my breath and I crumple the wrapper in my fist before stuffing the peanut butter cup in my mouth.

"What did you get?" Aiden asks.

"Oh, nothing," I say. "Came out clean."

"Yeah…" Carlitos nods, proud of himself. "That's what I'm talking about." He stuffs the perfect peanut butter cup in his mouth. "What about yours, Abby?" he asks, his mouth still full.

"No more monsters for me." She grins. "Thank God." Then she peers over Aiden's shoulder, her brow furrowing. "What's that?"

I peer over his other shoulder too, all of us staring at the wrapper.

"It looks like a dog," Clau says.

"Hey." Carlitos pats him on the back. "Maybe it means you're getting a pet."

"I thought you said it was supposed to be a bad omen," Aiden says, holding the wrapper like it might grow fangs.

"Not necessarily," I say.

"Yeah, we're still trying to work out the kinks," Carlitos adds.

"Oh good." Aiden sets down the wrapper before stuffing the chocolate in his mouth.

"Me! Me!" Chale knocks over Carlitos's candy pail as he reaches for a peanut butter cup.

"Okay, Chale, slow. Like this…" Carlitos shows him how to remove the brown wrapper.

Chale purses his lips, concentrating. He peels off the wrapper and then immediately tosses it on the floor before stuffing the peanut butter cup in his mouth.

The rest of us lean in for a closer look.

"It's uh…" Carlitos cocks his head.

"What is it?" Clau asks.

"It looks like"—I lean back, confused— "nothing. Just a normal chocolate blob."

"Maybe that just means there's more candy in his future," Aiden offers.

Carlitos sucks his teeth. "Lucky."

We finish sorting the candy before Soona gives Abby and Aiden a ride home. Then it's time to clean everything up, including ourselves. It takes me almost an hour to get the glitter out of my hair. By the time I get out of the shower,

Carlitos and Chale are gone too, even though the kitchen table's still a mess.

I toss an empty glitter bottle in the trash and spot the brown wrapper Chale left behind. I lean over it, getting a closer look. But it's changed. Melted, probably.

Then I touch it.

And it stings.

Suddenly, I see the face of something wild, its teeth bared, too big for its mouth. And I swear...I can hear it...*snarling*.

"Do you think she's trick-or-treating right now?"

I jump at the sound of Clau's voice and slam the lid closed on the trash can.

I step beside her. "Who?"

She smiles to herself. "Candela. Do you think someone dressed her up as a princess or a puppy dog or fuzzy avocado and took her around the neighborhood to get candy?" She meets my eyes. "Do you think she's with a family that does things like that?"

I smile back. "I'm sure she is. I'm sure she's stuffed full of candy and they're tucking her into bed right now."

"I just need to know that she's okay."

"We'll find her." I wrap my arms around her. "We'll make sure she is."

Abuela appears from the hallway and motions to the

kitchen table. "Ah, Omega, this mess isn't going to clean itself."

I roll my eyes so that only Clau can see. She laughs.

"I'm on it, Abuela."

She gives me a kiss good night. "And there better not be a speck of glitter on this floor in the morning."

"Sí, 'buela. Good night."

She hugs me. "Good night."

I scoop up some of the empty candy wrappers. "Clau, can you—?"

But when I look, Clau's gone. Of course she's avoiding chores right now.

"Knock, knock?"

I jump at the voice.

"I'm sorry," Luna says on the other side of the screen door. "Did I scare you?"

"No..." I toss the wrappers in the trash with the rest. "I'm fine."

I push open the screen door, but she doesn't come inside.

"I thought maybe we could chat for a moment."

"Oh..." I step out onto the porch, easing the door closed behind me. "Sure. Is everything okay?"

"Everything's fine," she says. "Thank you."

She moves to sit on the porch steps, and in the awkward silence I move to sit next to her.

"You know, the night I found Clau and Candela, I followed the ambulance all the way to the hospital. I went back to the accident before I saw what happened to her, where she ended up. But I'd like to help you and Clau find out."

"Thank you," I say. "Clau will be so happy to hear that." I face her. "But what do you mean you went back?"

Then she meets my eyes. "For Clau."

I go still. "You...you brought her here...."

She nods again. "I knew she'd be safe here."

"Because we can see her?"

Luna looks away and then she says, "Because she's not like other ghosts." She senses my surprise and finally faces me again. "I've met countless of them. But there's something different about Clau. Special..." She narrows her eyes at me. "You feel it, don't you?"

"Shinier," I say.

"Exactly."

"But what is it?"

"We don't know yet."

"We?"

"Your mother, Abuela, and I. Soona and Luisa too."

"And me...?" My throat clenches. "What have y'all figured out about me?"

Luna glances over her shoulder. But everyone else has gone to bed.

"Omega, before I say anything else, I want to thank you for what you did for me."

"Oh…" I feel myself blushing. "It's nothing, really. I mean…what are families for, right?"

"Right." The smile reaches her eyes and they well up with tears. "But they took some convincing."

"Just a little."

"You're special," she says. "But you already know that. You feel more deeply than the others. True things. Necessary things. Sometimes it might be easy to second-guess yourself, especially when no one else can see what you can. But you have to believe in your abilities, Omega. You have to believe in yourself."

"I understand," I say.

She looks up at the moon and it's just a sliver. Not the half-moon I saw in the palm of my hand.

"It's beautiful," she says. "Isn't it?"

"It is."

"You know, *feeling* things more deeply than others can be a blessing, Omega. You're alive in a way no one else is. It's exhilarating. But…there's also great risk involved."

"Do you mean how I keep blacking out and getting sick?" I ask.

"That's how it can sometimes start, yes." She looks down. "What happened to me…what I *became*…it was because I let myself absorb too much. Too much hate and anger and vengeance. This power I had to sense things, to feel them more deeply than anyone else, became a weapon. A weapon used against me until I was caged by my own wings."

"But then you broke free."

She smiles. "Because you helped me." She takes my hand and I feel her gratitude. "Because you're not just an empath, Omega. You're something much more powerful. The kind of witch that can manipulate the emotions of supernatural beings. That can control them. Heal them. The way you healed me."

"It wasn't just me," I say. "You fought hard too, Luna. You *fought* it."

She nods and then she's quiet for a long time before she says, "And you can too." Then she squeezes my hand, looks deep into my eyes, deep into my *soul*, and says, "When the moon starts calling to you, Omega…don't be afraid."

A shiver races down my spine. I feel watched.

I feel seen.

I feel hunted.

Then I fight my own fear and face the moon. It winks.

Acknowledgments

This story was my happy place at the height of the COVID-19 pandemic, the summer after my last year in the classroom, when my dream of being an author felt so close and big and fragile. When I wasn't sure what the future held, this story held me, reminding me that courage can look like all sorts of things and that even though big hearts may be more easily bruised, they're the only superpower worth having.

Thank you to my agent, Andrea Morrison, for being such a great champion and ally and continuing to help me find homes for each one of my stories (and there are a lot of them). Thank you to my editor, Sam Gentry, for believing in my work from the beginning, wholeheartedly, and for helping me hone my voice in this new category, which I have fallen head over heels for. And thank you to the entire Little, Brown Books for Young Readers team for giving each one of my books the introduction to the world it deserves.

I also want to thank my family, and especially my cousins, for helping me make the memories that inspired this book. Thank you to my two pups, who were my other saving grace during the pandemic and who reminded me how important it is to play in real life and in stories. Thank you to JD for lending me your humor for this project and for being the comedic relief in my own life.

Thank you to mis comadres in Las Musas, my brave friends who are still making a difference in the classroom, and to all the teachers and librarians I've met over the past few years. To the readers joining me on this new journey into middle grade, I hope this story makes you smile, your stomach growl, and your middle-school heart believe in magic again.